PAINTING THE DUKE

A NOVEL BY

GEORGINA NORTH

PEPPERBERRY PRESS

PAINTING THE DUKE | Copyright © 2023 by Georgina North

Library of Congress Cataloging-in-Publication Data

Names: North, Georgina, author.
Title: Painting the Duke: A Novel / Georgina North.
Description: First U.S. edition | San Diego: Pepperberry Press, 2023.

Identifiers: LCCN 2023914361 (print)
ISBN 978-1-959794-03-5 (paperback)
ISBN 978-1-959794-04-2 (hardcover)
ISBN 978-1-959794-05-9 (ebook)

Cover design by Robin Vuchnich

For my husband

 $\mathcal{V}$ ivienne picked up the old brush that had been in her collection nearly as long as she'd been painting—at least as long as she'd been disappointing everyone's expectations but her own—and impatiently swiped it through the flake-white paint on her palette.

Her frustration with this particular work had turned Vivienne into the very model of a tempestuous, passionate artist, the part of herself she worked hard to hide from society. She could not afford to be so. Not when she lived with her aunt and uncle, Lord and Lady Lane. Not when she moved in the highest circles of society, circles that believed women only acquired talents to acquire a husband. Not when oil painting, unlike watercolour, was thought an indelicate pursuit for females, never mind an occupation. That she dared have a viewpoint or even consider herself an artist raged against the feminine virtues of modesty, chastity, and obedience society expected from her.

But Vivienne was at least as much artist as she was woman. She'd torn apart a canvas or two. She'd snapped brushes, smashed jars of colour, slammed doors. Her emotions were always simmering just below the surface, and the more vexed she became with society, the harder it was to keep those feelings under control, to maintain the pretence of a genteel young lady with nothing more to concern her than who might solicit her hand for a dance at the next ball.

She set the palette on the chair next to her before dropping to her knees, brush in hand. With rapid, controlled motions, she dappled the sea crashing on the shore of her canvas, rolling her fingers to replicate the rugged beaches of Cornwall. Like most of her pieces, this one was crafted from a memory of the home she'd once shared with her parents, when they were still alive and she'd led a very different life. A life before the complications of moving, of making her come out, of living an artist's life in secret.

She stippled the brush again, and again, and again, until she could feel the sea foam running through her fingers as if her hand were a sieve, smell the brine, feel the shivers run up her spine as she imagined dipping her toe in the cool water of the Atlantic on a hot summer day.

Tilting her head this way and that, Vivienne rose and took several steps back. The water would need one more layer and the baby boy the woman was holding would need a little more colour on his bare backside, but for today, she was finished.

This painting had quickly become one of her favourites. It was of a young woman at the water's edge, her hair held back by a grey handkerchief, the hem of her brown linen dress rough from wear. Her arms were full—she was holding a baby in one and in the other clutching a small girl with long blonde curls hanging loose and wet down her back. She balanced both as she picked her way across stones scattered in the sand. But the woman was not looking at the infant in her arms or where to place her foot—she was looking out, pleading for something. Respite, perhaps.

A knock on the door of Vivienne's studio startled her as she cleaned her brushes. When she cracked it open, her uncle Nigel was peering back at her, mischief ripe in his eyes.

'Your aunt says the carriage will be ready in a quarter of an hour.' He nicked the bit of stormy blue-grey paint on his niece's cheek, and his smile widened. With a conspiratorial glance around, even though no one else was present in her rooms, in an exaggerated whisper, he asked, 'The next great work of art?'

'Next?' Vivienne retorted with a short, dry laugh, opening the door more fully for him to step into the room that had been converted into a workspace. 'I'd settle for one—right on the line. If a lady can only display her work at the Royal Academy during the Summer Exhibition, then it ought to be in a place of prominence, if she can manage.'

'All your pieces are excellent,' her uncle replied, but made an amendment at his niece's incredulous look. 'All right, perhaps not your very earliest, but what acclaimed artist ever painted a masterpiece on his first try? Besides, these last years, you and I both know…' He let the sentence hang in the air between them, as if unwilling to advance the inevitable discussion. Her paintings had begun to garner attention, and more attention meant more risk. 'When can we see it? Or are we not to have that pleasure?'

Vivienne didn't always show her aunt and uncle what she was working on. Not all art was fit for an outsider's eyes—some was just for her, to find her way, to practise a technique, to wish and dream on canvas.

'I need a little more time with her.'

'But she will be going to the Academy?' It was more statement than question.

Vivienne expelled a long breath. Over the last handful of years, some of her pieces had been hung within those august walls. Of course, no one knew it was *her* work. Society at large was not kind to women who dared to be professional artists. It was possible her paintings would stop selling, or she would be accused of having any number of affairs—with other artists, with Academicians, with any man who sat for a painting, all of whom would be given the credit for her work. Her livelihood, her reputation, her aunt and uncle's reputation, could all end up in tatters. And yet, it was everything to her just to know her paintings were there, seen by others; it was the thing she was proudest of and the secret she most closely guarded.

'Yes,' she finally answered, after a long moment. 'I think so, if they'll have her.'

'They will,' he said with confidence.

Vivienne's laugh was full of affection. 'You cannot know that.'

'Your work may be above the line, but it sells. Your name— well, what they think is your name—has been appearing in the papers slowly but steadily for years now.'

It was true. As more of the *ton* arrived in London for the season, and discussions around all the grandest events became louder and more common, the *Public Ledger,* the *Morning Chronicle,* and the *London Literary Gazette,* among others, began to speculate on what the main pieces of the Summer Exhibition would be, as the Royal Academy moved away from religious scenes and displayed more portraiture and genre painting. Vivienne was not so well known as some others, but her name, or the initials she signed, had been mentioned as an artist to watch.

'They'll accept what you submit,' her uncle assured her, cutting into her thoughts. 'Either way, I cannot wait to make her acquaintance. Now,' he added, with a comical little bow, 'I will take myself off, since you likely need every one of those fifteen minutes—perhaps more like ten now—your aunt bestowed on you.'

The pride on her uncle's face as he closed the door made Vivienne's heart swell with gratitude. She had lived with her aunt and uncle at their estate in Norfolk since the age of thirteen, and although her aunt didn't quite understand Vivienne's love of painting, her uncle very much did. Without his help, his connections, and the network he put in place to protect her, her work would have remained in her studio and not on the walls of the Academy. One day, she would see her paintings on the centre line, the place of honour during the Summer Exhibition, the placement coveted by every artist.

She stepped back into her studio, finished cleaning her brushes, put the lids on her paints, and checked her person for splatters of blue and grey and white, removing the spot on her cheek and the paint on her hands. The little break would do her good. The only way she altered her current perspective or discovered a new one was to put distance between herself and the work.

Taking a full, resolute breath, she removed her apron, closed and locked the door to her studio, and entered her own room, where she gave her appearance a critical glance in the mirror before ringing for Maria to help her change and ready herself for morning calls.

2

$\mathcal{B}$rick William Thomas Vesily, known in drawing rooms as His Grace the Duke of Hazelhurst and nearly everywhere else as a bit of a hellion, sighed, took a sip of smooth French brandy, and debated leaving the country once more, this time of his own accord.

He'd returned home a little more than eighteen months ago for no greater reason than he'd missed it. The work he'd been doing abroad had finally come to an end, and it felt like enough time had passed since the scandal that saw him sent away in the first place. There was only one person whose actual approval he needed, and Prinny, when applied to, had replied with a touch of impatience and an enthusiastic invitation to dine that made Brick's jaw muscle flex, his lips compress into a firm line, and the general cynicism that defined his outlook compound into a real distaste for the trappings of society.

During his first year back on English soil, he'd not bothered to come down to London for the season. An estate the size of Goldfinch Park, no matter how well managed in his absence, would always require almost more care than any owner could provide, to say nothing of the other eight estates he kept fully staffed year round. Brick had spent the better part of his time at home working. Working, and savouring the miles of footpaths winding through woods, or else fishing the lakes, or riding rolling downs. He thought he'd be content enough never to leave again.

When he'd arrived at the little soirée at the Jevingtons' several days ago, his first event in town in nearly seven years, he'd wished he hadn't left Goldfinch Park at all, dukedom be damned. The butler had announced him, and he'd strolled into the dazzling drawing room as a walking contradiction—confident he would be welcomed back into the throes of the *ton* because of his wealth, his status, and his title, and disgusted by it all the same. Men who eyed him with caution would seek his favour, invite him to their card tables, copy the simple and elegant style of his cravat. Women who circulated the gossip about his past, his present, his person would seek to secure him for themselves or their daughters, regardless how impulsive or cold or sharp a shot he was. He wanted none of it.

Brick could count on one hand the number of intimates he had and on two the total number of people he called friends; he had no need of more. As for the women, that was trickier. At thirty, he was far from being an old, beleaguered man, but at some point he'd need to marry and sire an heir.

The problem, of course, was that he could have his pick. He could have had any woman at the Jevingtons', at Almack's, in London, in the country, dark reputation and all. The problem with having everything available was that none of it then seemed all that appealing.

In that one night, no fewer than three matchmaking mamas and two determined grandmamas drew their demure relations near him to introduce the creatures to his notice. By the end of the evening, they had blended together, without a single distinguishing characteristic to set one apart from the other; they all played beautifully, spoke French, netted purses, embroidered pillows, and had not one unique thought among them.

'Care to join me at Watier's?'

The voice startled Brick, and he looked up to see his oldest friend, Lord St Germain, standing in the doorway to the library.

'Had I any notion how much you missed me, Saint, I would have returned sooner. I've hardly been in town a sennight, and you've appeared in one room or other of my house'—he looked up as he briefly counted out the days—'all but Monday and Thursday.'

St Germain chuckled as he moved towards the sideboard. 'Only because Ellena insisted I accompany her to the Royal Zoo and Vauxhall. Dashed annoying thing, having a sister make her come out.'

'Only because you wish to make her happy.'

His friend shrugged. 'Yes, well, it's a bad business having children when one is too old to see them out of leading-strings, much less the schoolroom.'

Brick's love for his own father had been profound, and it never failed to sadden him that his own friend had inherited his title at the tender age of nine. When they met, Valentine Ainsley had been Earl of St Germain for four years already. Brick didn't inherit until close to his twenty-fifth birthday and even that had felt too soon by half.

'Under whose aegis will she make her come out?'

'Franny's.' After a pause, he clarified, 'The second eldest.

Lydia is indisposed, again, and Catherine is in Belgium. Ah, but you know that, of course.'

'I do,' Brick confirmed. While abroad, he'd spent some time with one of St Germain's older half-sisters and her husband, who was a diplomat on the continent. St Germain had a whole pack of sisters. His father had three daughters in his first marriage, remarried after the death of his first wife, sired St Germain, and died at seventy-two while his second wife was pregnant with twins, Ellena and Edward. The latter was currently away at Oxford.

After helping himself to a measure of brandy from the snifter, Saint said in an offhand way, 'Lansbury will likely be there tonight. He will be disappointed you weren't drowned at sea by pirates or felled by fever in India. Best to see the quarrelsome cur and get the awkwardness out of the way.'

Brick once thought himself lucky to have a cousin so close in age, someone to call an ally, a confidante—things hard won when one had wealth and position and power. 'Lansbury is a fool. He has had an age or more to accustom himself to my return, and longer still to accept that which he cannot change without risking a murder charge.'

'Your return became apocryphal when you made no appearance in London last year.'

'Yet it was always inevitable. He has created a rivalry that can only exist in his head.'

'Easy to say when you're the duke,' Saint replied, a look of mild reproof in his eyes.

Everything was easy when one was a duke. Brick could do anything, say anything, have anything or anyone. 'A title wouldn't change his character. He'd be as much as he ever was, and more so with a coronet settled upon his head.'

'I've never seen you in a coronet.'

Brick lifted a nonchalant shoulder.

'His own father should have checked his behaviour years ago,' added Saint, with a shake of his head.

'My uncle thinks of little else beside his hunting dogs. He prefers to live quietly in ignorance rather than expend energy he does not have.' Exonerating his uncle, and his own father too, was something Brick had done long ago and without thought. He had simply never spoken to either of them of Lansbury's behaviour. When they were together at Eton, once that gentleman learned the truth of Brick's parentage and felt himself ill-used, entitled to what Brick would have, it had been insults, slurs, a streak of terrible pranks. For too long, Brick had hoped for the return of his friend, thought letting himself be the target of his cousin's jealousy would somehow help them find their way back to where they'd started as two boys catching frogs in the lakes at Goldfinch Park.

At the long break for Christmas and Twelfth Night, during Brick's last year at school, his father had given him the duchy signet ring. A symbol, the duke called it, of sacrifice, of strength. Of fate. 'If I had a hundred lives, I would choose you to be my son in all of them,' his father had said, as Brick slipped the ring over his little finger.

When Brick returned to school, Lansbury saw the ring, said it was too fine a piece for a bastard, and spat at Brick's feet. Brick reacted without thinking, landing a punishing left that sent his cousin reeling. The schoolmaster called him a hellion. The name stuck, but perhaps would not have done after Cambridge, if not for the duels.

'So, Watier's? No point in prolonging the inevitable, old chap.'

'You think I've been forgiven for leaving a hole in the wall?' Brick hadn't been to Watier's since before he left

England, and the last time he'd been at the club to gamble, some fool had accused him of counting cards. St Germain had taken the ace of hearts, held it by the corner between two fingers only eight or ten inches from himself, and Brick, from a distance of roughly twenty paces, shot the card right through the heart in the centre, before asking Sir Geoffrey if he was certain Brick was a cheat. Sir Geoffrey had recanted, once the colour had returned to his face, and fumbled through an apology.

'You may be sure of some sharp rebukes and idle threats,' St Germain told him. 'But you know how it goes.'

Yes, he did. He sighed and tossed back what was left in his glass.

3

*V*ivienne was perched on her preferred bench within the British Institution, gazing at her favourite painting, when a group of richly dressed women assembled in such a way as to obscure her line of sight.

One of these women stood out, in a chartreuse satin gown and turban of gold, with ostrich plumes bustling up and out. She stood at the front of the pack, a little separate from the rest, and when she spoke, they all nodded along, their quiet chorus of complaisance buzzing in Vivienne's ears.

A youngish woman, perhaps half a decade or so older than Vivienne herself, ventured to speak without being spoken to. 'Oh, I recognise this painter. She petitioned to join the Royal Academy several years ago and was denied. Seems rather hypocritical, does it not? They will display her work during the Summer Exhibitions and yet not allow her a place in the Academy?'

The turbaned lady, on the tall side for a woman, looked down over her shoulder. 'No. You may add your incorrect opinions to the long list of reasons you've not been able to find a man to take you on. Who does this woman think she is to insert herself into a man's domain? Of course they do not want her, and very likely she required a man's hand to finish this work, besides. Such is common practice, as we all know.'

We did not know. *We* speculated and perpetuated pernicious rumours, Vivienne thought angrily. The *we* being women with so little going on below the curls of feathers atop their heads that they believed themselves an authority on any subject for which a man had already given his incorrect opinion.

'If she is not married, she might as well do, and turn herself to more useful pursuits than being a *lady painter.*' The last words were delivered with a shudder. The woman looked around, then nodded in the direction of another painting, turning a shoulder to the one the group was discussing. 'Let us put our attention to this one. Similar colour palette, but no weakness of hand can be detected, and it's far more interesting in subject.' All the women but the young one murmured their agreement.

The paintings were by the same woman, which this lady would have known had she only bothered to compare the signatures. Vivienne should be well accustomed to such dismissals, the pervading belief a woman's purpose was to bear children for a man who would no doubt force her to put down the brush, as history had so often demonstrated. Yet, she still fumed. Fumed, but did nothing. The fact remained that there was very little she *could* do beside glare at the backs of the group as they retreated. It was hard enough fighting against men who didn't believe in women, but fighting against women who *wouldn't* believe in women was the more frustrating of the two.

She sat in silent indignation all the way home, while her

14

maid Maria, too familiar with Vivienne's sour moods, worried her fingers in her lap for the entirety of the carriage ride from the Strand to Grosvenor Square. Irritated by both the woman's words and her own perpetual inability to wage war against the many injustices women faced, Vivienne stalked up the stairs of Huxley House to her art studio. Oil painting was her passion, but in fits of pique like the one gripping her at present, it was often a blank sheet of paper for which she reached, a devilish smile pulling her cupid's bow taut.

As soon as Vivienne had been able to hold a pencil, she'd begun drawing. The result of this early practice was an ability to sketch with rapidity. Drawing the caricature of the woman took hardly any time at all. Her image showed the turbaned woman from the gallery, her head weighed down by ostrich feathers, entering the Grand Salon on the uppermost floor of the Royal Academy. In her wake was a trail of other women, strewn over the steps ascending to that prestigious top room. A glimpse inside showed paintings, each a variation on the woman—a hippo, a monkey, a snake. The woman's smile was wide, smug. Underneath, Vivienne penned the words: *She may have terrible taste, but her vanity is dressed to impress.* It would be taken to her uncle's man and sent off to one of her preferred papers for publication—if they accepted it, which she didn't doubt they would.

It wasn't money that drove Vivienne to draw satirical cartoons; aside from what she earned selling her paintings, she was heir to the money and property of her uncle's that wasn't entailed on the next Lord Lane. Caricatures were her opportunity to observe, to critique, to wield the only measure of power she had to push back against the same people who wished to see her kept in a neat, tidy box labelled '*Woman, Wife, Mother*'.

Last month, she'd drawn a caricature of George Lawton,

after overhearing him tell another artist that if a woman chose to do something so indelicate as to take up oils, she ought to at least stick to those subjects with which she was familiar—portraits of family and scenes of domestic felicity—rather than attempt to succeed where she must fail. In Vivienne's humble opinion, the works he had hanging in the British Institution were sloppy, derivative, and muddled, so she drew him with hooves for hands, and delighted when she saw it in print, imagining the pompous fool's outrage.

She'd signed that image, as well as the one in front of her now, with her standard 'VC'—Caldicott being her mother's name before marriage. The letters intertwined to resemble something like a 'W', the 'C' standing a little crooked and the 'V' catching its tail. All done intentionally, of course, to make it harder to identify the signature. Every time she signed her name, she wondered with a defeated sigh how many other female artists intentionally wrote themselves out of history.

It was two days before the cartoon appeared in the *Morning Chronicle*. Until her Uncle Nigel came into the breakfast parlour and blew out a low whistle when he lifted the paper, she had given very little thought to the object of her ire after venting her spleen via caricature. Her mind had already moved on to the painting on her easel so near completion, and she'd thought of nothing else beside where it would be placed in the Great Room and if she would ever see her work hanging on the centre line.

'The Dowager Duchess of Hazelhurst won't take kindly to this. Bold move, running it,' her uncle commented, as much to himself as to her.

Vivienne's ears perked up, and her cheeks pinked.

'Is this—?' Her uncle squinted and lifted the paper to

within a few inches of his nose, and she waited with all the patience of a guilty prisoner for her sentence. 'Vivi!'

Vivienne could only offer a sheepish smile. 'If you'd heard how she talked about Arnaud's work.'

Lord Lane gave her his best reproachful look, but his lip twitched, betraying his amusement. 'Your aunt will not be pleased with you, young lady.'

She loved that at four-and-twenty, her uncle still thought of her as a young anything, but he was right. Her aunt fretted endlessly about Vivienne having an occupation, about what would happen if she were found out. The jump from artist to woman of easy virtue was never a long one. 'No, I suspect for penance I'll have to promise no caricatures for at least a month, until the fervour of this one fades away, and agree to at least two days this week committed to nothing but shopping.'

'What are we shopping for?' Lady Lane asked, as she swished into the breakfast parlour. 'Or perhaps I should be asking why?'

Vivienne's uncle rose from his place. 'Take a seat, my dear, and let me make you a plate.' He placed a fleeting kiss on his wife's cheek as he settled her into a chair.

Vivienne sipped her coffee to hide her smile. Some mornings her aunt took a tray in her room, some she began the day quite early to visit charities, and while the ones where she joined them in the breakfast parlour were few and far between, they were Vivienne's favourite.

'Extra bacon, if you will, Nigel. Now, shopping.'

Without a word, Vivienne slid the newspaper towards her aunt. She watched the woman scan the page, noticed when her eyes landed on the caricature, and knew the exact moment Lady Lane discovered the perpetrator of such a piece was her own niece. Two unamused brown eyes pinned Vivienne with a displeased stare.

'Come now, ma'am. That woman is intolerably haughty, even for a dowager duchess.'

'We've given you painting. Must you do these base things as well?' The question was rhetorical. Lady Lane tried the only other tactic she could—guilt. Even if it never worked. 'Your father—'

'Would be horrified, certainly. He had very specific notions of what a woman and wife ought to be, I know. But my mother would be thrilled.'

The late Mrs Emory was the daughter of a man who owned coal mines, but she'd been everything she ought to be as the wife of a country gentleman. Vivienne's mother had accepted her role and its constraints but railed against the very same by raising a daughter who understood there was more than one path forward for a brave woman. Vivienne didn't think herself very brave, but unlike her mama, she knew how important it was to protect her independence.

4

'Have you seen this?' Brick's mother exclaimed as she charged into his sitting room and thrust the *Morning Chronicle* so far into his face, the paper tickled his nose.

Undeterred by the fury raging in his mother's eyes, Brick lifted his hand up and curled his long, strong fingers over the top of the paper to push the pages out of the way. 'I have, yes,' he said, a notable lack of interest in his voice.

The dowager duchess, against all possibility, turned a deeper shade of red. 'And? And!'

'Have you rung for tea, or should I?'

'How can you think of tea at a time like this, you insensitive child?'

Calling him 'child' was the only maternal sentiment his mother possessed.

'What's to be done? Who is this person?' She brought her quizzing glass up to better inspect the tiny signature in the corner of the caricature. 'Who is this—? What is that—? A

"W"? What kind of *artist* can't even sign his own name? Fraud. Here, you look.'

Brick took the paper from his mother, prepared to glance at it and thrust it back while agreeing with whatever nonsense she was spouting. When his eyes caught the signature, however, he sat up straight and pulled out his own quizzing glass to better inspect the odd little insignia. It was not a 'W'. Or maybe it was, he could hardly tell. What he did know was that the artist who'd drawn this excessively flattering portrait of his mother was the same he'd taken a keen interest in some years before.

'I'm sorry to be the one to tell you, ma'am, the gentleman who drew this is no fraud. His work has appeared in a number of Summer Exhibitions at the Royal Academy.'

'It should all be taken down.'

He didn't mention that the pieces wouldn't still be hanging. 'Perhaps you should make that suggestion to the Academicians,' he said, in a bland way, feeling fatigued by the visit already.

Ignoring her son's sarcasm, she pointed to the page. 'What is this, right here, supposed to be?'

Brick looked at where his mother's finger rested on the page. 'A donkey.'

Her eyes went wider than he'd ever seen, and he didn't bother to smother his laughter. While she was offended into silence, he took the opportunity to ring for tea and, when it arrived, poured her a cup, in the hope it would pull her from the sulks.

'Shall we talk of something less likely to result in your first fit of apoplexy?'

'Marriage?'

'Or my first fit of apoplexy?'

'Maybe Lady Felicity. It's her second year out. She's a beauty, and clever without being too intelligent.' There were many things the dowager countess couldn't abide in addition to artists who portrayed her as sundry animals. Overly educated ladies, as she considered them, determined to upset the natural way of things, also ranked high on her list.

'Your last choice of bride for me was a failure of magnificent proportions, or have you forgotten?'

His mother tilted her chin. 'Yes, well, that was quite your own doing. Had you made any attempt to replace that darkling look you wear—'

'This is simply my face, ma'am, now, as it was then.'

'—or restrained yourself enough to at least appear you weren't so deep in your cups as to require a life preserver whenever you met with her—'

'Three times in total before the wedding.'

'   and bark out orders at anyone within hearing—'

'As I was taught to.'

'—perhaps you wouldn't have frightened the chit off.'

'She wasn't frightened. She was "passionately"—her word, not mine—in love with someone who wasn't me.'

The dowager waved a hand as if shooing a street urchin who dared get too close. 'A daughter of a baron and all that.' In one short statement, Brick was absolved of all wrongdoing in that debacle and the blame placed squarely on a young lady with the misfortune of being born to a lower rank. He allowed himself a moment to marvel at the way his mother's brain worked. 'Lady Felicity is the daughter of a marquess and as dutiful as you.'

His jaw clenched. He couldn't remain a perennial bachelor, but he saw no reason to rush himself to what was tantamount to an early grave. 'How romantic.'

The dowager tsked. 'Romance is for poets and the poor.'

'Ask me in another ten years. If I'm lucky, by then I'll be senile enough not to notice how avaricious the mothers are and how tedious the daughters.'

'Ah, yes. Boredom. The motivation behind so many of your charming pursuits.'

Brick cast a sidelong glance at his mother but said nothing.

'I'm your mother, not some hermit living in exile. Of course I know what mischief you get yourself involved in. Racing, gambling, actresses and opera singers—I can only imagine what I *don't* hear.'

He hoped she didn't put much effort into trying to do so. 'I haven't raced this age.'

'Well.' That one word, a quick sniff, and feigned distraction with the bit of tea left in her cup, was the extent of her response.

His own teacup remained on its saucer, untouched, and he rose from the divan, signalling an end to their visit.

She looked up at him through narrowed eyes, but stood nonetheless. 'We'll have the pleasure of seeing Lady Felicity sometime in the next fortnight. Her mama writes that they're due in town no later than the first week of March.'

'What is that saying about pleasure and pain being bedfellows?'

'I don't believe there is such a one.'

'There ought to be.' Brick marched his mother to the entryway and saw her out himself, if only to be sure she boarded her carriage. When the equipage was out of sight, he returned to his spot on the divan, but the book he'd brought in from the library no longer held his attention, nor did the paper his mother had abandoned on a nearby chair, or the half-opened pile of correspondence he'd left sitting under a pearl-and-gilt snail paperweight on a side table that morning.

After consulting his pocket watch, Brick called for his hat and coat, and in little more than a quarter of an hour, he was bounding down the steps of his town home. He stopped for a moment at his club in St James's Square before strolling down Bond Street. He was debating as he went which invitations in the stack on the table he would accept, when he saw her. It was just a glimpse—she came out of a shop and looked only a moment in his direction before turning in the other.

It was enough for him to know her hair was the colour of polished copper. Her jawline and cheekbones angular and unconventional. Her lips bow-shaped, her eyes wide-set and the same pale green as the tourmaline he'd brought home from his time abroad. Her exquisite features had brought him up short, but it was her laugh, bright and ringing out like a sleigh-bell, that compelled him towards her.

He wanted to see her again, hear her again—and what Brick Vesily wanted, he got. Matching his step to theirs, he walked behind her and the older woman she was with at a careful distance, pausing to look in a shop window when they did. They passed several jewellers, haberdashers, and tobac-conists, eventually crossing the street in the direction of a dressmaker. He did not follow. Instead, he chose to wait a moment to see if they went in, taking the opportunity to observe this unknown Aphrodite, her long limbs and graceful movements giving rise to primal, base instincts within him. Over the years, he'd been with many women, but none with a face quite like hers.

The young lady paused in front of the modiste as the woman she was with pointed to something in the window. The younger tipped her head but then began to turn as if to look over her shoulder, her movement slow, methodical. Just as she may have spotted him, he raised his face upward towards the sky, pretending to study a passing bird, the architecture of the buildings, the cirrus clouds above that signalled fair weather. Brick could feel her eyes assessing him and found himself oddly curious to know what she thought, before the cynic within answered: tall, rich, the fox in her hunt.

He counted out several seconds in his head before chancing to look her way once more. The woman who had stopped his heart had disappeared inside the shop, although the sun beating on the glass window prevented him from seeing anything inside. For a moment he contemplated waiting or storming in and carrying her off. With a little shake of his head he cleared his mind, chastising himself for acting like a boy of fifteen caught by a pretty face and not a gentleman nearing one-and-thirty, and continued on down the street, taking a right towards Savile Row. He was, quite suddenly, desirous of a new jacket and waistcoat.

5

'Oh, these gloves are divine,' Lady Lane declared, pulling her niece's attention to the window display. 'Let's go in and take a look.'

'In a moment, Aunt, if you please,' Vivienne replied, as she scanned the reflections in the window, hoping it would reveal the person whose gaze she'd felt at her back. The flesh on the nape of her neck had prickled almost as soon as they left the shoemaker.

On a sunny winter's day like today, Bond Street was bustling with people. She watched the glass until the frenzy revealed one man—noble, purposeful bearing, dressed in a coat that hugged his broad frame—standing still, forcing others to move around him. She cocked her head over her right shoulder, a measured, deliberate movement. The kind one would make when hunting a frightened animal. As his person came into her line of vision, he raised his head to look up at something, in a careless sort of way that suggested the movement was anything but. She was only granted a moment to make her study of him, as her aunt, with a gentle tug on her arm, pulled her inside the shop.

'Madame Sandrine is expecting us,' Lady Lane said to the shopgirl who greeted them. 'But first we'd like to see the violet gloves in the window.'

The silk gloves *were* exquisite, with embroidery over the hands extending up past the wrist, and tiny buttons running the full length of the arm, but what kept Vivienne's attention was the stranger outside. He remained in the same spot, staring at the door to the shop she and her aunt had just come through. She watched him as long as he watched the door, which turned out not to be long at all. He lingered only another minute or so, contemplation or longing or something else writ upon his face, before making his way up the street and out of her sight, just as she was slipping the left glove over her hand.

'Vivi—Vi—Vivienne.'

Vivienne startled. She was standing on a little platform in the private room of the modiste, muslin pieces draped and pinned all about her person, her aunt looking at her with some expectation of reply, and yet she herself had no recollection of moving away from the window.

'I asked your opinion on the neckline. I feel it too high for a girl not in her first season.' Her aunt turned towards one of Mme Sandrine's seamstresses. 'It needs to be lower if she's ever to find a husband.'

'Aunt.' Vivienne kept her tone pleasant, but the word held a hint of warning. Her aunt knew quite well that Vivienne was not on the catch for a husband, this season or any other, not that it stopped the dear woman from worrying about her niece's future and what it might look like when Vivienne was eventually left alone in the world.

'And how about the garnet silk instead of the primrose? It will look divine against the rubies.'

On this, Vivienne agreed. Richer colours were always more flattering on her, but up until last year her aunt hadn't felt them appropriate for a young lady on the marriage mart. Although she received fewer offers now than when she first came out, requests for her hand had not altogether dried up, and she darkly suspected those who still pursued her did so because she'd become something of an unattainable object, a prize all the more attractive because it could not be won. Worse, that was all her own doing.

When they left the shop, she couldn't help but cast a hurried look around—uncertain whether it was relief or disappointment that coiled inside her when the man from earlier was nowhere to be found.

'All right, out with it.'

'I beg your pardon, Aunt?'

'You've been distracted this hour or more and would have bumped into Mrs Dalrymple outside the haberdasher's had not I nudged you out of the way. I'm certain you didn't even notice her rather substantial person.'

Vivienne hadn't. 'My apologies. It's only—' She broke off and teased her lip, weighing whether she wanted to mention a man of any kind to her aunt. 'I had the oddest feeling I was being watched earlier.'

'Watched?' Lady Lane got as close to screeching as a lady of quality on a public street could.

'No, no, not like that. There wasn't some nefarious character in a mask and cape waiting to carry me to the border.'

Everything about Lady Lane's countenance said it would take more than those reassurances to assuage her.

Vivienne shoved down a sigh. 'Did you by chance notice a

gentleman, quite tall, dark hair, coat of blue superfine, as we walked to Mme Sandrine's?'

Lady Lane looked at her niece, her expression turning from one of horror to one of repressed curiosity, an expression with which Vivienne was well acquainted. 'You're asking me about a gentleman?'

'Aunt.' Vivienne couldn't hold back the short laugh that bubbled up. There was nothing that would make her aunt happier than to see Vivienne married off to the kind of nonpareil who couldn't possibly exist among men of flesh and bone. 'I suppose I am. I can't understand why anyone would be watching me.'

Her aunt made a little murmuring noise. 'No?'

Ignoring this, Vivienne pressed on. 'I only saw him for a moment, but he didn't look at all familiar to me. While up to my neck in pins it occurred to me that perhaps he might have been known to you.'

'I can't say I observed anyone as you describe, and I find that's rather too bad, if he's tall, dark, and handsome.'

Vivienne attempted a stern look in her aunt's direction as they paused to admire some lace fans. 'Handsome, Aunt, is your word, not mine.'

'The season is only just beginning in earnest. If he's a gentleman of means, there is every likelihood we'll see him at some event or other. You've quite piqued my curiosity, and now I'm gone into distraction wondering who he could be. Was there anything else about him that attracted your attention?'

An unwelcome surge of curiosity and excitement rippled through Vivienne, and her fingers flexed as she thought of how his ink-black curls would wrap around each one when she combed them through his hair. 'The tailoring of his jacket was impeccable, and he was holding his hat under his arm.'

'I think one of the Cambry sons has just returned from some time overseas.'

'He wasn't so tanned as to have been abroad recently.'

The afternoon went on in this way, Lady Lane speculating about who he was and Vivienne offering reasons why it wasn't this man or that one but nothing else, much to her aunt's disappointment. To Vivienne's own dismay, she couldn't put the man's handsome face or his arresting expression from her mind. Nor could she ignore the itch of her palms or the desire to pick up a pencil and begin sketching.

Lord and Lady Lane, with Vivienne in tow, made their way through the doors of a palatial London home and took a place in the receiving line for their first ball of the season.

Vivienne scanned the great room while waiting, running a reverent finger over her necklace of petite round-cut rubies and delicate diamonds. With all the candles, she had no doubt the stones glowed as if on fire and was glad her aunt insisted upon her wearing the stunning set. She was not in thrall to pretty things, but she preferred to fit in with society, in that small way, since there were so many others in which she didn't. When it was their turn to greet the host and hostess, Vivienne accepted Lady Ballentine's compliments on her new gown, knowing her aunt was giving her a sly smile without even needing to look.

Her uncle announced his intention of finding the card room and departed, while Vivienne and her aunt moved deeper into the ballroom.

'Look alive, Vivi,' whispered Lady Lane. 'Sir Jackson Brooksbank is heading in this direction, and I doubt it's me with whom he wishes to dance.'

Vivienne was smiling when she turned to face the gentleman and noticed the warm, appreciative gleam in his eyes immediately. Sir Jackson Brooksbank, who held a baronetcy in Lincolnshire, had twice proposed to Vivienne, two years apart. When she turned him down the second time, he had said with a courtly air, 'I suppose my only hope is better luck in the ballroom.' He had not asked for her hand in marriage a third time, but he always solicited her for a dance. He didn't love her, of that she was certain, but he was kind and funny and good-looking—the kind of man many women would accept even without deep affection. She may have seriously considered his offer too, had it not been for her love of painting.

She had felt the first flush of exhilaration, accomplishment, purpose, at seventeen when the Hanging Committee of the Royal Academy had selected one of her works. In that moment, her cheeks pink with pleasure, her heart had filled with unbecoming pride, and Vivienne had known she would face the same unfair choice as generations of female artists who came before her: be the woman who played her role in society or be the painter she was desperate to become.

It didn't matter that she had to look above row after row to see her own work on the fringes of the Grand Salon, so high it touched the sash of the windows just below the ceiling. When she tilted her head back and saw her—the young girl with golden hair, braiding flower crowns without a care in the world, despite her shabby dress suggesting otherwise—she'd swelled with pride at having any place in the gallery. She'd known in that moment that the most important thing to her, more than having a husband or children or home to manage, was seeing her work on the centre line of the Academy walls.

'You're distracted this evening, Miss Emory.'

Vivienne offered a small, apologetic grin. 'I'm afraid I am. I shan't deny it.'

'A concern shared is a concern halved.'

'Oh, I'd hardly call it a concern. My life is too charmed for that,' she teased. 'But I'll own to poorly timed reflection.'

'Miss Emory, I'm afraid I'll have to ask you to keep that bit of information to yourself,' he said, with mock seriousness. 'How will I ever secure another dance partner if my conversation is so boring as to give way to *reflection*?'

She almost laughed. 'It's only because I am so comfortable in our friendship that I have the luxury of letting my mind wander and of confessing the transgression to you. I promise, however, my lips are sealed, and to make up for my inattention, may I introduce you to Miss Kent? I saw you watching her as we went down the line.'

'Am I so obvious?'

'Not at all. Only how many times have you been gentleman enough to stand up with me?'

'You say so as if there isn't a line of men forming for the same purpose.'

Vivienne was glad the dance parted them for a moment. Said by any other man, those words may have come out with a flirtatious undercurrent, but she knew them to be a tease. Still, the sentiment made little roses bloom on her cheeks. By all accounts, she should be on the shelf, set aside for younger ladies looking for eligible matches, but the *ton* and all their arbitrary rules extended a little courtesy to a pleasing countenance and a dowry.

It was fortuitous that when Sir Jackson led her from the

floor, both Mrs Kent and her daughter were in conversation with Lady Lane. Vivienne made swift work of dispatching him and was pleased to see Miss Kent's beaming countenance when Sir Jackson offered to take her for a glass of punch before the next set formed. Vivienne was watching them walk away, admiring her own handiwork—for she thought those two would deal extremely well together—when an imposing figure crossed her line of sight. She resisted the urge to stand on her tiptoes, but dipped and bobbed her head in an effort to confirm her suspicions as her heart ticked a wild beat in her chest.

'That sounds charming, does it not, my dear?' Lady Lane asked her niece.

Vivienne was forced to own her inattention to the discussion and explained it away by complimenting the richly decorated room. Her aunt darted a hasty glance in the general direction in which Vivienne had been staring but said only, 'Quite. Mrs Kent invited us to her Venetian breakfast the Tuesday after next.'

'How charming that sounds. I'm sure it will be a pleasure to attend.' Even as Vivienne responded, her thoughts were already being pulled away once more, and when the conversation turned to other topics, her eyes grazed over the hundreds of bodies creating a sea of satin and silk and superfine, looking for one in particular with a desperation she couldn't ignore or account for.

'Vivienne,' her aunt called to her, with a light touch upon her elbow and a meaningful look. 'Mr Flanders is asking if you'd like to dance?'

Mortified at being caught out twice, Vivienne realised as she looked round the little group of ladies with whom her aunt was engaged that Mrs Kent had departed and several others had joined. Feeling as if her incivility already knew no bounds, and with little other choice, she acquiesced with a slight smile.

As Mr Flanders led her to the floor, Vivienne resisted the urge to put a hand over her heart, which had begun to pulse and pump erratically in her chest, or to open her fan and cool the wave of heat washing over her.

The music began. Vivienne did her best to be an attentive listener as her partner talked at length about crop rotation and felt immensely grateful that the dance in which they were paired parted them often. But his words, which should have dulled her senses, only made her more aware—the swish of her taffeta skirt rang in her ears, flames from the thousands of candles burned too bright in her eyes, and there was an all-out war raging within her as she battled between the desire to flee from whatever it was overtaking her and to be seen again by *him.* To know his attention was hers.

They had completed a turn, and Mr Flanders had reached out a hand for her own, which she bestowed, to lead them down the line. As she faced forward, *he* was there, just beyond the edge of the couples dancing, in conversation with a gentleman with whom she was a little acquainted. The only view of him she was awarded was of his profile—that aristocratic nose, the commanding air with which he carried himself.

When once more returned to her aunt's side, it was much easier to locate him, and her eyes remained fixed on his person, the strong planes of his body. She was smiling in agreement with something Lady Ballentine was saying when she saw the man's head whip in her direction—sharp, decisive, as if someone had tapped him on the back. He stared out over the sea of heads separating them from one another and found her eyes immediately.

The contact was hard, penetrating, and a little voice in the back of her mind whispered a warning, but instead of demurring, she held his eyes with her own, revelling a little in the sudden flash of surprise upon his face. There was cynicism, hunger too, in the way he looked at her, and she felt a coil of warmth tighten in her belly.

How long they would have stood like that, staring intently at one another, was anyone's guess. She hated being the one to break, hated the satisfaction she was certain he felt as she turned away first for yet another dance. As she took her place for a waltz, she imagined the stranger's eyes on her, suspected it to be so by the tell-tale prickle of her skin. She thought of him watching another man's hand come to her waist, catching the rise and fall of her breasts shown to great advantage in her new gown, wondering what was underneath. The thought brought a becoming flush to her cheeks and more radiance to her smile.

Vivienne didn't see the man again until after supper. He was wending his way towards her, his enigmatic expression revealing nothing. She waited at her aunt's side, thankful for the gloves she wore that covered her hot, clammy hands. His movements were fluid, his whole being compelling. Her heart was in her throat, her breathing so shallow she began to feel lightheaded.

He stopped abruptly. A woman whose face she could not see had stepped into his path, dragging some young lady with her. Vivienne was captivated by the way his mouth moved as he spoke and startled to find him once more moving nearer, each step causing her stomach to clench with both uncertainty and anticipation.

'Come, Vivi. Your uncle awaits us. The carriage is ready,' Lady Lane said, all her attention devoted to releasing the diamond bracelet which had caught on the fine satin of her glove.

Vivienne flung her head around to her aunt. 'So soon?'

The hand that had busied itself at Lady Lane's wrist fell still. Her aunt quirked a brow and studied her niece a moment before making any reply. 'I've never known you to possess the desire to tarry at a ball.'

A cursory look cast over her shoulder told Vivienne there were still a dozen people or more separating her and this stranger, and another had stopped him. When she turned back, her aunt was peering at her, eyes bright with interest.

'Care to share what it is holding your interest? Or should I say who?'

There was a brief pause during which Vivienne considered confiding in her aunt, before deciding the answer to the burning question she so wished to ask wasn't worth the hope her aunt would extract from it. ''Tis nothing. I thought I saw Anabel's brother and was going to inquire whether she'd be down for the season, as she is still with her aunt in the north according to her last letter. Alas, I was mistaken.' Vivienne looped her arm through her aunt's, and without another backward glance, allowed herself to be steered from the ballroom.

At home in her bed, she wondered until the sun pushed its way through a crack in the curtains what would have happened if she had remained.

6

$\mathcal{B}$rick had thought himself alone on the top floor of Hatchards, but with one foot on the stairs, he caught a flash of Titian hair in one of the many rows of books fanning out from the landing. Beyond having learned her name at the ball, the young lady he'd first spied on Bond Street was quite a mystery to him. Although he hadn't seen her since, she was often on his mind, particularly in the small hours when sleep was elusive, and he'd resorted to tried and true methods for putting himself to bed.

Her head was bowed over the book in her hand, and she appeared as unaware of anyone else occupying the space as he had been. Rather than continue on to the lower floor, he moved back to the spot he'd just abandoned around the corner from the long row of books where she stood, the carpet beneath his feet muffling the sound of his steps. He quickly scanned the works available to him and selected a slim volume of poetry, placing it on the floor where the shelves from his side and hers came to meet at right angles. With the finesse and skill of an adept sportsman, he used the tip of his polished boot to scoot the book of poetry into her row, the movement making a hushed shuffling sort of noise, and then pulled back out of sight once more as soon as he was certain she'd be able to see it.

Brick waited a few moments and tried to quiet his breathing, which sounded loud and a little ragged to his own ears. He watched as a delicate gloved hand reached out and picked up the volume, but the lady herself didn't appear. A second or two later, he heard the sound of a book being pulled from the shelf, the ones around it collapsing into the empty space. He waited, his veins thrumming with anticipation, and was rewarded for his patience when the tip of a fashionable, feminine boot peeked out from around the corner, a sturdy book beneath it.

The exchange was delicious—intimate even—in its silence.

He relished the moment he pulled the book towards himself, his curiosity heightened as he wondered what she could possibly select for an unknown gentleman. The title was familiar, although he'd not read it, and when he opened it to read the first line, he had to force down a sudden laugh. *It is a truth universally acknowledged, that a single man in possession of a good fortune, must be in want of a wife.* From this, he surmised she was either unbecomingly forward, in league with his mother, or had an unexpectedly acute sense of humour. Rather than discover which and ruin their playful encounter, he dipped back and trotted down the stairs, hoping she had the good sense not to follow.

Exiting the bookstore, he made a left onto Piccadilly and another in quick succession to bring him to the steps of White's.

'I had no expectation of seeing you today, Hazelhurst,' St

Germain said with some surprise, when Brick sat down at his lordship's table in the corner.

Brick poured several fingers of brandy into an empty glass on a silver tray. 'I stopped at Hatchards on the way to visit my mother and realised it would be better to ignore the summons from her.'

'A summons. Heavens. Does that mean you were caught in conversation with an imminently eligible female or disastrously ineligible one?' St Germain asked, with a deep, rolling chuckle.

Brick couldn't do anything but smirk at his friend's question. 'According to my mother, ineligible, although I've not had a single conversation with the girl.'

St Germain held his glass suspended halfway to his mouth and raised both eyebrows in question.

'She was at the Ballentine ball surrounded by a pack of other women, young and old. Among the former, according to my mother, one quite a diamond, one excessively eligible, one who earned only a grunt, and two more who "would never do"—my mother's words.'

'If Lady Ballentine deems her worthy of an invitation, she can't be at all ineligible.'

'Miss Emory, by all appearances, is perfectly eligible, at least for a gentleman wishing to be leg-shackled, which I am very much *not*.' His mother, it seemed, had an entire roster of the ladies in attendance, and when she saw him looking in that general direction had provided the name of every lady in the cosy group. The only one he bothered to commit to memory was hers.

The guffaw from across the table earned the pair several curious stares from other men in the room. It was a full minute before St Germain was able to speak through his laughter.

'Miss Emory? Perfectly eligible? There must be a second lady by that name I've yet to meet.' When Brick's mouth pulled into a straight line, St Germain laughed harder. Wiping the tears that had formed at the corner of his eyes, he said, gasping as he attempted to take in enough air, 'I can't recall the last time I laughed till I struggled to breathe. I thank you.'

'You seem to be of a mind with my mother, a situation I never thought possible.'

'What does your mother know of Miss Emory?'

'Very little. There may have been something about her being an ape leader. You know the trouble I have listening to my mother speak. Something in her tone makes the words impossible for my ears to hear. Perhaps you'd care to let me in on your little joke?'

'Don't tell me she's caught your interest, old man. That's one nut that will never be cracked.'

'I beg your pardon?'

'Now, now,' St Germain began, in a false placating tone. 'I've had the pleasure of encountering Miss Emory on any number of occasions over these last few years, and she is everything fair, lovely, and eligible—that is, if she had any desire to be wed. It is well known, or so I thought in any case, that she has no intention of marrying.'

Brick's brows furrowed. 'She remains single by choice?'

'Looking like that? Of course. Since her coming out some years ago she's turned down'—St Germain paused, a thoughtful look crossing his face—'at least twelve offers. Those are just the ones I've been privy to hear about. Entirely possible, good fellow, that there have been plenty more.'

'Twelve?'

'Twelve.'

'*Twelve*?'

'Honestly, Hazelhurst, I know you were gone for a time, but how is it you've never heard any of this?'

Brick shrugged in response. He refilled his glass and stared at the liquid settling in it, thinking that in the dimly lit club it was the same bronze colour as Miss Emory's hair.

'From what I've heard, her rejections are nothing out of the ordinary, aside from the act itself. She too much enjoys her current way of living, and as she will inherit something from her aunt and uncle, she's no need to secure her future in that way. She may be viewed as a little eccentric. After all, what's a woman without a husband?' he said, his words replete with sarcasm. 'But for my part, I admire her all the more for it.'

'You must be the only one. Surely, a woman cannot turn down so many eligible offers without giving rise to some speculation—something carrying her beyond eccentric.'

St Germain lifted a lazy shoulder. 'There's gossip, as there always is. She lost her heart to a man lost at sea—a most romantic take on spinsterhood—and my personal favourite.' He took a long swallow from the crystal glass in his hand, impervious to Brick's tapping his foot under the table in impatience. 'Shortly after she turned down Lansbury—'

At the mention of his cousin, Brick's eyes snapped up before narrowing with the certainty he wouldn't like what would be said next.

'—a rumour went round that she remained unattached because of an illegitimate child she was unwilling to give up.'

'Jesus. That daft prig.'

'You may calm yourself. The girl may be a trifle unusual, but she's a paragon of respectability.'

'I see.'

'You're piqued.'

'Am not.'

'By Lansbury?'

'Gentlemen! Did I hear my name? How flattered I am, Hazelhurst, that you deign to speak of me.' No one present missed the sarcasm in Lord Gareth Lansbury's voice as he dropped into an open chair at the table, ignoring the ferocious glare of his cousin. Their first encounter since Brick's return home had been frosty and fraught. Each one since had been filled with disdain on one side and bitterness on the other.

'We were only discussing the one woman in the world no man can entice to matrimony, as you are well aware,' added St Germain with a bite.

Anger flared in Lansbury's eyes. 'I'm afraid you've got me bested. I can think of any number of ladies I could have and none I cannot.'

'Come now, Lansbury. It wasn't so long ago the lovely Emory chit refused your offer.'

'I'll be sure to compliment her on her good sense next we meet in a drawing room,' Brick drawled as he raised his glass to his mouth, ready to be done with his cousin.

Lansbury poured himself a drink from the decanter on the table, threw it back in one swallow, and said with a belligerence suggesting it wasn't his first glass, 'Naturally, you would think yourself an exception. That prime article is a prize to be won, but I doubt even your title is enough without the bloodlines to accompany it.'

Brick heard St Germain's sharp intake of breath at such a blatant affront, but Brick had never known Lansbury to hold back an insult when opportunity presented itself. And his cousin wasn't wrong. Well, he was wrong about Brick not being able to win whatever it was he wanted, but he wasn't wrong about the bloodlines.

When Brick was born, his parentage had been a source of

delight for the gossips. Once he inherited, it became a matter of no importance to matchmaking mamas, and thanks to his accuracy with a pistol, it was now the thing everyone knew but rarely spoke of: Brick's father was the man who raised him, but not the man with whom he shared the same eye colour, or the same Roman nose with its subtle bump on the bridge, or even a passing resemblance. The way English law worked, it mattered not. His mother had long been married to the duke when Brick was born, and so a duke Brick would become. Lansbury felt robbed of his birthright—if not for Brick, the title and wealth passed down through more than twenty generations of Vesilys would have gone to Lansbury's father, and eventually Lansbury himself. Brick had spent the first half of his life trying to befriend a cousin who was only kind because he coveted what Brick had, and the second half needling that man whenever opportunity presented itself.

'We both know any woman with discerning taste would decline your offer, regardless of your position,' Brick said. 'As Miss Emory has in fact demonstrated, given you have never been deprived of wealth nor connections, despite your petulant lamentations.'

Mischief, spite, and rage warred on Lansbury's countenance. 'How about a wager?'

'To what? Steal a kiss on a darkened terrace? That's hardly a challenge. Compromise her? Which you know I will not do. Use my charm to convince her you're a catch? Impossible even for me.'

Lansbury took a slow swill of his drink, glaring over the rim of the glass at both men sitting across from him. 'I'll wager you cannot get her to say yes to *your* proposal.'

Brick's expression grew taut with contempt. 'I've no interest in taking a wife at present.'

Lansbury's smile held no humour. 'You've no interest in losing, in learning there is something beyond even your golden grasp.'

'Lansbury, you fool.' Brick's voice had turned to silk but kept its steel edge. '*When* she says yes, because of course she will, do you propose I ruin her reputation by reneging? That's more aligned with your character than my own.'

'Hazelhurst.' St Germain's voice cut in as a warning that Brick disregarded.

'You need not concern yourself. She'll never accept you.'

Brick scoffed. 'It matters not. I've no interest in accepting such a wager.'

'Not even for Milwell Lodge?'

The duke maintained a placid countenance despite the sudden feeling of heaviness in his chest. Milwell had been a favourite retreat of his father's, but as one of the few properties unentailed, the previous duke had left it to his brother, who in turn had given it to Lansbury while retaining a larger property in Kent for himself. A sense of foreboding settled over Brick. He had always been too impulsive by half and was only beginning to consider what Lansbury would ask for in return if the lodge was what he was willing to risk.

'I'll be generous and give you till the end of the season to try your luck. In fact, the months between now and then will be all the more entertaining for watching you fail.'

Brick was quick to do the maths. That was roughly four months—or three months and three weeks longer than he would need. He knew what women saw when they looked at him: more pin money than could ever be spent, playing hostess at an estate that rivalled most royal homes, how fine it would be to sign their correspondence *Duchess of Hazelhurst*. Even before inheriting, he hadn't met a single woman who didn't take pains to display her accomplishments, mention her connections, hint at her ability to manage an estate the size of Goldfinch Park. Miss Emory may be in possession of a well-developed mind, but she was still a woman.

'You want Milwell, I know you do.'

Lord St Germain's voice, lower and with a trace of disapproval, came again from Brick's side. 'Don't, Hazelhurst.'

But Brick did want Milwell Lodge, for the memories he had there with his father, hunting in the autumn, swimming in the summer. He hated thinking of that place being used by a man like Lansbury, sullying his father's memory. Brick knew what was going to come out of his mouth no matter how he fought it or how ill the prospect of the wager made him feel. 'Fine.'

'Don't you want to know what I get if—perhaps I ought to say *when*—you lose?'

'I won't lose.'

'*When* you lose, you will give me that handsome band on your little finger.'

Brick ran his thumb and forefinger over the signet ring, a heavy gold thing with an alder tree emblazoned upon it and a half-circle of tiny diamonds under the roots. The words *Courage, Duty, Honour* were engraved inside the band. It was more than a piece of jewellery—it was identity, authority, lineage moulded in gold.

There was nothing Brick valued as much as this ring. When he'd been a child of just nine or ten he had overheard two houseguests talking about his parentage and he'd repeated the conversation to his father. His Grace had taken Brick by the shoulders and had said, without equivocation or prevarication, 'In the ways that matter, you are my son, and I your father. Nothing and no one will ever change that. Words can only hurt if you let them. Do you understand, my boy?'

At the time, he didn't, not truly, and he wouldn't for several years. What he understood now was his father was the best of men, and he would sink his ring in the large lake at Goldfinch Park before he saw it worn by the likes of Lansbury. Brick could not wager his title. To Lansbury, the ring was the next best thing. He held out his hand, and Lansbury shook it.

'What's this? A wager?'

All three men at the table turned to see Mr Roberts walking by wearing an open expression of curiosity.

'Follow us to the book if you'd like. We're just on our way to record it,' Lansbury announced, making to rise.

'No,' Brick interrupted. 'We keep it out of the book.' He didn't truly think the lady's reputation would suffer—she came from a good family, and they weren't the first and would certainly not be the last men in the history of White's to wager on a woman. All the same, he preferred not to have it recorded for posterity. 'We have one witness, or two if you care to include Roberts.'

Roberts' only response, once brought into their confidence, was a sharp whistle that hissed in Brick's ear. 'Well, best of luck, old fellow. You know she turned me down once—three, maybe four years ago.'

St Germain shot a glance his friend's way, saying in a low, amused tone, as he did, 'Thirteen.'

7

*J*n the quiet of Hatchards, it had taken Vivienne a moment to discern where the odd shushing sound had been coming from. When she saw a boot so shiny it could light the dark pushing a book her way, she knew it was him, would have staked her life on it. Four, five long strides perhaps, would have taken her around the corner. It would have been so easy, and yet, she had remained rooted until the boot disappeared, held her breath as she pushed her own selection towards that same spot, vacillated between fear and hope he would appear.

Vivienne recognised something in herself that wished to be displeased with the book the unknown gentleman recommended to her, but she found herself lost in the poignant poems for hours at a time. There were even a few lines that helped her discover something that was missing from *Woman at Water's Edge*. It wasn't her preferred title for the painting that had become so dear to her, but *Wife, Mother, Drudge* might raise eyebrows, and she was already conflicted over the interest her work was beginning to garner.

Being acknowledged for her talent was everything she imagined ever wanting, but she harboured concerns that some curious person would wonder why the artist had never been seen, determine the 'W' was, as a matter of fact, a deformed 'VC', and dig and dig and dig until their shovel found her person. If history were to be held up as an example, there was every possibility the public response to such a reveal would be dreadful. People would accuse her of sleeping with other artists, simply because she dared to exist in the space. The work critics praised would be torn to bits, or worse, be called good 'for a woman'. She knew of some successful women painters, but only a few were English and none came from the gentry—at least none who dared do more than miniatures.

'Miss?'

'Yes, Maria?' Vivienne was seated in front of the mirror, her maid styling her hair for a musicale that evening.

'Is something on your mind? Only there was such a scowl upon your face just now and the lines...'

Vivienne reached up a forefinger to rub the little space between her eyebrows. Her aunt worried about wrinkles marring Vivienne's countenance, as she tended to furrow her brow when thinking over something.

'I'm quite all right, Maria.' She added a smile to punctuate her point. The little maid was very dear to her, having come with her from her parents' home, where she'd been taken on very young on account of her aunt being the Emorys' cook. 'We settled on the apple-green satin, but what think you of the blue silk instead?'

Like any good lady's maid, Maria had mastered stoicism and betrayed not so much as a flicker of interest when her mistress suggested a different dress than the one laid out for her—a first in all the years of Maria's employ. 'Certainly. When I finish with your hair, I'll see to it.'

Since the book exchange with the stranger, Vivienne had been to four dinners, two card parties, an opera, Vauxhall Gardens, and several routs. An empty schedule, in her aunt's opinion and compared to most of the *ton*, but the deadline for submissions to the Summer Exhibition at the Royal Academy was looming, and the sketch she'd started to get the stranger's face out of her mind had quickly turned into something more —something she wished to see hanging in the Great Room.

At one dinner and the rout, she'd indulged in a brief look about her. For the rest, she was quite proud that by and large she'd forgotten all about him, aside from the book of poetry that moved from her nightstand to the chair near the window, and the many sheets of paper in her studio celebrating his handsome face.

The unknown gentleman and her odd encounters with him had been neatly put aside in her mind that night when she entered the salon of some over-decorated townhouse in Curzon Street alongside her aunt and uncle.

Mrs Hempstead, their hostess and a woman who seemed to know everyone in London by name or face, was clutching one of Vivienne's hands, imploring her to exhibit on the pianoforte—which Vivienne declined on account of having no musical talent—when a prickle of awareness began at her neck and ran down the length of her body.

'It's quite all right, no need to quake. I like to offer all the young ladies the opportunity, but I would never dream of forcing any one of them into a situation that wouldn't show them to the best advantage. Ah!' Mrs Hempstead's face brightened, and she held out a hand, gesturing to someone behind Vivienne. 'Hazelhurst, come here, dear boy.'

Vivienne knew it was him; she could feel his warmth at her back, and it wasn't just the hairs on her neck now at attention, but every inch of her being suddenly awake to his presence. She was rooted in place and waited for him to come round, her discordant breaths verging on violent as she saw the intricate gold embroidery of his white waistcoat and followed the pattern up his solid chest. It was her first true look at him, and his proximity made her body feel heavy and hot. There was a moment's hesitation before she met his eyes, a moment to tuck away that ominous feeling that everything was about to change. When she did finally look up, it was like light from a dream passed between them. His eyes were sharp, vivid—the ephemeral blue-grey of water off the Cornish coast after a storm—and so compelling she felt as though she ought to step back beyond his reach.

'Your Grace, allow me to bring to your notice Lord and Lady Lane and their niece, Miss Emory.' The party exchanged greetings, mentioned the weather, offered pleasantries expressing their false delight in the evening's entertainment. Vivienne, however, was not listening. There was something about his name that echoed in the back of her mind, only she couldn't place it. Her aunt said something about a charity, and on the word, Mrs Hempstead recalled another pair she wished to make known to Lord and Lady Lane, whisking them off and leaving Vivienne to linger behind.

She put a steadying hand on the fluttering space below her breasts and turned to the duke, who had remained at her side. 'You are to be commended on your tastes, Your Grace.'

'Should I assign your compliment to the blue superfine I'm wearing, that happens to match your dress, or to the volume of poetry?'

Of course he was a flirt. That ought to have been expected.

What wasn't expected was how his voice—low, smooth, certain—sent a wave of awareness through her. She schooled her expression into one that was bland, unimpressed, and answered in an even voice, 'I'd like to say it's the coat so we may disagree on the writer's skill and merits, but I found myself rather enraptured by certain turns of phrase and the image he painted so clearly of him brushing his wife's hair in the poem about his grief when she died.'

He smiled. Her body seized, her mind raced, an image conjured from nowhere—him gazing at her in a crowded ball-room, some secret between them, a feeling that now she'd met him she could never *not* see him again.

She pressed down a thick swallow. 'Your turn, Your Grace. Tell me, how are you faring with your new book? It's a partic-ular favourite of mine, but I promise I won't hold it against you if you don't find yourself half as engrossed as I was when I first read it.'

When he spoke, there was laughter in his voice. 'Will you hold it against me if I tell you I stayed up late two nights in a row because I couldn't possibly wait another day to know how it was all resolved?'

'Not at all, but since I've already commended your taste I suppose I ought to admire your honesty for admitting so.'

He flushed so quickly it was gone before she was even sure she noticed anything.

'Tell me, Miss Emory, do you feel a connection with the heroine? Are you hoping to catch the eye of your own Mr Darcy?'

Vivienne didn't even trouble to contemplate the question. In her experience, no man was ever earnest in wishing to discuss opinions on literature, particularly if one was both a duke and a flirt, so she answered, 'I feel a connection with any lady who trims bonnets and enjoys dancing.'

The words brought the whisper of a frown to his lips and something like disappointment to his eyes. Perhaps he would have preferred her to swoon at the suggestion of a Mr Darcy for herself. Well, if he didn't like that response, he wouldn't like the next one either. She couldn't say what compelled her to go on, but in a flat voice she added, 'No, actually. As a matter of fact, I feel sympathetic toward the youngest girl.'

If he had hoped to hide his surprise, he failed, although he settled his raised eyebrows after hardly a moment. 'The one who eloped? Who very nearly ruined her entire family and all her sisters' chances of happiness?'

'She's a product of her environment, of a lack of care and concern and parenting. The mother provides a poor example, but the father provides none at all.'

'Be that as it may, is not a girl of fifteen old enough to understand the consequences of her actions?'

'Certainly, but what business does a man of eight-and-twenty have running off with her to begin with? There's no denying she's foolish, but she's also full young and no doubt intoxicated on the attention and experience of a first season. Still, she set her mind on something. She knew what she wanted and got it. There's something admirable in that.'

'Is there?' His question was all dubiousness.

'Compare her to the neighbour who we are told is in love with the eldest sister. How easily he's persuaded away from her. He's a man with all the power to do as he pleases, who knows what he wants, and yet doesn't take any steps to secure his happiness until nearly a year has passed and he's encouraged by the same friend who first discouraged him. There's a weakness of character in that, that the youngest sister, for all her faults, knows nothing of.'

Vivienne worked not to fidget under his penetrating stare. It was not her habit to speak so, to display the parts of her that had no part in polite society.

As he made to reply, a spark of roguish mischief flashed in his eyes. 'If it's debate that would please you, Miss Emory, perhaps you'll accompany me to the painting hanging on the far wall there,' he said, with a nod in its general direction. 'It's much admired among the *ton*, and I believe Mr Hempstead paid quite a fortune to secure it for his wife, but every time I stand in this room, I feel further from seeing in it what others must.'

She nodded once. The duke held out his arm for her to take, despite the short distance between where they stood and where the painting hung. Vivienne was too aware of how the hard muscle of his bicep filled her whole hand. All her attention, or so she convinced herself, was on the painting now in front of them.

'I'll own there are few landscapes I count personal favourites, but there's a lot to admire in this work.' She glanced at the painter's name in the corner before adding, 'He's well known for these pieces—one of the Devonshire pastureland series, I believe.'

The duke, without looking at her, challenged her assertion. 'What is there to admire? It's a pastoral scene—the view, the prospect, not exceptionally interesting or pleasing, and surely most of us have seen such before.'

'Yes, but have any one of us ever seen it through his eyes?' Vivienne heard the slight exasperation rising in her voice and took a breath. 'Look how he captures it with such detail, such care.' She used the opportunity to untangle her hand from his person and moved a step closer to the painting. 'Look at the minute brush-strokes he uses here to create the rain falling in torrents, blown back by wind we can't see but can feel by the movement he created. And here,' she said, bringing her hand towards the middle of the canvas, pretending she couldn't feel his assessing, intelligent eyes on her and not on the painting. 'See how he finds the right balance of light and dark to shade this inlet as the clouds begin to move across the land? We can see sheep, and right there is a shepherd watching the storm. We know he's nervous through his rigid posture and can share in his worry because, as you said, many of us have seen this exact scene before in our own counties.'

Vivienne studied the painting; the duke studied her.

'You didn't tell me you were a bluestocking. Had I known, I would have selected alternative reading material for you.'

She flustered a little, realising far too late how much she'd given away in their exchange, and asked with some asperity, 'Can a woman not appreciate art, sir?' As soon as the question was out, a flash of recognition flared in her memory, and she knew exactly why his name was so familiar to her.

His smile was a little queer but not malicious when he replied. 'What you just displayed was not appreciation, Miss Emory. It was *knowledge*.'

Vivienne, her thoughts in disarray as she matched this man to his odious mama from the British Institution, could make no immediate reply and was spared from the necessity of doing so when the call came for people to move to the music room. Her aunt and uncle came over to collect her, but the duke threaded her hand through his arm, and without much choice, as her uncle had already begun moving away with her aunt, she accepted it and allowed herself to be led to a back row.

'Do you play, Miss Emory?' the duke asked, dipping his

head towards her as he did so and sending a caressing puff of warm air down her exposed neck. Vivienne worked to keep her focus on Miss Turner, who had begun to plunk out a lively Scottish air, and not on the proximity of his lips to her ear.

'Very little and quite ill, much to my aunt's despair.'

'How shocking for a lady of your station.'

She suspected him of teasing her and added, 'As a matter of fact, I'm also deficient in netting purses, embroidery, and the harp. Although I'll own to speaking both French and Italian fluently.'

His only reply was a lilting close-mouthed smile, and when he made no other, she ventured to say, 'It's odd, is it not, the ways in which females are expected to be accomplished?'

'You are saying proficiency on the pianoforte serves no other purpose than to entertain? I am all shock.' His voice was full of mirth, and her own lips twitched as she repressed a grin.

'I am saying we praise men like the one who painted that pastoral scene and call them artists, but a young lady who plays as well as any of the renowned composers will only ever be allowed to be accomplished.'

The duke turned his head a little in her direction, a curious, uncertain look upon his face, and she chastised herself for expunging the levity from their exchange. Never before had she allowed herself to challenge such accepted opinions or to speak so freely to someone in whom her own understanding was deficient, and she could not account for her behaviour.

'You would compare Miss Turner to Beethoven?'

'I would compare any lady of talent to a man considered by society her better and be unsurprised to find her talent equal to if not in excess of his.'

'You wish to attend a concert and watch a woman bowing a

violin? See that pastoral scene with Eliza or Anne or Mary scrawled in the corner rather than John or George or Edward?'

'Would not you?'

The duke was silent for a long moment—too long for Vivienne's pleasure, and she was beginning to think the son was much more like his mother than she first gave him credit for.

'I suppose that must depend on the woman in question. If a woman has not been given the same opportunities as a man, the same education, tutors, travel to study the masters and build upon her own abilities, is it truly possible for her skill to exceed his?'

'Then perhaps we ought to provide equal opportunity. Certainly a woman could have penned Shakespeare's plays had she been the recipient of the same education.'

'You desire my agreement, but who am I to make such decisions?'

Red-hot anger flooded Vivienne, but rather than cry out in outrage, she dragged her eyes over him from leather shoes to cravat, lingering a moment too long on his firm, full mouth, which had settled into a tense, tight smirk.

'My mistake, Your Grace. It is true you dress the part, but perhaps you prefer to wield the power you hold for personal advantage rather than greater good. I see now you are one of *those* people.'

'I beg your pardon?'

'People who believe women are the intellectual and artistic inferiors of men—therefore incapable of excelling beyond the four walls of her home—and who attribute any skill in her playing or painting, or whatever else, to a man, whether a father, a husband, or a lover.'

'How do you suppose a man can play for a woman at the pianoforte? Does she sit upon his lap, her hands atop his own?

That's a rather different kind of exhibition, Miss Emory, although one I am happy to be part of if you'd care for a lesson. I'm proficient enough on the pianoforte for us both and happy to be your teacher.'

Two red spots formed on her cheeks. Not because she was awash with indignation, although she would have given a little huff of annoyance had she been able to breathe. It was the immediate and detailed image his words called to mind. His chest of stone and arms of marble wrapped around her, his fingers threaded through her own and gliding their hands as one over the black and white keys. She swallowed a little cough, the pause not long enough for her to form any witty reply, and so she settled for a haughty 'I refer to composition, *obviously*.'

'Obviously,' he repeated dryly.

They sat in silence for the rest of Miss Turner's performance, but for the entirety of the lengthy display, Vivienne was too aware of the duke's presence—the large thigh threatening the seam of his breeches, the broad shoulders grazing the sleeve of her dress because they could do no less, the jaw carved by Michelangelo. He was—physically, anyway— perfection. As an artist, *only* as an artist, she was desperate to thumb his hard edges, pluck out something in him no one else could see, immortalise his sharp angles on canvas. Somewhere in the middle of the performance, his eyes skidded over to find hers firmly fixed his direction. A subtle pink hue rose from her chest to her hairline, but the duke's lip pulled up at the corner as if he knew there was nowhere else her attention would be besides on him. *Insufferable*.

When the young lady had finished, Vivienne excused herself on account of needing to speak to her aunt and walked away from the duke on a silent wish that their paths would never again cross. Not just because she found him exasperating, but because despite him being so, he was like a magnet drawing her near. She knew enough of the female artists who had come before her to know the danger in desire, in wanting to be both a woman who softened for a man and a woman who must always remain hard to compete with them. It was impossible to be both. She had already made her choice—but half an evening spent in company with the duke, and he had begun to unravel her. Vivienne despised him all the more for it.

8

'*N*o, Brick, not her.'

'Not who, ma'am? And for what? If you ever want me to understand you, you must give up speaking in riddles,' the duke teased his mother as his carriage rumbled down the road. Already he was blessing the very short distance between the Hempsteads' home and his mother's own.

'That Emory chit. You were in her company far too long tonight.'

Brick levelled an empty look at her. 'She's interesting company.'

'Which is nothing to the point. I made inquiries—discreet, of course—and she's not a match for you. There is nothing wrong with the aunt and uncle with whom she resides, but niece to a viscount is not good enough for you. That's to say nothing of her mother or father. Her father was a gentleman, but her mother was the daughter of a tradesman.' The dowager puckered her mouth as if the word trade were as sour on her tongue as a lemon.

Brick refrained from pointing out the hypocrisy of her obsession over lineage and ran a hand over his face to keep the thought in. 'Really, Mother, we need not have this conversation.'

'We do. You need to marry. You need an heir. Better to start with a young wife, one in her prime who has plenty of years to fill Goldfinch Park with children.'

'Jesus.'

'Will not help you now, nor will a woman in her twenty-anything years. Lady Felicity will make you an unexceptional wife. You have only to trust a mother's intuition.'

'Yes, that worked so well last time.' The remark was beneath him, but he didn't regret making it, even when his mother rapped her cane on the floor of the carriage in frustration and exasperation.

'Enough, Brick! Your sisters never gave me so much trouble.'

'You too often indulged me.' It was the truth. As her only son and the heir, he had been fawned over and given a long rope on which to run. His sisters, on the other hand, had been raised to be dutiful daughters who did as their parents wished, and, once married, did as their husbands wished. He liked his sisters as well as any brother could, but he hated spending time with them. They were all dreadful bores with the exception of the youngest, who had passed away from a bad bout of scarlet fever almost ten years prior. She was the only one he ever missed.

'Now I must reap what I sow is your point, I suppose. It matters not. You're not a child, and you have a duty to this family—to me, to your father, God rest his soul—and I am out of patience with you. Find a wife, a suitable one, or I will find one for you.'

'And your plan for forcing my hand? Running a notice in *The Times*?'

'Yes.'

'Remarkably flawed, coming from you, ma'am. Ought I be concerned for your faculties?' He need not have said so. It would be awkward to cry off, and he would wish to do so without damaging the reputation of whichever poor young lady had been browbeaten into agreeing to the scheme, but both he and his mother knew he would suffer no ill effects in doing so. It was her only threat, and a weak one at that. He had a title. He had an estate. He had wealth.

'You cannot continue to tarry as you have been doing, Brick. Your uncle appears stout enough, but so did your father, and Lansbury—' She cast a beseeching look towards the heavens. 'Only imagine what he would do to Goldfinch Park. He'd sell the silver and the tapestries, lose the Rembrandts and Ruysdaels in a foolish game of chance. It wouldn't surprise me in the least if he gambled away the whole pile while your grave was still fresh.'

'A little melodramatic, ma'am, do not you think? Besides, if you were on this mortal coil and I was not, I'd hope you would be too deeply drowned in sorrow to notice.'

Her eyes narrowed. 'You jest as if I know nothing of what goes on. I know everything, and I'll not go to my own grave until the succession is settled, with a whole brood of stout boys running through the halls of Goldfinch. Enough for an entire regiment.'

A minute later they arrived at the steps of his mother's home, and when she was safely inside, Brick sent his carriage home and opted to walk the half mile to his club in St James's.

'You did not tell me,' he said, taking a seat between St

Germain and Roberts in one of the card rooms, 'about Miss Emory's most notable quality.'

'What's that?' Roberts asked.

'Her intelligence.'

His lordship didn't look up from his cards, but there was a hint of casual interest in his reply. 'Is she? I had no idea.'

'It's rather a shame she opened her mouth and ruined the illusion.'

'Illusion of what?'

'Perfection,' Brick replied in even tones. He signalled to the man holding the bank and avoided eye contact with his friend, in a bid to appear unaffected by his encounter with Miss Emory. 'You must tell me, Roberts, whatever possessed you to make an offer for a woman with such prodigious intellect?' He went on, 'I had thought you more interested in finding an unremarkable, placid wife to please your mama.'

'Who's that now?'

'Miss Emory. I cannot conceive how a woman so free in her displays of opinions and ideas, one who shirks the very notion of duty and with no desire to marry, has managed to secure as many offers as she has.'

'You've seen the lady, have you not, Hazelhurst?'

It seemed all the explanation Mr Roberts was capable of offering, so Brick prompted him further. 'I have had that pleasure, yes, as well as the more dubious one of engaging her for the length of a conversation.'

'Is that so? I spent some little time in company with her at any number of events and even took her out driving once or twice and feel we must be talking at cross purposes.' After a thoughtful moment, Mr Roberts added, 'In fact, I'm quite sure we are. Talked of the weather, the theatre, her time in Norfolk with her relations, and the easy ways she spends the days in the country. Nothing of consequence. She was everything the gentle sex is expected to be.'

This admission, in creating so different a vision of the woman in his own mind, gave Brick pause.

'The bet is going well for you, then?' St Germain asked, entering the conversation once more. 'I'll own to feeling a little surprised, Hazelhurst, as I consider you a man with rather forward ideas. Besides, a spirited woman—'

'There's spirited, and there's Miss Emory.'

'You can't punish an entire sex for the sins of one.'

Brick cut St Germain's thought short with a withering glare in his general direction before focusing once more on the cards in his hand. 'That's just the thing, isn't it?' he said, scorn, not pride, in his voice. 'I can do whatever I please.'

Saint's gaze flashed with something like compassion but didn't waver. 'Then do something that makes you happy.'

Brick was not, as much as he wished to be, indifferent to his duties as Duke of Hazelhurst, which meant he would eventually take a wife, as much as he enjoyed teasing his mother into believing otherwise. His father was the best of men, and Brick, even in his worst moods, never considered for a moment doing anything but carrying on the legacy of the Vesily name. That dedication was how he'd found himself standing alone at the altar in St George's seven years ago at three-and-twenty.

When Brick next opened his mouth, he surprised himself as much as his two friends. 'It wasn't really her fault, *The Honourable* Amelia Bromwell. She was raised to do her duty to her family, had likely been told as much of the weighty expectations she bore even before understanding what it meant. When you think of it in such terms, is it not impressive she left me at the altar?'

'What are you getting at, Hazelhurst?' Saint asked, both his cards and his glass on the table and all his attention riveted to his friend.

'Nothing.'

It wasn't nothing at all. Brick had only just realised he'd been looking at the matrimonial state, and the candidates, all wrong.

ith a frustrated little growl, Vivienne pressed her thumb into the centre of the charcoal pencil in her hand until she felt the satisfying snap of the wood splintering away from itself, the sharp crack filling the silence of her studio as she let the two pieces fall away.

She clipped a fresh sheet of paper to her easel and picked up her favourite pencil for sketching, beginning with a long vertical mark in the centre on which she could hang the rectangle that would turn into his moulded shoulders and chest. After first seeing the duke in the street, she couldn't get his face from her mind and so did the only thing she could: she began to draw him. But what she thought of him, how she saw him on paper, had changed with every interaction, and now she couldn't get his proportions or the planes of his face right. She went through half a new rubber trying, and still, his lips were too thin, his jaw too hard-set, the expression in his eyes too open.

What was supposed to be a simple sketch after seeing him in Bond Street rolled over into a new day, required a new sheet of paper. Another after seeing him at the Ballentine ball, and again when they first met. By the time the remainder of the rubber was gone from erasing and erasing and erasing, Vivienne decided to tuck the sheet away altogether.

She was debating which was more irritating—the man in real life or the man on paper—when a knock at the door of her studio put an end to her struggle.

'What?' The one syllable snapped out of her mouth as she wiped her hands on her apron and went to see what was so important that her dedicated work time was being interrupted.

Her aunt greeted her with pinched lips, surely unappreciative of Vivienne's sharp tone. 'Miss Boyton is downstairs with her mama.'

'Anabel!' Vivienne exclaimed, with a mix of surprise and genuine joy. She untied her apron as she moved to pull the bell for Maria. Anabel Boyton was Vivienne's dearest friend, and it had been an age since they'd last seen one another. They exchanged letters, of course, but it was never quite the same as walking arm-in-arm, whispering confidences, sharing gossip, laughing over absurd little things that never seemed quite as amusing when put in writing.

'I thought perhaps you girls might care for a stroll while her mama and I take tea? You've hardly left the house in some days, and you two must have lots of news to talk over.'

'Certainly. I'll be down directly.'

Maria helped Vivienne with her hair and into a fresh dress —one she didn't wear for work, that didn't reek of turpentine, and wasn't covered in paint splatters. Her sweet maid knew Vivienne perhaps better than anyone. On occasion, when Vivienne was forced to leave her art behind and return to the present, she found herself the object of Maria's perceptive stare, as if her maid knew which subtle signs precipitated a change in mood and was simply exercising great patience with her mistress.

For Vivienne, the more challenging the project, the harder it was for her to switch from her artist self to her society self and to ignore the thing that continued to occupy her mind as she smiled, discussed the weather, nodded as some gentleman exhausted the merits of hunting in the Midlands compared to the north country.

Even with Anabel, Vivienne kept this part of herself a secret, but on days like this one, she longed to walk downstairs, take her friend's hands in her own, and tell her of the struggles that had darkened her mood. Instead, she worked her grimace into some sort of a smile and greeted her friend with 'I thought you weren't due in town for another week at least!'

'Aunt Mary is *so* unpredictable. There we were, cosy as you'd like by the fire, hardly eight days ago, when she proclaims over her coffee that she's had enough of the quiet and is quite ready for town. She put every maid and footman to work, had our trunks packed, and two days later the house was closed up. I hardly had time to get a letter off to Mama. Who, by the bye, didn't even let me settle in before parading me out.'

'Still worried you're destined for a sharp decline if you don't marry soon?'

'It seems to me that marriage is the greater risk. I saw Mrs Patchett only last night, and let me say, Vivi, that she may have given her husband an heir, but her figure will *never* recover. Oh, and the new Lady Cameron! Do you recall how everyone thought it was a love match? Well, Lord Cameron was seen at the opera with a woman who most certainly not his wife, unless her ladyship sprouted up six or more inches and dyed her golden locks a sallow brown.'

'Haven't you only just arrived? This may be a record, even for you,' Vivienne teased, always amazed at the volume of information her friend seemed to gather with very little effort. Perhaps that was merely an effect of not locking oneself away in one's studio.

It had taken mere minutes for the two of them to make the short walk from Grosvenor Square to Hyde Park, with Maria behind them at a little distance.

'Oh!' Anabel exclaimed as they meandered down one of the wide lanes, nodding to acquaintances here and there. 'That's not even the best bit. Guess who I saw only last night at the Jevingtons' card party? Have you any idea? No, I don't think you do.'

Vivienne's mouth curved into a wide, happy smile for the first time in at least three days, and she tugged Anabel, whose arm was linked through her own, a little closer so their shoulders bumped. There was no one so enthusiastic as her friend, and she was only realising how dearly she had missed her and how backward she sometimes was in showing her appreciation. Anabel's exuberant nature balanced out Vivienne's own, which tended toward the serious more often than not.

'Then why don't you tell me, or we'll be walking until the morrow.'

'He who was banished and has only just returned. Well, to town, anyhow.'

Vivienne, not at all following along, lifted one brow in confusion.

'The Hellion,' stated Anabel, staring at her friend as if the answer were the most obvious in the whole of England.

When Vivienne remained silent, Anabel said with an edge

of impatience, 'The Duke of Hazelhurst. Goodness me. You're familiar with the man, are you not?'

'I made his acquaintance for the first time several days ago,' she replied, clearing her throat a little and hoping the bit of heat she felt in her cheeks wasn't outwardly noticeable. 'What? What is it?' she asked, in response to the odd look Anabel was giving her.

'Are you blushing?'

'No.'

'You are! It's no matter. You're not the first young lady to flush when his name is mentioned, and you certainly won't be the last, although I personally prefer Lord St Germain. That man is a treat to look at, has been as long as I've known him. He went to school with Frederick, you know, and came to Woodruff Abbey several times,' she added with a faraway look. 'But I digress. Tell me about you and the duke.'

Questions of her own were forming in Vivienne's mind, but she said only, 'There's nothing to tell.'

'Your countenance suggests otherwise.'

Vivienne chewed her bottom lip and drew in a deep breath through her nose, noting with a passing thought how the air smelt of dirt after a good rain. 'All right. If you must know, we sat next to one another for a performance at a musicale, and I find he is not at all to my taste.'

Everything about Anabel's person, excepting her clothing, suggested disbelief. 'Be serious. He is to every woman's taste.'

'His countenance is fine enough. But his manners and his way of thinking are not.'

A little bubble of laughter burst from Anabel before she could smother it with her hand. 'Fine enough? You proclaim a desire to remain unwed—very credibly, too—but I never thought you so odd as this! Who gives two figs what his manners are like?'

'I do. Or I did when trapped in his company, which I plan to avoid in future.'

'The other young ladies will thank you, I'm sure.'

Vivienne came to an abrupt stop, tugging her friend's arm as she did so. 'What did you mean when you said he was banished?'

'Oh.' The one syllable came out in accents of airy artlessness. 'I had not thought you interested in him.'

'Not interested.' Vivienne looked straight ahead, chin jutted upwards. 'Curious.'

'I'd thought every lady from sixteen to sixty knew him by report, if not in other ways.' Anabel giggled, giving her friend's arm a little squeeze.

A sidelong glance and a little lift of her shoulder were all the reply Vivienne offered.

'Well,' Anabel began, looking skyward. 'I suppose you weren't quite out when he was conquering town, and this, I believe, is the first time he's come down for the season since returning to England.'

'If I wasn't out, neither were you. How do you know all this?'

'It's what elder sisters are for. That, and buying all the pretty new ribbons for the younger ones to steal. There was one time—'

'Anabel.'

'Oh, yes, where was I? He was sent off to the continent some years ago for killing a man in a duel.'

'What?' The word came out nearer a shriek than Vivienne had intended, but her shock at the statement was more than her composure could withstand.

Anabel hushed her friend. 'He was betrothed to some girl —goodness me, what was her name?' They took a few steps forwards in silence as Anabel tried to recall the other party of this story. 'Well, it will come to me. The point being, he was engaged and presented himself at the wedding, as a groom ought, only *she* did not.'

Vivienne gasped, the amount of air she inhaled nearly choking her.

'I know, I know. What lady lucky enough to land him would dare do such a thing? It gets worse. It wasn't just that she didn't arrive—she ran off with another man, some Scottish lord she'd fancied herself in love with. Something she did rather often, it seems—fall in love, that is. The man had already inherited, too. Not that *that* had anything to do with it.' Anabel's look suggested it very much did. 'I'm not at all clear on the specific details beyond what I've shared. I only know that the duke pursued them all the way to the border, felt the slight too great to be let go of, and so met the man on the field of honour. The duke, even then, was purported to be an excellent shot; very likely he could shoot a quizzing glass out of your hand from fifty yards. Well, the handkerchief was dropped, both men fired. The duke was wounded, but it was the other man who sustained a fatal injury. And before you go feeling sorry for the lady, it was not so long after she was carried out to sea on a wave of her tears that she was once again in love, this time with some Italian count. She married him, if I remember the story correctly, and moved to Milan.'

Vivienne's head swam, the figures of those walking nearby turned to blurry shapes of muted colours, and if not for the support of her friend, she might have gone so far as to faint.

'His papa—oh, which is another thing, but never mind that. His papa,' Anabel began again, without a care for her friend's bemused expression, 'was still alive then, and their title is an old one. *Very* old—handed down by Henry I. The whole affair was hushed up, and the king sent him to India in service to the crown by way of turning a blind eye. Of course, things like that are bound to get around, one way or another.'

Several minutes back, Vivienne had put a hand to her open mouth, where it remained.

'Now he's returned to town for a season, and the poor man can't sneeze without everyone speaking about it.'

'That's awful.' Vivienne's tongue had been stuck to the roof of her mouth and the words were hard to get out.

'Indeed. To have your betrothed leave you at the altar! I would positively die of shame.'

'Anabel! Who cares about that? What of the poor man who died?'

Her friend tilted her head a little as if considering the question. 'As far as I know, 'tis a perfectly acceptable reason to issue a challenge.'

'How can you be so glib?'

Anabel tutted her. 'You wish me to feel badly for a man I've never met who did wrong. Meanwhile, the duke is the one who suffered all the mortification of the moment and whose dark, brooding countenance is handsome enough to make any young lady question the true worth of her virtue.'

'Anabel!'

'My apologies. Any young lady except you.'

Vivienne smiled at the tease but said nothing. Virtue was the only thing a genteel young lady possessed that was worth anything, and being a painter made her even more aware of the importance of maintaining an air of impenetrable respectability, as if in doing so she could shield herself from the kind of rumours that would connect her name to a man's, if ever her identity became known.

'How is it you're utterly unaware of all of this?'

'I've not a gaggle of older sisters to inform me of the best gossip.' It was half true. She'd heard the duke's name mentioned once or twice in conversation but always assumed he was of an age with her uncle and was never much interested in someone she'd no notion of ever meeting, except perhaps for a brief introduction in a drawing room. Beyond that, when her nose was in the papers, it wasn't to read about some terribly handsome man shooting someone. She leafed through caricatures, art critiques, reviews.

The two settled into silence, taking a left turn towards the Queen Anne Garden by tacit agreement. It was one of their favourite places within the great big park, and the best, they agreed, for watching people come and go. Vivienne was relieved Anabel said nothing further on the subject of the duke. The man had intrigued her, irritated her, and now incensed her. There was something hypocritical in his behaviour—a kind of passion he was able to display that he would censure in others—that bothered her, to say nothing of his callousness in mortally wounding another man.

She had recently excused herself from a number of engagements with her aunt and uncle on account of work, the deadline for the Summer Exhibition at the Royal Academy always at the forefront of her mind. She told herself her desire to avoid a certain duke and the dangerous ways in which he provoked her played not the smallest role in her absence from society.

And still, there was nothing she could do to prevent her eyes, her mind, her hands, from returning to the sketch of his person. The challenge of capturing his innate confidence, the powerful masculinity at the core of his being, the slate blue eyes that were at once wild and discerning. The mouth that was frowning or smiling or knowing but somehow always sensual, always beckoning her.

'Vivienne? Vivienne?'

Vivienne responded to Anabel's singsong voice with a little murmuring sound, her thoughts not yet returned to the present moment.

'Am I right to think you'd rather not cross paths with the duke again?'

'Not if it can be helped,' she replied, with no little asperity.

'Then perhaps we ought to walk on.'

Her friend's words filled the air between them just as a tingling sensation began to crawl up the back of Vivienne's neck.

10

*B*rick felt the impossibility of keeping his eyes from wandering in the direction of Miss Emory—her fine figure, the graceful curve of her neck, the mouth that betrayed her as a woman of more interesting parts than she let on. Not for the first time, he regretted the ruin of their delightful, delicious beginning.

The dreary little article perched next to him in his phaeton was prattling away about something so boring he'd stopped listening before they ever entered the park. For this piece of bad luck he cursed his mother, who'd sent a note asking him to come and see her that morning, failing to mention she wouldn't be alone. He had hardly set foot in the front parlour before the dowager suggested he take Lady Felicity for a drive.

'Then Miss Breason asked if I'd seen the awful dress Lady Rose was wearing, which of course I had, because how could anyone not? Only at that exact moment we were both taken by surprise when the lady herself came over, but she only remained with us a moment, because no sooner did she arrive at our side than Mr Alvaney came up asking her for a dance—

her!—in that hideous cherry dress, which isn't even a colour a girl in her first season should be wearing, and as we watched her go...'

Brick wondered if his ears were bleeding, or if they only felt as much, and did nothing to prevent a gusty sigh from escaping him. Lady Felicity would never hear it over her monologue.

'Ought we converse on something beyond ladies and their raiment?'

Impatience strained the elegant young lady's features, and when she cast a reproachful look his direction, Brick was forced to repress a derisive chuckle.

'What else is there to discuss, Your Grace? The weather is fine; the theatre was boring; neither of us are in possession of a cough or gout or some other ailment that may be of interest.'

'What think you of *First Impressions*?'

'Did you not only just say you wished to speak of something beyond ladies and fashion?' Lady Felicity asked, not with confusion but with exasperation.

'I did, which is why I sought your opinion on a novel.'

'As if I've time to read more than a few lines of poetry, to stay current, you know. Besides, Mama believes novels are for those too poor or too ugly to pursue other enjoyment, and that is to say nothing of the ideas contained in them, which, if adopted by a young woman, must materially lessen her attractions, or make her so stupid as to think *romance* the most important thing in a relationship.' The young lady nearly gagged on the word.

'I see.'

'Oh, I do beg your pardon, of course,' she cooed, peeping up at him through her lashes. '*You* must know something of the word, to hie off to Scotland as you did, although it was undoubtedly a lesson learned.'

'Tell me what lesson that was, my lady?'

'Not to trifle with romantic females, of course.'

'Ah, I thought perhaps you might mention the discovery that a man could shoot another and still be the season's best and biggest catch.'

'As if one has anything to do with the other.'

To Brick, it seemed as though perhaps they should. Driven by boredom or disgust or something else altogether, he steered the phaeton down the lane where Miss Emory now walked, pulling up alongside the lady and her companion. It didn't go unnoticed by him as the little gig came to a standstill that neither looked surprised at his appearance.

'Miss Emory,' he said, tipping his head in acknowledgment. 'A pleasure.'

She and the woman next to her curtsied, although he was certain he heard her say under her breath something rather like 'For whom?'

'May I present Lady Felicity Wright, daughter of the Marquess of Burlingham?'

'Charmed.' The word was as flat as the ribbon tied round Lady Felicity's waist.

'How do you do? This is Miss Anabel Boyton.'

'Of the Devonshire Boytons?' he asked.

The young woman responded in the affirmative.

'I was at Cambridge with your brother, Frederick.' They spoke casually of her family for a few moments, and Brick could feel Miss Emory's observant eyes upon him. When he glanced her way, her expression rested somewhere between impatient and annoyed. It made his lips tip upward in the barest hint of a smile.

His next inquiry was directed at her. 'Are you enjoying the unseasonably fine weather?'

'I was.'

Brick's mouth twisted wryly, but he managed to smother a whole grin at her sharp response.

The crunch of carriage wheels as they passed and the murmur of slow conversation happening all around them was not enough to take the awkward edge from the quiet.

Miss Boyton, with too-cheery a voice, said, 'Lady Felicity, what lovely lace on your dress. I noticed it as soon as you approached.'

The young lady next to Brick looked at the lace as if it were the first time she were seeing it and scrunched her nose a little.

'Yes, I suppose it is.' She brushed an imaginary piece of something from her blue kid gloves before adding, 'It should be, at any rate. It's the same as the Duchess of Avondale uses on all her walking dresses.'

'The duchess is known for her exquisite taste,' Miss Boyton replied, with incredible diplomacy.

'Mama believes it the responsibility of a lady of rank to follow the example of her betters so she may demonstrate the foremost principles of fashion, character, and decorum to her inferiors. As the daughter of a marquess, I am, understandably, limited in who I may look to.' The lady said the last with her nose so far in the air as to make it a wonder she was able to see those standing on the ground at all.

'What a charming sentiment,' cooed Miss Emory, with a pleasant, innocuous smile, 'to compliment the charming picture you two make.'

Brick felt, rather than saw, Lady Felicity preening next to him. In a show of possession, she would have looped her hand through his arm had he not held it tight against his side.

'How kind of you to say so,' he returned, his tone droll. 'Miss Emory has quite the discerning eye.'

'Some shades are not so obscure as others. It hardly takes a discerning eye, as you would call it, to see the grass is green and Lady Felicity's dress yellow.'

'You cannot convince me *you* see only green when you look at the grass, yellow when you look at her dress, or just blue if you look towards the sky.'

A muscle twitched at the very edge of her lip, but he noticed it all the same and pressed on.

'The shade is jonquil, actually,' interjected Lady Felicity, to the notice of no one.

'Tell me, Miss Emory, what is it you truly see when you contemplate the heavens?'

She ran her tongue over her lips as she considered the question, the movement momentarily distracting him. 'A gradient of colour not unlike the changing shades of blue in your eyes and an infinite expanse that reminds me of my own smallness against it.'

'Really, Miss Emory, you grow odder by the day,' sneered Lady Felicity.

'No doubt it seems that way to you,' Miss Emory replied kindly. She flicked her eyes briefly in his direction. Brick wasn't fooled. He saw the amusement—the mockery—in those pools of sea green. It struck him for the first time how very alike they were in some ways.

'Ah, I see my aunt waving. You'll excuse us.' Miss Emory dropped a curtsey, and her friend, looking a little bewildered, did the same, before the two stepped back from the phaeton.

He was almost certain he was being lied to, but he was diverted rather than upset by the idea and sent the gig in motion once more, a little smile playing about the corners of his mouth.

'I would positively *die* if I were unmarried at her age. Have the decency to be widowed, at the very least. My eldest brother was thinking of making her an offer last season and I suppose thought better of it, since I cannot conceive even her turning down the heir to a title and a tidy fortune. Can you imagine?'

He could. 'You are familiar with the lady, then?'

'Only by reputation. I've overheard my brother and his idiot friends mention her name when they're in their cups and think themselves well alone.'

Brick couldn't tell who bore the brunt of the young lady's judgement: the men for doing what men do, or the lady for the indecent crime of being *mentioned* by them.

'She seems to me one of those women who seeks to set themselves apart by being outrageous.'

'Remaining unwed is hardly outrageous.'

Lady Felicity turned her fine-featured face towards him, her pert little nose wrinkled and her pouty lips curled in distaste. 'You may say so. There is nothing outrageous about a man remaining a bachelor, particularly one who may choose to wed when and where he pleases.'

The purring way she said so made Brick's skin itch.

'Men hunt and gamble and travel. They have more opportunities for enjoyment than a woman. Besides, men take mistresses. A woman cannot do the same until she's provided her husband with an heir.'

The forthright and matter-of-fact way she said this caused Brick to choke on the breath he'd just taken.

'You speak as if that's a certainty.'

'Is it not? Oh!' Lady Felicity clapped her hands. 'Let's make it a game. One of us names the society couple, and one of us names their lovers.'

Brick had not taken a mistress since he returned to England, although he supposed he would eventually once he married. Sooner, perhaps. But he had not expected a woman vying for the role of duchess to approach the subject with open and unabashed delight, nor was he prepared for how repugnant he suddenly found the idea. When he married, it would be a union of two hearts, two souls, two bodies. There would be no room for outsiders.

'It would not distress you to know I was seen at the theatre with my mistress or that I gifted her an extravagant set of sapphires?'

She looked at him as one might a confused child. '*We* know that marriages are made to join fortunes, land, connections. Certainly it won't be a punishment to give my husband children, and I would expect the gifts he presents me with to outshine those he bestows on a mistress, but otherwise what would I care how he spends his time? Oh, look, Miss Fletcher and her awful little dog!'

He was content to let Lady Felicity prattle on as he drove them back to the dowager's home, where he went so far as to see her up the steps before making his escape. He would determine how to punish his mother later. In the meantime, there was a letter in his pocket from his middle sister, who had written asking him to send her favourite combs, along with her favourite scent, as she was unable to come to town this year due to the impending arrival of her fourth child. He turned his horses towards Jermyn Street and was before long stepping through the door to Floris.

A few people tarried at the front of the shop, but there at the back, with russet curls framing a face bent over a low mahogany case, was Miss Emory. He walked to the other side of the case, standing directly across from her.

'Where is your charming friend?' Brick asked, the intensity in his lowered voice startling her. Miss Emory's hand flew to her chest as she whipped her head up to look at him.

'Home, I imagine. At least, that's where Maria and I left her on our way here.' She gave a nod towards her maid, hovering near the entrance of the shop. 'And your charming companion? Has she returned to her post guarding the underworld?'

Brick let a slow grin part his lips, appreciation blooming within him, but instead of answering, asked, 'And your aunt?'

The light in the shop was too dim for him to notice any discernible colouring of her cheeks, but the narrowing of her eyes, the contemptuous pursing of her lips, were evidence enough that he'd been right in his earlier supposition. She set down the glass bottle she was holding and pretended to consider the selection of scents laid out before her.

His eyes roamed, catching on her narrow waist, the gentle rise of her breasts, her graceful neck. He licked his lips. 'Your restraint, by the bye, was commendable.'

'Some people are simply too stupid to bother with.'

'Is that a compliment to my own intelligence?'

Miss Emory's head jerked up in a sharp, sudden movement, and her hands came to rest atop the glass counter. 'Not at all. That's exactly the kind of female I'd expect you to marry.'

He leaned forward a little over the case between them. 'A stupid one?'

A young man working in the shop approached, but one look from Brick sent him back to whence he came. From the corner of his eye he noted the same man shake his head a little when another customer made to walk in their general direction.

'Men do like their wives to be at least a little ridiculous, I suppose. It gives them a sense of superiority, real or imagined, that must give the union a better chance of being a happy one. You must end the suspense and tell me, Your Grace, has she one original thought behind her pretty brown eyes?'

'She had her opinions on the latest fashions. Marriage, too.'

'Let me guess,' Miss Emory said, putting a delicate finger to her chin. 'She hated the dress Lady Rose Allsopp wore two nights ago at Almack's.'

Brick pressed his lips together but schooled his features into casual boredom. 'Do you know as much about scents as you do about inferior landscapes? Perhaps you'd care to tell me which top notes are present in this fragrance?'

'That landscape was not inferior just because *you* lack the taste to appreciate it.'

'You think you understand my tastes?'

'I do now.'

'Forget the top notes then, and tell me more about my preferences, Miss Emory,' he demanded, as he came around the glass case between them, 'and the kinds of things I *do* appreciate.' He watched her gaze slide to where his hand was on the counter, his fingertips a hair's breadth from her own. He inched his hand forward, his fingers stroking hers for one second, then two.

She was still, her eyes unblinking, watching the sensual movement, letting him linger a moment too long before yanking her hand away. Fury brightened her eyes. It mattered not. Those seconds were more than he needed to know her fingers trembled under his own, to observe the uneven rhythm of her breathing, to imagine the way her pulse skittered.

'You forget yourself, Your Grace.'

'On the contrary.'

'What is it you want from me?' she hissed.

'Everything.'

'What a luxury, to speak in absolutes.'

'Luxury,' the word slipped from his lips like a knot coming undone, 'is choosing where to marry—or choosing not to marry at all.'

'Or trimming one's outerwear in ridiculously expensive imported lace one doesn't even like.'

'You would mock Lady Felicity for using the means at her disposal?'

She scoffed. 'Is that what you call it?'

'What of you? Are you not now at this very moment doing the same? To shop? To do as you please with your day? To avoid marriage? You mock her for thinking herself superior to others, but are you not now standing here thinking yourself better than her because she's accepted a fate you deem repulsive?'

'Accepted a fate?' An ugly laugh freed itself from her mouth. 'You mean doing her parents' bidding and basking in the envy of the *ton* by accepting a duke?'

'I've no intention of offering for that chit.'

'Ah, yes. We forget the luxury of being a man—a titled one at that. The luxury of doing what one pleases without consequence.'

A muscle at the corner of his mouth twitched; his jaw set in irritation. 'You speak as if you aren't a part of this world, as if you face anything more than the occasional quizzical looks and a whisper or two about remaining unwed, as if growing old alone is an accomplishment worth being proud of. I suppose it must be, when it's your *only* accomplishment.'

Miss Emory's words snapped out like a whip. 'You know nothing about me.'

'I know you like art and literature, and detest frivolity, although your dress and bonnet are of the latest style. I know the night-scented jasmine is the perfume you'll leave here with.'

Her nostrils flared.

'I know you liked how my hand felt on yours.'

He watched her lips first clamp tight then part, as if she would say something, but no sound came out. Without a word, she pushed past him. He watched her go, wondering if he ought to toss his ring in the lake and tell Lansbury he may dive for it if he so wished.

---

11

*V*ivienne flew out of Floris, snatching Maria's arm as she did so, and plotted her revenge on the duke as she covered the streets from St James's Square to Grosvenor Square.

After she'd left the park with Anabel, she'd been irritated, exacerbated by her friend's easy ribbing—*'I rather enjoyed the show, however I don't think it was to Lady Felicity's taste'* —but her low opinion of the gentleman had undergone no significant change. The way he spoke to her in the shop, however, and the judgements he felt himself entitled to cast, infuriated her.

'I'll be in my studio, Maria, should either my aunt or uncle have need of me.'

The little maid bobbed a curtsey and hurried away, too familiar with her mistress's dark moods to have any desire to linger longer than it took to see Vivienne out of her walking dress and into one designated for work.

When the door had clicked closed behind her, Vivienne stalked into her studio and tore the sketch of him to pieces. Little good did it do. She spent the succeeding hours outlining his face once again, tracing his body, thinking of how his hand had felt on hers. Had it been up to her, she would have remained locked in there, drawing him out of her system for however long it took. Unfortunately, she had committed herself to a ball in the evening.

'You look lovely, my dear,' Lord Lane said, placing a kiss on his niece's cheek just as her aunt came down.

'I'm quite in agreement with your uncle. Lovely, if a little stormy-faced.' Vivienne's aunt reached up a hand, gently turning her niece's head this way and that.

A blaze of anger flickered in Vivienne's eyes—acute, disdainful, and gone before either her aunt or uncle could notice. 'Not at all. I've had a'—she paused for a thoughtful moment, selecting her next word with care—'constructive stretch of uninterrupted time in my studio. What could make me happier than that?'

'Dancing every dance tonight?'

Vivienne regarded her aunt with amusement. 'My apologies, ma'am. I thought we were discussing my happiness, not yours.'

'Everyone will be at the Lievens' tonight, and you have not suddenly failed to remember our agreement, I trust?'

Lord Lane steered the two ladies towards the door where the carriage waited.

It was impossible for Vivienne to forget the deal she'd made with her aunt. Unless ill, she had to attend six events a week, excluding calls, and say yes to every gentleman who asked her to dance, provided he wasn't a known libertine or scoundrel. Those were her aunt's terms if Vivienne wished to remain in their home and continue to paint.

'You need not worry I'll turn into a hermit or a wallflower. I shall dance.' She always enjoyed a turn in the ballroom, and the men who weren't bruised by her refusals saw her as a safe partner. It meant the sticks of her fan were most often filled with the names of gentlemen with whom she could converse freely—or relatively so. The rest were the idiotish men who saw her as a challenge, or a prize to be won.

There was a long line of carriages winding down the street that held the Lieven townhouse, and the longer they were forced to wait their turn, the more effort it was for Vivienne to avoid thinking about the possibility of seeing the duke. Encountering the man twice in one day felt punishment enough; a third was impossible to countenance.

Over her hands she wore the long violet gloves she and her aunt had purchased the first day she'd seen him. She ran a finger over the embroidery before folding both hands in her lap, the light lilac of the gloves set off against the pale green of her dress.

'I believe we're next.'

She gave a smile to acknowledge her uncle and forced it to remain on her face as they stepped down from the carriage, up the few stairs to the door, and ascended to the ballroom on the first floor of the home.

There were at least three hundred people already present, with however many more still waiting their own turn in the street below. From a distance Vivienne spotted Anabel with her mama, at least one of her brothers, and two of her married sisters and their husbands. She easily found Sir Jackson and was pleased to see him in conversation with Miss Kent; not far from him was Lady Felicity's brother, Lord Daly, whose proposal Vivienne had turned down last year and who was as spiteful as she suspected the sister to be; and in another corner, Mr Roberts, who always had a smile and a kind word for her.

Vivienne was taking inventory as her aunt led her through

the crush, not bothering to ask if there was a destination in mind, when a tall, broad form blocked her passage. In such close proximity it felt as if the duke towered over her, and she noticed, much against her will, how the hard outlines of his well-developed shoulders and arms appeared to fight against the fabric in which they were contained.

When she looked up, he was unsmiling, and just as she opened her mouth to ask that he move his odious person out of her way, he said the most unexpected thing.

'May I have your first?'

She could not see behind him, and therefore couldn't be certain if her aunt was near enough still to have heard the invitation or not. Vivienne gave her agreement with a small frown, worried the effort of looking pleased would do more damage to her face than scowling ever would.

He held out his hand.

'The musicians have not yet begun, Your Grace.' As she said it, she heard the first notes dance through the air.

'A waltz.'

With a reluctant sigh pressing at her lips, she placed her hand with as light a touch as possible on his and allowed herself to be led to the floor to join the other couples.

They stood across from one another, and she regarded him with impassive coldness as he took his fill of her in an unhurried manner and with a face made of stone. Her whole body stiffened when he stepped nearer, and she tensed further still when, with his right hand, he put her left on his shoulder, and with his left hand held her waist.

'You have waltzed before?'

She started to answer that she had, but the words fell away as the duke pulled her so close not even her gasp could fit between them. The unexpected movement caused her to miss a step, and her fingers dug into his hard shoulder as she righted herself—or perhaps it was he who righted her. Vivienne's back burned where his hand rested, and the music was difficult to hear over the thrumming of blood in her ears.

'Are you all right, Miss Emory?'

She blinked, trying to focus on anything but him.

'Quite.' After a heavy swallow, she added, feeling more herself, 'Only I cannot account for you soliciting my hand for a dance.'

'Can't you?'

The intensity in the quietly spoken words sent a little wave of anticipation rippling through her, and she wondered if he could feel the way her hand quaked against him.

'I didn't at all care for how we left things after the park.'

Vivienne didn't want to look back up at him until she knew if she preferred seeing sincerity in his countenance or a lack thereof.

'You condemn me to silence? It's no less than I deserve, so I will accept the punishment and carry the conversation. Let us look about as we turn. You will agree, I think, that Mr Allen has chosen the wrong colour for his waistcoat. I cannot be sure you've sampled the champagne yet tonight and therefore may have no opinion—ah! There was a painting in the anteroom where we discarded our outerwear, surely unnoticed by most, but I suspect it came under your scrutiny. Presumably a countess of generations past and her children The signature on it, however, was unfamiliar to me.'

Vivienne bit down hard on her lower lip, annoyed by the duke's affability and its effect on her. When she finally dared bring her eyes up to his face once more, she tried for an expression that managed to be both aloof and stern. He was seeking out her opinions, working to pull a smile, a word, from her, and her desire to enjoy herself in his company would never do.

'You *did* see it, and'—he cocked his head as they made another turn—'no doubt have thoughts. Won't you share them with me?'

'No.'

'Then I'll tell you what I think, knowing what I do of the family. That woman never smiled and certainly wouldn't have done so surrounded by her eight children.'

'The deification of motherhood is nothing new.' The comment ought to have remained in her mind where it belonged but escaped before she could prevent it from doing otherwise, and she felt all the displeasure of giving him satisfaction, clear from the way his lips eased into a pleased grin.

'It feels incumbent upon me to tell you, after such a comment, that I've heard an account of you I've yet to reconcile with my own experiences. My source, who I will not name, but who is the epitome of credibility, said he's only ever heard you converse in what I'm certain you'd consider trivialities, polite topics. I cannot account for how you speak to me.'

Her lips turned down in a gentle pout. 'You provoke me.'

He dipped his head, and she could feel the intensity of his words cascade over her body when he spoke. 'Tell me you don't enjoy it.'

His fingers exerted more pressure where they rested on her back, and Vivienne glanced up once more, immediately regretting her decision to do so. She wished to remind herself how much she disliked this man spinning her about the ballroom, but the longer she spent in his company, the longer she wished to remain. They were silent too long—the quiet playing havoc on her nerves and her thoughts, which had strayed so far from where they began as to be nearly unrecognisable.

'Shall we return to the offensive puce colour of Mr Allen's waistcoat? Abominable choice for someone with a shock of red hair.'

He was so excessively dramatic she couldn't help but smile and didn't realise she was doing so till he said, 'You have a lovely smile, Miss Emory, and seeing it gives me more pleasure than it ought.'

'I've also a shock of red hair.' She hoped, in ignoring his compliment, the feeling of a thousand birds flapping in her belly would also cease.

'That's not what I'd call it at all. Yours is the colour of freshly polished copper glinting in sunlight. If my hands were burrowed in it, I wager it would feel as smooth and slip through my fingers like fine silk.'

Everything he said made her stomach swoop, her limbs tingle. 'You might have better luck turning your charms on Mr Allen.'

'You think I'm charming?'

'That's not what I said.'

He raised both eyebrows.

'Fine,' she said on a huff that broke into a light chuckle. 'Once, or perhaps twice, certainly no more than that, you have had a moment where some might consider you charming. Are you satisfied, you horrid man?'

'A horrid man that made you laugh.' The pleasure in his smile was like a light scratch of nails gliding all the way down her spine. 'Now, what else might I say to repeat the effect? Ah, I have it.'

Vivienne couldn't tear her full focus from him, even if she wished it, and hated how curious she was for the words to follow. The duke, while they completed a turn, looked round as if he were on the brink of revealing a government secret, then whispered with mock reverence: '*She Walks in Beauty*.'

The hasty tug of her lips wasn't enough to keep the airy giggle inside.

'I knew you would not fawn over Byron's tripe like all the rest.' His words were sharp, but his eyes were warm with appreciation, and Vivienne realised then how easy it had been for her to slip into this moment with him. Easy, and dangerous.

'Say something else.' Her demand came out little more than a whisper.

'What would please you most to hear?'

'Something odious, provoking.'

He studied her and she was positive no one else existed in that moment except them. 'Why?'

'Because.' She watched his chest expand with a deep pull of air, the makings of a sensual smile tipping his lips upward.

'Very well.' His mouth lilted with mischief. 'Marry me.'

Had his hand not been so secure around her, she may have wilted right there in Princess Lieven's ballroom. 'I said odious, not insane,' she replied after a long moment, feeling a little revived but excessively disconcerted as her heart jumped from chest to stomach to throat and back again.

'You think it a jest?'

'Of course.'

'If it isn't?' There was a probing, insistent quality simmering in the rich timbre of his voice.

'Then you ought to consider Bedlam.'

'That's not a real answer.'

'And that wasn't a real proposal.' Vivienne couldn't work out how they went from needling one another to discussing marriage in the space of a waltz, but the rapidity with which her feelings were jumping from one state to another was causing her head to pound. 'Let us remain silent the rest of the dance, lest one of us say anything else we may regret.'

He did as she asked, and that was the most unnerving thing of all.

For the rest of the night, Vivienne was determined to remember how insufferable he was—how arrogant, how backward, how apathetic—and scolded her traitorous heart for how hard it hammered in her chest every time his bold, unnerving gaze slid over her, which it did an excessive number of times. There was no logic, no sense in their exchange and his awful jest about marriage. The Duke of Hazelhurst most certainly did not want to marry her, but even as she convinced herself of what she knew to be true, she couldn't stop thinking of how his hand floated at the small of her back when he led her from the floor, how his words sent shivers through her body, how she imagined, only for a moment, the beautiful raw musculature that must exist under his jacket.

12

'Winning our wager may be harder than I anticipated,' Brick confessed to his friend, overcome by a feeling so foreign it was not immediately recognisable: guilt. Their horses were trotting up to the Red Lion Inn some fifteen miles outside of town. Once a sennight, or thereabouts, the two of them rode out, exercising their horses in a way impossible to do on Rotten Row.

'Don't tell me you're giving up already, old chap. I'll have to reconsider my unflinching faith in your abilities to get exactly what you want.' After a pause, and with a steady stare and serious tone, St Germain added, 'You were a fool to wager your signet ring.'

His friend was right, of course, but Brick was impetuous—he always had been, which was how he'd ended up needing a bone reset after jumping out of a tree on a dare, how two barn cats ended up sleeping in his room every night when he was a child, and how he'd found himself in a mad dash to the Scottish border all those years ago. His besetting sins were an extreme confidence and the assumption his title could succeed where other men had failed, because it always did. There wasn't a single woman he could name between eighteen and eighty who would reject him on any grounds, much less for the simple reason that they wished to. It wasn't how society worked. Plenty of members of the *ton* had whispered behind his back, but when it came to their myopic ideals of importance, Brick had what mattered: a title, money, and power. When he made the wager, he couldn't have known Miss Emory had carved herself from a different mould, one that had him questioning everything he thought he knew about himself.

'Not giving up. Rather, reconsidering my approach.'

'Don't tell me she's immune to your attractions.'

'Immune, no,' Brick said, his voice flat. 'Repulsed, more like.'

St Germain was still laughing when the pair walked into the coffee room to take an early luncheon. 'Now that you mention it, she didn't seem best pleased to partner you at the Lieven ball. At least at first.' He raised a mischievous eyebrow but continued, 'Next time we are in company I'll have to request her hand for a dance myself so I may compliment her on her taste.'

'Not a day goes by that I don't reconsider our friendship.'

The coffee room was mostly empty, and they took up a small table at the window, ordering bread, cheese, and two tankards of ale. The Red Lion was one of the duke's preferred inns, as the quality of food and drink was always dependable.

'Is that the only complication?' St Germain had frank, open brown eyes that often compelled his friend to reveal things he otherwise wouldn't. One look across the table, and Brick was certain Saint already knew the answer to his own question.

There was no risk to Brick of being caught by something so trivial as a pretty face, which Miss Emory undoubtedly had; it was, after all, the very thing that first drew his notice. Brick had known he was looking but not what he was looking for until…well, when exactly? When she recommended a book that became a favourite? When she took his opinions and smashed them to bits? When he discovered a side of her no one else knew even existed?

The moment he had taken her in his arms for the waltz, he'd been undone by a rush of longing both immediate and more potent than anything he had ever experienced. Beyond a fervent need to take her to bed, to possess what others had tried and failed to obtain, he found himself in the midst of a most astonishing awakening, which had left him reeling. It was very much as if he'd chanced upon his soul and it had been waiting patiently for him to recognise its absence.

'Have you a copy of the *Morning Chronicle*?' St Germain asked the owner as he set the two tankards down on the table.

'Aye. I'll grab it for ye.'

A moment later, Brick's friend was scanning the pages for nothing and everything. St Germain was worse than most matrons, always waiting to eat up the latest gossip and exclaiming in delight at anything printed in the scandal pages, even if he was already personally acquainted with whatever 'news' there was.

'Good Gad, Hazelhurst.'

Brick, who'd allowed his gaze to grow unfocused as he stared out the window, turned an inquisitive look on his friend.

'Miss Emory may be the least of your problems.' St Germain folded the page in half and turned it towards him.

On it was an unflattering sketch of a man bearing an awful

resemblance to himself, looming over a long line of waifish golden-haired women who looked nearly identical. He read aloud the little caption underneath: '*Finding a wife isn't the hard part…*'

Brick cleared his throat. 'A little on the nose, don't you think?'

'I think it surprising this is the first mention of your past since you've returned to society at large.'

'You mean the first time it's appeared in such a way. The whispers began the moment I set foot once more upon English soil. If there is a benefit to killing a man, it must be that people are more careful to keep those whispers from my ears.'

'Jesus, Hazelhurst.'

Brick shrugged and slammed back his beer. 'If he didn't wish to be shot, he ought not have run off with my betrothed.'

'Have you considered the possibility that *that* is why Miss Emory holds you in no high esteem?'

'No.'

'Then I am all out of ideas. What does it matter, anyway?'

'It doesn't.' But even as Brick said so, it didn't ring as true as it had before. He allowed the conversation to wander to less troublesome topics, and although he was happy for his friend's company, by the time they rode back into London sometime later, he found himself desirous of being alone with his thoughts.

The duke was not a man prone to reflection. He was a man of action, a man too used to getting what he desired, and those two things together left very little need for musing. That was how he liked it.

But he could not set aside thoughts of Miss Emory, of her sharp tongue, her eyes alive with mischief, and how he'd felt he could wrap his whole hand around her waist as they moved through the waltz. He could not set aside how *he* felt with her: alive, happy, himself.

With a groan he rolled onto his back and took himself in hand.

13

*A*fter breakfast and several strong cups of coffee, Vivienne found herself perched in a window seat of the yellow drawing room that overlooked the street, a book left open and unread in her lap, while her aunt chatted with several of her friends over their second pot of tea. Vivienne made no effort to keep up with what they were saying, and they were content to leave her be, a little removed from the small party. She startled herself and them when she jerked up, causing the book to tumble to the floor.

'Heavens, Vivi!' her aunt cried out. 'You scared us half to death. What is it?'

'Nothing. It's nothing,' Vivienne answered, working to still her pounding heart and even her breathing. It wasn't nothing. A curricle had pulled up outside Huxley House, and even before he'd turned his steely blue eyes her way, she knew who it was. A moment later he would be ushered into the room where she stood, looking like a frightened, guilty deer. After the Lieven ball, she'd drawn a rather unkind caricature of the duke as if doing so would make her feel better, remind her why she couldn't let him in. Only she found it much harder to stand by her work when the subject of it was coming to call.

She counted: one, two, three, fou—

'His Grace, the Duke of Hazelhurst, your ladyship,' the butler announced in placid tones, before retreating from the room.

All the ladies stood, and Lady Lane held out a hand, welcoming him with all the warmth of long-time friends. 'To what do we owe the pleasure?'

His eyes found Vivienne's then, and she struggled under his strange, indecipherable stare. 'I was hoping to persuade Miss Emory into a visit of the British Institution.'

'With you?' Surely he wasn't serious.

The corners of his mouth quirked, and Lady Lane responded for her niece before he could say anything further. 'How lovely that sounds. Much better, I'm sure, then sitting around listening to we old ladies discuss charity business.'

A chorus of agreement swelled around them, and Vivienne, with the grim-set mouth of someone who had no authority to make her own choice, left the room to don her outerwear. Minutes later, she was beside him as they rode towards Pall Mall.

'I cannot fathom why you wish to punish me, and yourself by extension, by doing something as foolhardy as forcing me into your company.'

'I did not force you—'

'As if I could have said no when surrounded by a room full of ladies who would delight in sharing the tale that I rebuffed an invitation from *His Grace*, even more than they would in spreading the news that they watched me being driven off in his phaeton.'

'You, of all people, cannot care about whispers carried on the wind by bored matrons.'

'You mean because there have been so many about me? Or because in placidly accepting spinsterhood I encourage them?' It was true: she didn't care overly much about those rumours that swirled anytime a gossip caught wind of a proposal offered and declined—the rumours distracted from and concealed the real reason she remained alone. 'It does not follow I must be unaffected by the gossip.'

'By the bye, I don't find being in your company a punishment at all.'

She didn't hold back the laugh that rippled through the air up at such an absurd statement. 'Well, that is one of us then.'

'It's too bad you should find my company so revolting.'

Vivienne thought he would say more, and although she didn't want to ask, it was only a second before she inquired as to why he should think so.

'Because I have every intention of repeating days like today.'

'You are a sick man.'

'A determined one.'

'Often one and the same. Why are you bringing me to the gallery?'

'Looking at paintings gives you pleasure.'

'Impossible with you at my side.'

'Come now, Miss Emory, I think you quite like educating me about art, among other things.'

Vivienne sewed her mouth closed, refusing to be provoked into saying anything further, but she couldn't prevent herself darting her eyes in his direction. She hoped her look was a cross between boredom and displeasure.

'What else do you like?' He waited a full minute for her to

answer, and when she didn't, he went on. 'Ices? Starry nights? Thunderstorms in August?' The duke paused, took one sweeping glance over her person, and amended his statement. 'Allow me to retract my last guess. A lady who dresses as you do surely wouldn't appreciate a midsummer squall.'

She didn't, mostly because in the summer she enjoyed painting out of doors—not that she would say so.

He was looking at her, she could feel it, but she wouldn't turn to meet him.

'It is lucky for me we approach the gallery. I don't think you'll be able to maintain your dignified silence when faced with some boring scene fêted by the masses and described as art.'

The duke, she hated to admit, was right, although she didn't say a word the first quarter of an hour after they arrived.

'I noticed two paintings at your uncle's house—one in the long entry hall and one above the mantle in the drawing room —both quite good, not unlike this one,' he said, studying the painting before them. 'Is it the same artist? Or perhaps they attended the same school? You won't fool me into thinking you don't know,' he added, with a boyish smile that made her stomach clench.

'I think it unlikely you're familiar with the artist.'

'Because you believe me indifferent to landscapes?'

'Because the artist is not well known.' Vivienne didn't miss the way he worded his challenge, but further reply was made impossible by the passing of a mutual acquaintance, and the two of them soon moved down the gallery and on to a wall of portraits and other subjects.

He nodded to the nameplate of an artist who used the

initials JL. 'It may interest you to know that the true identity of the painter was only recently discovered to be a woman.'

Vivienne knew all about the piece, and the crisis the discovery caused in the art world. After being passed off as the work of a famous painter's less esteemed brother, the discovery that it was in fact by a woman entirely unrelated to the family was as scandalous as if the woman herself had walked naked down St James's. Reparations were paid to the museum, the piece passed through any number of hands, and for a protracted period of time, nothing else was said of it. Certainly, there was no celebration of the woman's talent. It was half a miracle the piece had resurfaced and found its way to this gallery at all.

'Does that affect how you view the piece?' She caught the twinkle in his eye when he looked at her.

'Yes. The painting as a whole feels a little naughty. If painted by a man, it would feel as if she's flirting a little, letting me in on some joke, beckoning me to her side.'

'But by a woman?'

'It feels as though *I* am the joke. She's not desirous of laughing *with* me because she is already laughing *at* me.'

'Perhaps because art in all its mediums so often reinforces women as objects of desire and possession. Paintings like this have always been defined by the viewpoint of the male gaze. Acknowledging its provenance is to question the accepted perspective. You have just discovered how uncomfortable that can make one feel. It's no wonder others are so reluctant to welcome women into the ranks.'

The duke looked as though he had a rejoinder, but Vivienne didn't wish to give him the opportunity to respond, and so said, 'You mentioned her true identity only recently surfaced. I take that to mean this work was thought to have been originally completed by a man.'

'Indeed. Part of Rousseau's collection, I believe.'

'And so what of her ability? It was good enough to warrant comparison—nay, attribution—to Rousseau.'

'You wish for me to invalidate her talent on the basis of her sex?' he asked.

'*You* questioned whether a woman could ever be equal in talent to a man.'

Recollection flickered in his eyes, and she was sure he remembered their first meeting with as much clarity as she did.

'I questioned whether a woman could equal a man's talent if she'd been deprived of the same opportunities for study. This particular artist is the daughter of a well-known Flemish painter under whom she trained. No doubt that level of unimpeded access to a master allowed her to develop skills comparable to a great many respected painters, or this work would never have been attributed to Rousseau in the first place. If the work was good enough to warrant the comparison when it was believed to be done by a man's hand, it must still be good enough after discovering the true artist. The painting itself didn't change, only our understanding of its origin.'

Vivienne was so surprised by his speech, she did little more than open her mouth to respond, only to close it immediately upon discovering she wasn't at all sure what to say.

'As a youth I saw several other works by this artist on a trip with my father. At the time, those who moved in august artist circles had begun to assign the work to Rousseau, despite the unusual signature in the bottom, at odds with how he'd signed his other pieces. My father, who was an avid art collector, asked my opinion. I said the colours, the soft lines, and the use of a palette knife weren't at all reflective of Rousseau's style. The works could have been a sort of experiment, which might also explain signing them differently, but to me, even then, those characteristics suggested an artist with a delicate hand— a more refined style in direct conflict with what I believed Rousseau capable of.'

Vivienne cast a sidelong look of disbelief at the man next to her, whose attention was all on the painting. 'Her work is admirable—the mirthful light in her eye captivating—but you overlook additional complications for others who don't have the luxury of familial connections.'

'That word again.'

'What woman without connection to a successful man may partake in success or acclaim herself? She,' Vivienne said, nodding to the painting, 'had those connections, and still it's a wonder her work is here, available for us to see, to discuss, to dissect. How many artists like her are overlooked or undervalued? That is to say nothing of the confines in which a woman must work if she wants her share of success.'

As one, they moved on to another piece.

'Such as?'

'How many paintings have we passed already?'

The duke, without looking about them, answered, 'Three dozen or thereabout.'

'Just so.'

'I don't follow.'

'We have seen history paintings, landscapes, portraits. Of those, the only ones completed by women are portraits, and no doubt we'll see some miniatures as well. That style is the only one available to women who wish for commercial success. The only style deemed acceptable for the delicate nature attributed to our sex.'

'I'll own to having never made that connection.'

'Because you're a man. You can be certain of things a woman cannot, such as having access to the male form, which is a necessity for history paintings.'

'You're telling me you've never laid your eyes upon the male form? How reassuring.'

His tone, as much as the dark, simmering stare he gave her, heated her cheeks.

'Certainly not. With the exception of paintings and the like, of course.'

'Of course.'

Vivienne pushed a hand to the space where her ribs met, trying to still the flutter in her belly, and wished she hadn't said anything. 'A woman artist must choose between two iden-tities: being a woman as defined by society, or being an artist. But even as an artist, she is not given access to education in the same way as a man.' As she said the words, she felt the ground give a little beneath her, realising how close she was to revealing too much.

The look on his face was more thoughtful than suspicious, but still, her breath wouldn't come easily.

'Must she choose? Why cannot a woman be both?'

'Because a woman who marries can only ever be what her husband wishes.'

'What is it you wish to be, Miss Emory?'

Her throat tightened on her words. 'Only myself.' Panic was beginning to rise within her, and she was desperate to correct the dangerous course they were on. 'Even men who espouse liberal ideals and think themselves great champions of equal treatment for women, struggle to maintain that view if their wives wish to shirk the duties to home and family in favour of other employments, whatever those may be.'

'Surely not all husbands.'

'Perhaps not, but history has made an example of women who took the risk.'

'Most women find security in marriage, but now we come to the reason you remain unwed.'

Vivienne felt hot all over and knew her cheeks were overcome with colour.

'I beg your pardon, Miss Emory. Your reasons are your own. I only meant that perhaps to you marriage feels the greater risk to your current happiness, as you are in the fortunate position of being financially secure without a husband.'

She forced her hand to stay at her side and not press her cheek, refusing to acknowledge the visceral reaction she'd had to his words, particularly as he hadn't meant them as a direct comparison. Naturally, he didn't think her an artist. No one did—she had not the connections or credentials as society saw it, nor was she born to that life. She was born to run an estate, raise children, host parties.

Next to her, the duke said with a resolution that made her grateful, 'We've established my father is the one who taught me about art and helped me refine my own eye. Your turn.'

'Same.'

His eyebrows rose a fraction. 'I've not heard you speak of your family before—your parents, that is.'

'They are dead. What else ought to be said?' The statement was a callous one, but better to be harsh than to blubber in the middle of the British Institution.

'Do you miss them?'

'Do you miss your father?'

'Every day I am lucky enough to wake.'

'As do I.' The words snagged on her lips. She was appreciative of the life she led, but it had not become easier for her to discuss the one that no longer existed. 'My father was kind but not much at home. My mother was a Cornwall Caldicott. Her father owned mines, and my father took over when my grandfather died. My mother was lovely, brilliant on the pianoforte —truly accomplished as would be said of her.'

'But you don't play.'

'No. Her talent was wasted playing Scotch airs for young people in the neighbourhood who wished to clear the furniture and dance at dinner parties. I had no talent on the instrument, but had I such a one, she would not have allowed the same fate to befall me.'

'You speak with such certainty.'

'My parents are one of the few things of which I have always been sure.' Her eyes focused on the painting before her, the edges blurring until one colour ran into another. It was one of the last pieces from this artist before her husband put an end to her work. 'This life is too short to live in a marriage where you're not seen.'

Both were standing still in the profound silence that had settled between them when another couple walked up to stand beside Vivienne.

'It's not uncommon for females to emulate the masters,' the gentleman was saying. 'But such vigorous brushstrokes as a man can make are beyond the capability of a delicate woman. Here, you'll notice a certain weakness in the feminine hand.'

The silly girl next to the man spoke as if that was all the insight she needed into this particular artist, and Vivienne, who had turned a little to inspect the nitwits next to her, felt her hand picked up and laced through a thick, strong arm. The latent strength in the duke's hand sent her feelings spiralling from comfort, to curiosity, to certainty that those fingers could set her ablaze if they breezed across her bare skin. The very thought made her pulse throb, and she wondered if he could see it thumping in her neck.

'Let it be.' The duke had tipped his head to whisper in her ear, and his warm breath sent a chill rippling through her.

She bit her tongue and dug her nails into his arm as best she could with gloves on and layers of fabric between them. He flexed the muscle under her hand, and she tensed at the thrill of it.

'Do not you feel women have the advantage when they sit in front of a canvas?' said the duke, scrutinising the man as he addressed him over Vivienne's head. 'Mr Keen, I believe? Cousin to Lord Cromley?'

The gentleman, upon realising who was speaking to him, turned and bowed. 'That's correct, Your Grace, although I cannot agree with you that women have the advantage.'

'The lady who painted this particular piece is not demonstrating weakness of hand. Rather, exquisite technique and truer mastery of fine strokes, and softer lines than any man can claim. Pick up a paintbrush yourself and tell me—is it easier to cover large swathes of canvas in broad strokes or define every blade of grass? She is not seeking to emulate masters; she's proving her own superiority.'

Mr Keen looked a little dumbfounded, but the young lady on his arm had stars in her eyes by the time the duke was done speaking. As for Vivienne, she didn't know if he meant a word of it, but that he said it all the same filled her whole being with almost unbearable tenderness. She allowed him to guide her further down the long hall, not realising until much, much later that she never reclaimed her hand from his arm.

14

'*You*'ve been hiding from me.'

Brick looked up from his book as his mother swept into the library of his house in Grosvenor Square.

'I've been hiding from the insufferable ladies you no doubt have coming and going from your home with all the regularity of a girls' school.'

'Lady Felicity is perfect for you.'

'Lady Felicity has Medici blood.'

'You say that as if it's a bad thing. She'll bring wealth and connections. She'll do as you ask.'

Brick turned the page in his book.

His mother let escape an impatient huff. 'Lady Celia? Lady Gwen? Lady Judith? Any will do. Perhaps it would serve you to spend less time in company with Miss Emory.'

'You cannot call meeting one another at a function attended by hundreds of other people spending time in one another's company.'

'You had her in your curricle. I saw you on my way home from paying a call on the Countess of Rangail.'

'And how is your dear cousin? Still the terror of all her children? A common interest shared between you.'

His mother walked to the bell-pull and ordered tea from the footman who answered the summons.

'Can I interest you in tea, ma'am?' Brick asked after the fact, his voice bored and teetering on annoyed.

'You were brought up better than to keep an old lady waiting.'

'Yes. My governess, or the several, did a commendable job.'

She ignored his comment and took a seat on the sofa, propping both her hands on her walking stick in front of her. 'Lady Gwen is attending a loo party this evening. You will go as well.'

Brick groaned. 'As if there were anything more insufferable.'

'Viscountess Becksley is hosting. Her husband is a friend of yours, is he not? No doubt you have the invitation buried on your desk, under all the others you don't deign to respond to.'

Brick knew exactly where it was. Contrary to his mother's supposition, he sifted through all the invitations he received, only he wasn't one to commit to accepting, on account of preferring to do what he chose when he chose. If he fancied showing his face at a loo party, he would turn up whether he'd confirmed his presence or not.

'Very well. Now drink your tea and go. No doubt securing my agreement was the only reason you came, so I feel no compunction in sending you off. If my evening is to be disturbed, I'd like to spend the rest of my morning enjoying what little peace I may.'

His mother saw herself out, and from his seat on the sofa,

Brick stared across at one of his favourite paintings. He had acquired it before being forced to the continent and he'd purchased it because the young blond girl perched on a cliff, her serene countenance, her enjoyment in the simple pleasure of braiding a flower crown, reminded him of his youngest sister, Elizabeth. When he sat in this particular spot and stared at this particular painting, it was easiest for him to remember her: her talent at the harp; the way she ran through the fields of Goldfinch Park, no matter how furious it made their parents; the way she laughed freely with tenants' children or nobility alike. It was as if all the best parts of the rest of them were saved up and given to her.

In a few months, she would have been twenty-eight, doubtless married with a child or two. He was sure she would have thwarted all their mother's attempts at making an illustrious match for her, and he wondered what kind of man she would have chosen for herself, what she would say to him if she could see him now, what she'd think of Miss Emory. Elizabeth would have been delighted, no doubt, to make the acquaintance of another nonconformist—a young lady who saw through the thin veneer of society, who lived a life of subtle, unwavering courage.

He sighed and ran a hand over the length of his face and back up through his hair. His sister would also have been horrified at his wager. It mattered not that all other kinds of bets were in that book—bets on whether the Duke of Clarence would have a legitimate child, if a certain fellow would be transported, what someone would name their next horse— Brick knew better, was better, than that. But Lansbury had a talent for stoking his impulsive nature and had offered the one thing he wanted and couldn't have—or at least, that was true before he'd met Miss Emory. She deserved honesty, but telling her meant forfeiting the bet and therefore his signet ring. Keeping the wager from her twisted Brick's stomach into knots as much as the idea of sacrificing the most important reminder of his father's love.

If he had known how difficult it would be to keep his mind from turning towards Miss Emory, he may not have sent his mother off with such swiftness.

That evening, Brick refused to look for her, but realised he hadn't been able to help himself when St Germain pointedly asked him if it were a certain lady for whom he searched.

When he responded with only a glare, Lord St Germain's eyebrows rose an inch. 'I don't mind admitting that I find myself in the unusual situation of being lost for words. I didn't realise your interest in her had roots.'

'Nor did I.' He had been attracted to Miss Emory from the moment he saw her, but he had also been equally in possession of the idea that he preferred an easy, biddable wife, which she would never be—nor would he want her if she were.

'If that's so, it may be worth considering why she's opposed to marriage, not just to you,' St Germain added, with an air of true concern.

'What are you getting at, Saint?'

'Down, boy. Bet or no, if I were in possession of anything to help your suit, I would share it. I only meant that the obstacle you need to overcome might be something insurmountable. There are a dozen other things that could prevent her from plucking a husband from the punchbowl at Almack's.'

'Such as?'

'A clause in her parents' will; stipulations by her aunt and uncle if she's to be their heir; a buried scandal or family secret she wants to protect others from. Hell, maybe she doesn't like men—or children.'

'Stop being ridiculous.'

'Me? Hazelhurst, I will own to being entertained by the reversal in your situation. Although I would much rather see you happily settled than pining away for the one lady you can't have, I find I'm looking forward to watching her lead you in a pretty little dance.'

Brick saw Lansbury approaching and so withheld any reply.

'Could it be even the golden one has met his match in the intractable Miss Emory?'

'Stow it, Lansbury,' replied Brick, his voice rife with world-weariness, 'and take yourself off in the direction from which you came.'

'I've only passed by to say how right, how fine, that pretty little ring will look upon my finger,' Lansbury sneered, his avaricious eyes gleaming as they beheld the Vesily family heirloom on Brick's hand.

'On this we must disagree. The ring represents qualities you can never possess, exemplified by the very wager you made in your quest to obtain what's not rightfully yours.' On that brutal note, Brick turned from his cousin, and alongside St Germain, made his way to another corner of the room, leaving Lansbury to suffer his anger in silence.

Despite his harsh words, Brick could imagine the disapproving glare of his own father, who would be equally ashamed at Brick accepting the wager as he would at the terms of the bet, even if Miss Emory were unlikely to suffer any lasting effects. If the *ton* at large came into the knowledge of the wager, half would be pleased she wasn't swooning at his feet because they wanted him for themselves or their daughters. The other half would delight in his struggle and see it as the closest thing to him being taken down—rightfully so for having such audacity, such good fortune, as to be the natural child of a woman wed to a duke.

Boys in school had teased him when he was much younger, nearly all of them except Saint. 'Jealousy makes people behave in ugly ways,' a wide-eyed St Germain said at just thirteen, while they swam in a lake near school. That day, Brick had decided to eat up the nasty comments, to use them against those who dared to speak with such thoughtlessness. He had begun to understand what society valued, how they would treat him for being undeserving by their measuring-stick, how swiftly the tunes they played would change when he inherited.

In fundamentals, he was unchanged, but he now felt certain that with Miss Emory in his life, he'd never be the same.

15

The Duke of Hazelhurst occupied a disproportionate amount of Vivienne's thoughts, by her way of calculating things, and she did not at all care for the amount of time she spent standing in her studio staring at the sketch of him. After every encounter with him, she was compelled to change something in it as he unfolded more of himself.

While she was still caught in the thrill of time before the first words were spoken between them, he was tall, rich, aloof. At Hatchards, playful, teasing, mysterious. The musicale proved him to be rude, arrogant, a flirt. In the park, provoking. At Floris, equal parts infuriating and exhilarating. The Lieven ball was the first time she'd seen him as dangerous, as a threat to her person in how much her body thrilled at his touch. It was the first time she'd noticed the wolfishness in the way he looked at her, and the first time her body physically yearned for more of another person.

After their day at the British Institution, she knew him to be a threat to more than her body.

Vivienne reached for her pencil and a rubber. She softened the tense edges around his mouth, sharpened the tip of his nose, and let more light into his eyes. He was just as beautiful on the page as he was off it, and even the black-and-white version of him staring at her like she was the only thing he could see made her heart flip. Black and white, however, were no longer enough. She was going to bring him to life with her oils, suffuse colour into his being. What had started as a small sketch now occupied a half-length canvas roughly forty inches by fifty.

There was a soft knock on her studio door. 'Miss?'

Vivienne repressed a groan. 'Yes, Maria?'

'His Grace, the Duke of Hazelhurst, is here.'

When Vivienne entered the bright and airy parlour, she expected to find the duke within. She did not expect to see him intently studying the landscape that hung along the wall, one she'd finished two years previously, during a time she was feeling a particular longing for the Cornish coast.

The sun streaming into the room from the windows illuminated his perfect profile; his long, straight back; the individual waves of his hair; little bits of light sneaking in under and over the curved strands.

Without looking at her, he said, 'I noticed this painting last time I was here. There is something familiar in the prospect or the sharp strokes used here and here.' He gestured at the grass. 'It draws me in.'

'You don't like landscapes.'

'I like this one.' He took a step nearer the canvas, leaned his head a little forward, and looked for a signature he would not find. 'How odd for an artist not to sign their work. Do you know its provenance?'

She hadn't signed it because she didn't know how. It

concerned her to sign it with the same signature she used for her publicly displayed works, but it also felt risky to sign it with her own initials.

'It's embarrassing to admit I do not. The painting has hung there as long as my memory serves. I suppose I assumed it some piece that had been with the house longer than myself.' The lie was flimsy. Despite the need to conceal her occupation, she had never been great at fibbing. The odd look he gave her —half-amused, half-confused—worried her he would press further.

The duke looked to the painting again, and Vivienne glanced at the wide-open doorway, wondering what was keeping her aunt from greeting their guest, as Lady Lane was never backward in attention. There was no sign of a footman, much less her aunt, although she thought she caught the subtle swish of silk somewhere just beyond the parlour.

'You left a card yesterday,' she said, hoping to draw his attention once more from the painting.

'I did, and you know, Miss Emory, I think you were home then, too.'

She had been—working…on her painting of him. A muscle at the corner of her mouth quivered. 'No matter. You've found me at my leisure this morning.'

'A pleasure which I cannot describe but hope to extend.'

With some difficulty, she tried to clear her painfully dry throat, and when she spoke, it was as if the bristles of a paint-brush were dragging along inside it. 'You may.' Her eyes swung to the clock. 'For twelve more minutes.'

His lips parted in a smile, the kind that seemed to imply he knew something she did not. 'Have you remained at home the entire day?'

'I have,' she replied, thinking of the paint drying on her canvas upstairs.

'Come to the park with me.'

'I thank you, no.'

'You've just admitted to not having been out all day, and the weather is fine, despite the light rain that fell at the breakfast hour.'

Inwardly she grimaced at having provided him the exact reason he needed to invite her out of doors.

'Yes,' Vivienne said, walking towards the long window that overlooked the square of green, just beyond the road running along the row of houses on the west side of Grosvenor Square. 'And how fortunate I can enjoy the warmth of the sun from this spot, where I stand.'

She sensed him moving and expected him to come and stand next to her, but he stopped a little behind her shoulder.

'You see that house there, with the colonnades?' He raised his arm to point to a townhouse on the north side of the square. He was leaning down a little, so when he spoke, the words ruffled the tiny hairs at her neck. 'The white brick with curved windows?'

Vivienne nodded.

'That's my home.'

'How is it then I've never seen you?'

'There are more than forty residences on this square, Miss Emory. Do you know who resides in all of them? Have you had the happy chance of crossing paths with every neighbour?'

She frowned a little at how easy he explained this away. 'No.'

'Exactly so, and when one considers my long absence from

England…' He let the rest of the thought hang in the air, and she did too.

Despite feeling him close at her back, she hadn't realised how little distance remained between them until she turned and found her chest nearly flush against his own. Her hands flew up of their own accord, as if to keep her from knocking into him, but the effect was that they landed on his solid chest, and she felt the jump of a muscle beneath her palm.

'I beg your pardon,' she said clumsily, stepping back only to knock her legs into the windowsill.

The duke reached out to steady her, the skin of her arms on fire from the touch of his bare hands. 'Excuse me,' she said, a second later than she should have. She stepped to the side, chastising herself for acting like a schoolroom miss and not a lady already on the shelf.

'You need not apologise. Only say yes to a ride. My horses are outside and excited at the prospect.'

Her eyes narrowed, but further protestations were interrupted.

'Those are your matched greys, Your Grace,' Lady Lane exclaimed, sailing into the room, a beaming smile on her face —the kind that made her look younger than her forty-three years. 'Such beautiful creatures. I was admiring them from the window of my sitting room, where I was occupied with some correspondence.'

Vivienne looked at her aunt, hoping her expressionless stare said everything she couldn't.

'Thank you, Lady Lane. It is my hope to persuade your enchanting niece to accompany me on a ride in the park.'

'What a wonderful idea. How nice it is to spend a little time under the sun when the city has seen so many gloomy days all in a row. Do not you agree, dear?'

Vivienne knew exactly what her aunt was doing but agreed all the same. The weather had in fact been quite dreary for nearly a sennight.

'You ought to fetch a pelisse,' her aunt added, 'although I hardly think you'll need it.'

'I had thought to remain indoors, ma'am.'

With a meaningful look, her aunt said, 'You've spent the entirety of the day thus far cooped up. Young people ought to get out as much as possible, before gout and shopping lists take up all their time.'

With a valiant attempt at smoothing out the grimace she felt forming, Vivienne said only, 'Let me retrieve my outdoor things,' and swept from the room, letting her face twist into displeasure as she ascended the steps to her bedchamber, taking longer than was necessary to secure her bonnet and pelisse.

Sitting by the duke's side in his curricle, Vivienne let the burden of conversation fall to him, content to remain silent for the duration of their time together, however long that may be.

He began with a comment on the weather, to which she made some sound of agreement but no meaningful response. He followed this with a question about a forthcoming event, at which she could neither confirm nor deny her presence, as it had not yet been decided, and he finished by letting them lapse once more into silence. Just when Vivienne was feeling satisfied with her efforts to fend off all conversation, he said, 'What think you of *Fordyce's Sermons*?'

So surprised was she, that Vivienne whipped her head around to look at him. His countenance was as bland as unseasoned potatoes, but there was a flash of mischief in his eyes she was beginning to recognise, and she couldn't suppress the ripple of mirth rising in her throat.

'You are ridiculous, Your Grace.'

'Hazel.'

'I beg your pardon?'

'Brick is what my mother calls me. Hazelhurst is what my friends call me. Hazel is what I'd like *you* to call me.'

'We are not friends. We are not anything, really.'

'No? All the same, I am not *Your Grace*. Not to you.'

She studied him, his earnest eyes, and quelled the pulse of emotion surging through her. 'I don't think Fordyce would care for you overmuch, with the exception of your being male.'

He chuckled. 'I don't think he'd care for you at all.'

'On that, I'm afraid we must agree, for I am neither meek nor submissive. And I cannot twist my rational mind into agreeing that if a woman is a paradigm of modesty and duty—according to everyone, not just Fordyce—the loss of her virtue must be an irretrievable thing. It seems quite unfair that only one false step, whether one's own or someone else's, must decide one's fate. We have only to turn to Wollstonecraft to see such in practice.'

'If your desire is to unfold your faculties, you have succeeded, at least where I am concerned.'

She started at his direct reference to the woman's work, but recovered her place in the conversation by saying, 'Her legacy has been tarnished, but what of the man who got her with child and left her? Ought we not to speak of *his* sins? Of *his* loss of virtue? Surely claiming a woman as one's wife, without the intention of making her so legally, and abandoning the child that resulted from that relationship, is a greater moral failing than believing oneself in love and giving over to the physical expression of such.' Only after the words were swirling in the air between them did Vivienne realise exactly what she had said, and despite her best efforts, she felt heat creep over her skin. When she chanced to look at him, his expression was a curious mix of surprise and desire, and a heat that warmed her more than the sun filled her belly and sunk down into the space between her legs.

'You don't speak this way to others.'

'No. I should not have—'

'Don't. I like that you are so free with me.'

Vivienne most certainly did *not* like it. The duke, his person, his being as a whole, was a distraction. More than that, without effort, he was able to make her say things she ought not say aloud, much less to a man whose gaze landed on her like a bolt of summer lightning.

She hated how she always knew when he was looking at her with his penetrating stare, how her skin tingled and her senses heightened.

'What's that?,' he asked, transferring the reins to one hand and lifting the other, his finger reaching round the shell of her ear and the soft leather of his glove grazing a sensitive little bit of skin. 'Right here. It almost looks like a spot of paint. How singular.'

The spot he touched prickled, and the sensation fanned out from there, her body coming alive at his touch. Vivienne reached a hand up to her neck, knowing she needed to explain away what was surely a remnant of her morning's work and chastising herself for being so careless.

'Without being able to see myself I cannot say, although Maria, my maid, uses all manner of powders, pomades, and potions to achieve such a naturally elegant look.' Her bright, cheery tone a sharp contrast with how she normally spoke to him. She dared a look his way to see if her jest was as distracting as it was intended to be.

128

On his face was an expression of feigned horror. Whether from relief or discomfort, she laughed, too loud and too long, but the duke's smile was wide, warm, and she felt his pleasure down to her very core.

16

*M*iss Kent, well on her way to securing an offer from Sir Jackson, was hosting a small picnic in the open green space in front of her home, having cancelled her original Venetian breakfast some time ago on account of bad weather. There Vivienne met with many familiar faces as well as some new, but it was the hair on her exposed neck coming to a stand that heralded *his* presence.

When she turned from her conversation with Anabel, she saw the duke on the far end of the veranda. He was engrossed with a Mr Thomas, but his eyes were intent upon her. She shivered.

'Are you cold?'

Vivienne blinked as she looked at her friend. 'Only the breeze,' she answered, making a show of pulling her shawl a little tighter around her shoulders. It was one of the finest days of the season so far, sunny and warm, and only a faint chill in the air as summer grew nearer. Air which, it ought to be said, was quite still.

'I see.' Anabel's eyes slipped behind Vivienne and back

again. 'Miss Kent is getting up a game of pall-mall. Shall we join? Unless you prefer—'

'Yes, let's.'

Not ten minutes later, Vivienne brought the mallet back and gave the little wooden ball a hard whack, revelling in the satisfying crack that echoed through the trees. Pall-mall was one of her favourite games to play when she was at her aunt and uncle's country home.

'You've thwarted my plan, Miss Emory.'

She jumped as the duke's deep voice folded around her. 'What plan was that, Your Grace?'

'Hazel,' he whispered, the word landing like a featherlight kiss on her neck. As he came round to face her, the fine fabric of his coat brushed the bare skin of her arm. 'It was my earnest hope you wouldn't even have seen a mallet, much less know how to handle one.'

'Perhaps if I were less competitive and a better actress,' she replied, with a nod to Anabel, who stood wedged between Lord St Germain's arms as he guided her through the swinging motion. The duke raised an eyebrow in question. 'Anabel and I have been playing pall-mall a decade or more,' she explained. 'It is she who should be giving your friend lessons.'

His pleased, rough laugh rumbled through her. 'How did the two of you become friends?'

'Her mother and my aunt are quite close. When I moved from Cornwall to Norfolk to live with them after…' Her lips twisted as her sentence trailed away and she swallowed the rest of her words. 'It was then Mrs Boyton brought Anabel down. I suspect it was all a ploy to distract me, and I suppose it worked.' She gave a smile, hoping to bring some levity back to the conversation.

'The Cornish scenery is some of the most spectacular I've ever seen.'

She turned to him, eyes wide. 'You've been?'

'You're surprised?'

Vivienne tipped her head. 'It's rather out of the way for most.'

He stared down at her with a curious intensity, his eyes flicking to her lips. She could feel herself being drawn in but was powerless to stop the attraction from rooting within her and was grateful when Anabel and Lord St Germain came breezing past them, the latter inquiring as he walked on to his ball, 'Are you two waiting for the season to change before taking your shots?'

'Only for the two of you to finish your lesson,' drawled the duke, before moving away from her side and leaving her with an unexplainable ache in her chest.

Without bothering to look around to gauge how much interest they'd attracted, Vivienne wandered to where her ball was and did her best to avoid the duke's company for the rest of the game. The number of people present made it easy to do so, but her tenuous sense of safety crumbled as the party was breaking up. She was once more with Anabel, whose brother had gone to call for the carriage, when the duke approached and offered to take her home.

'As my own home is in Grosvenor Square, it would be my pleasure to escort you, Miss Emory, and spare Miss Boyton's brother the necessity of going out of his way.'

'Mr Boyton doesn't mind,' she protested.

'Not at all,' agreed Anabel, 'but it's too kind an offer to pass up, is it not?'

Vivienne *wanted* to go with him, and that's what made her most desirous not to. 'As kind as it is unnecessary. It would be inappropriate for me to be alone in a closed carriage with you, anyhow.'

'I drove my curricle, which has already been brought round.' He held out his arm for her to take.

Her body shook a little as the deep timbre of his voice cascaded down her, and she felt, not for the first time, a pressing sense of danger. There was no other protest she could make, so she nodded, bid her friend goodbye, and allowed herself to be helped into his waiting equipage.

'Mrs Kent could offer a lecture on matchmaking,' he began, as they set off from the little party.

'You may give me the credit for Sir Jackson and her daughter. It was I who introduced them.'

'I congratulate you on what appears to be a success. We are sure to see an announcement any day, it seems. Will I see you at the Seftons'? Or perhaps Almack's on Wednesday?'

'I believe my aunt and I will be present at both.'

Silence grew between them and might have been awkward if not for the noise of the London season—phaetons and carriages carrying people and their packages, the bustle of streets crowded with ladies shopping for a new bonnet or parasol or ball gown, gentlemen discussing horses they'd seen at Tattersall's.

'You don't attend as many events as other young ladies.'

'Have you been looking for me, then?'

'Being in your company is the best part of my day.'

'Your practised words won't work on me, Your Grace,' Vivienne said, even as her breath came and went faster than before.

'Hazel.'

Her eyes flicked his direction.

'Surely you must know my words are in earnest. I'm quite the catch, yes, but not a flirt.'

A flash of amusement crossed her face, and her lips quivered against the desire to smile.

'I wish you would let me in, if only a little.' After a pause, 'Will you at least tell me why you refuse every offer of marriage? Surely there is one man in all of England who suits your tastes.'

She shook her head; the very thought of trying to articulate any response that wasn't the sob so suddenly formed in her throat had brought on a headache.

'Miss Emory?'

Her voice trembled a little when she spoke. 'I have let you in.'

'You have not, and I don't want to hear the untruths you've managed to pawn off on your other suitors.'

Your *other* suitors.

'You wouldn't understand.'

'Come now, Miss Emory, you cannot know that.'

She thought he sounded a little worn when he said her name. 'I can. I do.'

'That's rather vague, and a trifle unfair to me, don't you think?'

'What can a man know of fairness? It costs you nothing to be a man. Your greatest sacrifice in taking a wife is the pin money you settle on her.'

'Yes, and a woman sacrifices so much in marriage—hosting parties, shopping, taking tea.'

'You, who wants a wife so entirely dependent upon her husband as to require guidance on how she must feel— whether you're gambling away your estate or discussing how much you like the duck served at dinner—cannot know anything of what a woman must give up when she marries.'

'As a matter of fact, I'd much prefer a wife capable of forming her own judgements. I find I rather enjoy a spirited debate. You think I would expect anything from you in marriage other than for you to be exactly as you are?'

'We are not speaking of us.'

'What if I am?'

Vivienne faltered a little. 'I am not. Not now, not ever. Did you think I would fall at your feet because I am on the shelf, and you are such a matrimonial prize? Should I be so grateful to you for the attentions you've paid me?'

'That is not what I said.'

'But it is what you meant. It's what every man means.' The din of London had been left behind, and she dropped her voice so as not to be overheard by any passing acquaintance. 'I have a life, one I quite like, no matter how odd that may appear to you or anyone else, and I have no desire to give up what matters most to me.'

'I don't expect you to.'

'You do. The very idea, ingrained in every gentleman from birth onward, is such a part of your make-up that it's impossible to see and harder still to change.'

He made no further comment, and when the curricle came to a standstill in front of her aunt and uncle's home, he handed her down in silence.

She knew he waited to see her admitted to the house before driving off, but not once did she look back.

Inside, she went to her room, flung her hat and gloves off, and collapsed onto her bed to scream into a pillow.

a dark cloud appeared over Brick when he left Miss Emory on the doorstep to her home. He was a man who decided what he wanted and got it, and yet here he was, unable to pry even a direct answer from the lady.

When he strode into White's after eleven that night, even St Germain, who noted with a small frown the tension and anger in his friend's bearing immediately, would not push to discover the cause of Brick's dour mood. It took several hours, half a bottle of whisky, and two bottles of wine before the duke's sullen state showed signs of abating. The improvement was short-lived.

'Duke, gentlemen,' said Lansbury, as he took the last open chair at the table.

'Lansbury,' replied Mr Roberts by way of greeting. Brick and St Germain remained silent.

'I was on my way to make a wager but thought I might come to see how Hazelhurst gets on with his own,' Lansbury said, in his grating, nasally voice, the smell of spirits ripe and rolling off his person.

'Quite well.'

'If that's so you are to be congratulated. I'd begun to think perhaps the ageing Miss Emory isn't fond of men, if you take my meaning.'

It was St Germain who responded. 'Naturally you would think so. There could be no other reason the young lady wished to avoid having you as a tenant for life.'

Lansbury ignored this barb. 'Your Grace, might you give me some insight before I make my wager? Should we expect Miss Emory to take a lengthy sojourn in three months' time, or are you a little out of practice?'

Brick stood up so fast, the motion of pushing back from the table caused the bottles upon it to rattle.

'Hazelhurst,' Saint warned in a low voice. He looked round at the other men in the club, whose attention had turned towards them.

Brick sat back down but leaned across the space between them so no others beyond his own party could hear. 'I'll see you at dawn, Lansbury.'

His cousin's colour drained considerably, except the ruddiness of his cheeks. 'He doesn't mean it.'

'I assure you, I do.'

'Because I'm right?'

Brick's voice was deathly calm as he replied, 'Because you're wrong.'

'Ah,' his cousin said, a mocking little smile playing about his lips. 'How stupid of me not to see which way the wind blows. You're dangling after the chit.'

'I daresay, Lansbury,' Mr Roberts interjected, 'I've never met a man so determined to put a point to his own existence.'

Lansbury scoffed as he pushed back from the table. 'I've always wished for an excuse to get what's mine.'

When he was gone, St Germain turned to Brick. 'Really, man, what are you thinking? I know he is the most foolish man alive, but when word gets out—'

'It won't.'

'It most certainly will, and when it does—'

'It can't.' Brick was already reproaching himself for his rash challenge, but he would never regret defending Miss Emory to the likes of Lord Lansbury.

St Germain, his voice reproving, continued. '*When* Miss Emory learns of it, because she will, along with the entire rest of the *ton*…And what if you kill him? You go abroad again? Far be it from me to cast judgement, but that seems an unsettling way to live.'

Mr Roberts, for his part, was saying nothing except to mutter what sounded like a slew of prayers.

Brick ran a hand over his face. It was badly done when her honour wasn't his to defend, and if the gossipmongers learned of it, there wasn't a member of the *ton* who wouldn't assume an understanding between himself and Miss Emory. But a rat like Lansbury didn't deserve the privilege of even speaking her name. To say something so vulgar—well, it was more than Brick could countenance, and he wouldn't pretend otherwise. As it was, it would take all his control not to put a bullet through that man's heart on the morrow. Even that was a nod to his impulsive nature. No one actually met at dawn. Seconds sorted out details for days, sometimes weeks, and the challenged party was given a chance to issue an apology. 'Lansbury would never offer an apology for the slight.'

'You say that as if you would accept one if he did.'

Brick took a sip of wine and looked down at the claret reflecting the soft candlelight of the dark room, wondering how furious Miss Emory would be when she found out.

~

JUST AS THE sun rose on the following morning, both St Germain and Mr Roberts were present with Brick at Wimbledon Common, St Germain as the second, Roberts as a spectator. Lansbury was fifteen minutes late, a little wobbly, and browbeating his fearful second into silence. Each man brought a surgeon, with these preferring to remain in their respective carriages at some distance.

The whole affair, from beginning to end, was over in a matter of minutes. St Germain offered Lansbury his choice of pistol from the case Brick supplied, both seconds counted out twenty paces for the principals, and Roberts held a crisp white neckcloth in the air. The neckcloth dropped, the duke found his mark, and pulled the trigger.

His bullet would give Lansbury a bit of a limp for the rest of the season, something with which he could remember his stupid words and poor decisions.

Unfortunately for Brick, getting shot wasn't something a man ever got used to, and the pain when a bullet pierced his left shoulder took his breath away. He dropped the pistol and reached his right hand up, idly curious if Lansbury had meant to hit his heart, and he would have had he been a better shot. Both surgeons made for their men, as did the seconds, the latter shouting concerns as they ran.

'It's fine. I'm fine.' Brick's tongue felt thick, and he sounded as if he'd just ran from one end of his estate to the other.

Mr Wickwork, a man who'd attended the duke since he was a child, forced Brick down to the ground, removing his coat with help from Roberts and not bothering to spare his shirt from the scissors.

'Doesn't appear to be any major damage, but the bullet is in there well and good,' Mr Wickwork said, as he cleaned around the wound. 'I suggest you bite on something, sir. This will be unpleasant and may take a few moments.'

Brick's eyelids were heavy, and he half-opened them to watch Wickwork select a pair of long pincers, which he doused with something that smelled like brandy. Roberts held a sleeve of Brick's coat in front of his mouth, but Brick shook his head and turned away from it.

'Hold him as best you can.'

Four hands pressed down on his body, as if he could move even if he wished. Every limb and bone felt as if it were weighed down by rocks. The jerk when the pincers dug into his torn flesh, and the howl accompanying it, were entirely involuntary.

Mr Wickwork poured some of the spirits over the wound, but by that point Brick was so close to the edge of unconsciousness as not to notice the stinging sensation. He could hardly make sense of the conversation happening around him.

'Get him home and keep him in bed, where he'll need to remain at least a sennight. I'll come to check on him before dinner and tell him myself, but he ought not to be alone, lest he wake up and think himself capable of moving about. Any motion of the arm could lead to fever and irreparable damage.'

'Understood,' responded St Germain.

'These bandages will need to be changed in'—Mr Wickwork checked his pocket watch—'two to four hours, depending on the bleeding. As I said, I'll come round before dinner, but if you're seeing much red before then, or if he becomes delirious, send a note immediately.'

Brick attempted to mount a protest, but the pain finally had its way with him, and the last thing he remembered before passing out was being lifted between two people.

---

18

*V*ivienne appeared at Almack's on Wednesday with a smile on her face and apprehension knotted in her heart.

She had seen neither hide nor hair of the duke in the five days following their tense exchange after Miss Kent's picnic. He was absent at Lady Lacyday's rout, the Harewoods' ball, a large dinner party hosted by the Seftons, three card parties, and his box at the theatre had remained empty on the two occasions she was present during the week. Scanning the ball-room, it seemed he was not, after all, present at Almack's, either. Her brows pulled together. For all the faults she felt comfortable assigning to him, he didn't appear to her to be a man who said one thing and did another.

'Who are you in search of, my dear? Or do I already know the answer?' Lady Lane asked slyly.

'No one, ma'am. I was only looking to see which of my acquaintance is present tonight.'

'Has your survey returned the desired result?'

'Anabel is here with her mama and brother, and just over there I see Miss East with her parents. Were not you desirous of speaking with her mama?'

'I am. She and I are on the board of a new charity that supports widows and orphans, but we will hardly talk business in a ballroom. Oh, but I did wish to discuss the particulars of the benefit performance by the soprano Catalani.'

'Lady Lane, Miss Emory.' Lord St Germain bowed before them both, and Vivienne suddenly felt more alert. She knew him a little, most recently as a close friend to the duke. 'I was hoping you would allow me to lead you out for the next set.'

Vivienne nodded and moved with him towards the floor.

'You and I have a friend in common, Miss Emory.'

'I imagine we have many.'

'Yes, but I speak of one in particular.'

He paused as they crossed the velvet ropes and took their place across from another couple. The opening steps of the quadrille parted them, and it was some time before they could be still as the other two couples who made up their set took their turn.

'It is my understanding,' Lord St Germain began, in a quiet, languid tone, 'that our friend wished to be present this evening. He is, however, come down with a cold that will see him at home some days yet.'

Vivienne couldn't picture such a well-built man languishing abed with something as trifling as a cold, but the image of the duke in bed at all caused two matching red blooms to stain her cheeks. They deepened when it occurred to her that his lordship had very likely been tasked with delivering the message.

'Well, you need not have gone out of your way to tell me as much—in fact you need not have delivered it at all. I should wish everyone good health, of course, but there can be no cause for you to suppose that *his* health must be of particular interest to me.'

They were parted again, and when he was once more at her side, he spoke only of the size of the ballroom, the number of dancers, and the very fine weather.

By the time St Germain returned Vivienne to her aunt, she was feeling a little guilty for the sharp way she'd spoken to him, and said, 'I thank you for the dance and think you a credit to your friend.' She thought his lordship looked a little embarrassed, but he thanked her for being a delightful partner, bowed, and wished her a pleasant evening, before taking himself off.

It wasn't until the second set formed that it occurred to Vivienne her next had yet to be secured. In all her years being out, she could count on one hand the number of times she'd sat out a dance, and never before at Almack's. Even her aunt seemed to take note, pausing in conversation with some grey-haired woman whose gloved hand was covered in rings and bracelets, to lift a questioning eyebrow. Vivienne gave a bewildered little shake of her head and stood by feeling somewhat stupid as she watched the other couples begin a lively Scottish reel. By the fourth set, her lack of partners had become conspicuous, and she received several confused and pitying looks from other ladies. Relief washed over her when Sir Jackson appeared at her side to partner her for a country dance.

'I was beginning to feel like a leper, and you quite saved me.'

'Yes, well—' He cleared his throat, and she noticed some deficiency in the usual ease between them.

'We have been friends for some years now, have we not?'

He nodded in confirmation.

'Then tell me what you know, because I am certain you know something. Why am I treated tonight as a wallflower?'

'I don't know. At least, not for certain.'

'But you have suspicions. A guess.'

Sir Jackson shook his head before they went down the line of the dance, and for several minutes no more could be said.

'Tell me,' she demanded hurriedly as she went round him.

'Rest assured, it is not a slight against you.' He crossed in front of her, meeting another young lady in the middle, before returning again to Vivienne's side.

Her reply was steeped in sarcasm. 'How reassuring.'

She let the subject drop, sure in her belief that if he felt at liberty to say more, he would, and by tacit agreement they conversed on safer topics for the remainder of their set. The thread, however, was picked up once more when Anabel finally took a break from the dancing.

Vivienne was lingering at Lady Lane's elbow and doing her best to avoid appearing as confused as she felt. 'I would beg my aunt to take me home, only I fear leaving would lend credibility to whatever it is that's preventing any gentleman from partnering me. Have you heard anything?'

'I have not, not even from the ladies. Whatever it is, the men have closed ranks, it seems.'

'For now, anyway. It won't last long. Only, I'd like to know what I may be facing, at the very least.' Her worst fear, of course, was that someone had discovered her identity as 'VC', the painter the *Post* considered '*An upcoming talent and an artist worth adding to one's collection*'—praise that would never be given if those critics knew she was a woman. However, aside from sitting out more dances than she was used to, there was nothing so very different about the evening, which puzzled her most of all.

'Mr Carlyle is coming to claim my hand for the set,' said Anabel, glancing over her shoulder, 'but when my brother comes out of the card room, I promise to ask him. If he knows, he will tell me.'

After watching her friend go, Vivienne spent the dance standing at her aunt's side, smiling and nodding along with the conversation the women were having, and trying to look as if her presence in the little group, instead of in a pair on the floor, was not just normal, but entirely by choice.

In addition to Sir Jackson, her hand was solicited for a dance by a nephew of her aunt's friend, a young man who appeared to be just past his majority, and by Mr Roberts, who had proposed to her once some years ago and remained friendly whenever they shared company. He, like Sir Jackson, seemed not quite at ease at her side and desirous of saying no more than was necessary, although his manners were pleasant and his smile genuine.

It wasn't until Lady Lane blessedly announced she had called for the carriage that Anabel once more returned to Vivienne's side, joining her while she was donning her cloak. This time Anabel had a look that would have been comical if not for the way it made Vivienne's stomach drop.

'Do not be angry,' was how Anabel chose to open the conversation.

'What is it?'

'*Do not* be angry.' She repeated as she clutched at Vivienne's hand, squeezing so tight it hurt. 'I will not tell you here unless you promise to keep your countenance—and Vivienne, I warn you it will be a struggle to do so.'

'I'd rather you tell me, lest I stay awake contemplating whatever horrible fate is about to befall me.'

Anabel's face grew a shade paler, and Vivienne could see her swallow with effort.

'Anabel.'

Her friend nodded in what appeared to be an attempt to rally herself.

'Quickly, if you please.'

All at once Anabel blurted out the words, 'The duke shot Lord Lansbury in a duel. I've no other details, but Frederick believes that is the reason you were relegated to your aunt's side tonight.'

'But I've naught to do with either.'

'Accuracy of that statement aside, the gentlemen at least feel His Grace has enough of a claim on you to keep away.'

Anabel's face blurred, the entire room tilted, and it felt as if Vivienne's ribs had squeezed every last bit of air from her lungs. She put out a hand, hoping for a wall or anything to steady herself, and hit a hard body. Strong fingers clasped her shoulders, keeping her from dropping to the ground.

'Good Lord, Anabel. Did I not tell you only a moment ago not to tell her? At the very least not in a crowded ballroom? Here,' Mr Frederick Boyton said, lacing Vivienne's hand through his arm. 'Your aunt is just there. I'll see you to your carriage.'

Mr Boyton took a step and was stopped by his sister.

'And Vivi,' Anabel whispered, 'the duke was also wounded.'

On those final words, Vivienne was led away from her friend and out of Almack's. She couldn't recall if she thanked Mr Boyton and didn't notice if her aunt was talking at her.

Panic was rioting within. A sheen of sweat developed at her hairline and in the crevice between her breasts, and she had the uncomfortable sensation she was on the verge of casting up her accounts, which she did—twice—once home and in the privacy of her rooms.

---

he worst part about a bullet ripping through layers of flesh and lodging itself in his shoulder was not the pain, which was like a hot bee sting, or the constant presence of the surgeon or the nurse St Germain hired to ensure he didn't develop infection or fever. It was the lazing about in bed. Mr Wickwork urged him to remain an invalid for a week complete, but Brick was now on day four, and aside from the soreness in his arm and the need to keep the dressing clean, he felt very much himself and able to resume his usual activities, with a few exceptions. He was debating how he might spend his first day out of his rooms, when St Germain came wandering in, suggested to Brick that he send his valet, Halliwell, away, and sat in the chair that had been moved nearer the bed.

'I'll not dally with pleasantries, Hazelhurst. The sooner you can see Miss Emory, the better.'

For a moment, Brick had the odd sensation he was drowning. 'Ought I to ask why?'

'Saw her at Almack's, danced with her even, but I was one of the only gentlemen to do so. Word is out, as we knew would happen, and men know enough of your reputation to suppose Miss Emory at the root of the duel. The ladies present seemed keener to discuss Miss Ronan's sudden departure to the country in the middle of the season, but it's only a matter of time before your little escapade is general knowledge, and once the gossip begins in earnest...You're lucky it hasn't already, but I doubt you have more than a day, maybe two, now that everyone has borne witness to such curious behaviour. Poor girl looked quite confounded to be left standing at her aunt's side.'

Brick let out a long sigh. 'Damn it all to hell.'

'Just so.'

'Get Halliwell back in here,' Brick said, easing himself from the bed.

Saint did as he was bid, wished his friend good luck, and saw himself out. An hour later, Brick was being announced in the drawing room of Lord and Lady Lane's townhouse.

It was not one of Lady Lane's at-home days, thankfully, and she was alone when he entered, although she didn't seem surprised to see him or do more than blink when he requested a private audience with her niece.

'I believe she's in the music room. If you care to sit, I'll send her in directly.'

His brow furrowed at the mention of her being in the music room, but Lady Lane left before he could make any reply. Once alone, he paced. From the door to the window, the window to a little table stacked with books, the little table to the mantle. At the mantle, he paused to study the painting he'd noticed when he was last in the room and was once more struck by something familiar in the type and quality of the work. Taking a step closer, he leaned further forward still to study the brushwork, the prospect of the painting: a stormy sea in the background and lush, rugged, green cliffs in the foreground.

He was still looking at it when she walked in, the movement catching his eye. Brick turned to face her and was met with a hostile glare. As he spoke, he noticed her hands were balled into tight little fists at her sides.

'Miss Emory—' He stopped speaking as she marched over to him and stood still as a statue as she inspected his person. She cast a long look over each of his arms, ran her eyes over his chest, walked behind him and was there for several interminable seconds as he imagined her inspecting his back and lower. She circled again to the front, rising on her tiptoes to get a closer look at his face. Inches. That's how little distance separated them then, and his body was acutely aware of it.

With each inhale, he took in the scent of her, and as her head tilted, he eyed the tender spot of her neck, wondering if it would feel as soft beneath his lips as it looked. Softer, more likely. He imagined leaning in, the throaty whimper she would make when he nipped and sucked and kissed—and then she poked him. Hard.

Caught unawares, he let out a little grunt as she stabbed him in the middle of his chest. She jabbed him again, this time in one side of his ribs and then the other. She poked his right bicep, and then the left. He flinched.

'Ah.' It was the only sound she had made so far, and her eyes, lit with impotent rage, met his own as she prodded again, this time a mere inch from where the bullet pierced his skin.

Brick cried out. He couldn't help it.

'I beg your pardon, Your Grace. Does this hurt?' she asked,

stabbing her finger into him, the sharp tip of her nail pushing against the ridge of his sewn-up wound.

When she made to do it again, he reached up with his right hand and caught her wrist tight in a strong grip. 'I will thank you to keep your hands to yourself.'

'I'll wager that's the first time you ever made such a request. Let me assure you, I'm happy to oblige.' She wrenched her wrist from him and turned to cross the room, putting as much distance as possible between them.

'We need to discuss—'

'*We* need nothing.'

'I'm sorry—'

'Oh, are you?' she asked, in an airy, singsong voice. 'Well, then, it's quite all right you've made me a pariah. The gentlemen at Almack's would scarcely look at me; Mrs Roberts' drawing room fell silent when I walked in with my aunt to take tea. I've yet to make sense of any of it, but somehow people seem to hold *me* responsible for *your* actions.'

'I did not mean—'

'It matters not.'

'Will you let me—?'

'No. I will never—'

He crossed the room in a flash, wrapping his good arm around her to pull her body against his and lifting his left hand to cover her mouth. When he opened his own to speak, the heady, delicate smell of night jasmine filled his lungs. It was as if he could taste her when his tongue skimmed his bottom lip. Her eyes, angry and clear and curious, dropped to his mouth. The yearning that wrapped around every bone of his body threatened to pull him apart, and Brick listened to the grind of his own heart as it began to beat a rhythm only for her.

'Miss Emory, I *am* sorry, whether you choose to believe it or not, even more so as I know what I must say next will be repulsive to you.' He took a breath and tried to focus on what words he needed to string together, rather than how warm and pliable her lips felt against the flesh of his palm. 'We must announce our engagement.'

She jerked against him and snaked a hand up between them. The pressure of her touch, right in the centre of his chest, closed a void where he'd not known one existed.

'I will release you, but for your own sake, you must set aside your anger with me for the space of a conversation.' Brick did as he said, letting her go in an instant and feeling the absence of her immediately. 'We've been in company too much to avoid rumours.'

'Then perhaps you ought not to have defended your honour at the expense of mine.'

Brick swallowed hard. 'There was no choice but to demand satisfaction.'

'Why?'

There was irony, he knew, in the situation. By defending her honour, he gave rise to gossip about the very thing, but he was as incapable of appreciating the irony as he was able to explain to her why her honour mattered so much to him.

'What I propose is this: we announce our engagement so the *ton* will see the duel as something that brought the event forward rather than the cause. We go about as a happy couple. I will escort you to events, and Lord and Lady Lane can host a dinner party.'

'Have I not been clear?'

Her words stung like a pinprick between his ribs.

'You have.'

'Then you must know my answer.'

'And you must know there really is no other choice at

present.' *What can a man know of fairness?* Her earlier words struck him then, sending a quick, sharp pain straight to his gut. 'In some months, perhaps when everyone has retreated to the country or Brighton for the summer, we might put it about that I was ungenerous with the marriage articles or some such thing, and the wedding has been called off. I will shoulder all the blame and do my very best to absolve you of fault whenever and wherever I can.'

Her eyes narrowed in suspicion, and anxiety pulled her delicate features taut. 'You promise you will release me from this engagement?'

Trying to hide the hurt and disappointment he felt, he answered solemnly, 'I promise.' He meant it. As much as he'd come to understand his feelings for her, his desire to be with her always and in every way, he would never take this choice from her.

Miss Emory studied him with wary eyes, teasing her bottom lip with her teeth as she did so. 'Very well.'

Her frustration was palpable, and yet relief coursed through him. Relief and a little trill of excitement, of hope. Even a false engagement was reason enough to fill all his hours with her. 'You are of age, but we ought to inform your aunt and uncle. I'll see that an announcement runs tomorrow. What plans have you this evening?'

'A loo party, a musicale perhaps.'

'We can ask your aunt. If possible, we ought to be seen together tonight. The loo party hosted by Lady Linden?'

Vivienne nodded and went to pull the bell, and they stood in silence until Lady Lane arrived. Brick let Miss Emory say what she pleased to her aunt, which was the whole of it, and he didn't even interject when she referred to him by turns as a blackguard, a coxcomb, and a hell hound without a care for anyone or anything but himself.

He turned down an invitation to stay for tea but left with a promise to arrive promptly at ten o'clock to escort her to the Linden home on Brook Street.

20

Up until the party, they had been seen together often enough, as people in the same circles so frequently are, but they had never *arrived* together. Doing so, her hand sitting prettily—possessively—on his arm, his eyes warm with admiration only for her, was tantamount to the announcement that had not yet run. They walked into the spacious drawing room of Lord and Lady Linden's home together, and like sand washed away at the water's edge, the chatter died out as one person noticed them, and then another, and another. Eyes went wide, mouths hung slack, and silence reigned for several seconds before curiosity was raised to a cacophony of sound.

Brick took a glass of champagne from a tray held out by a footman and handed it to Vivienne before taking one for himself. 'Perhaps when you reach the bottom of the glass you'll have forgotten how angry you are with me,' he said, a half-smile lilting his lips.

When he'd arrived once more at her aunt and uncle's home, she'd kept him waiting in the entry hall a quarter of an hour, no doubt on purpose, judging by the annoyed sideways glance she'd shot her aunt while descending the stairs—much like the one she was giving him now. He suspected she would have lingered longer, or simply not come at all, had that been an option.

'All the champagne in France is not enough to achieve such a thing.'

'How about all the champagne in the cellars of Goldfinch Park? It's at least enough to rival the country, if not more.'

Her eyebrows furrowed. 'Goldfinch Park?'

For a beat he was nonplussed, then he shook his head and chuckled. 'My home in Hertfordshire. The cellar is nearly the size of France. The eighth duke might have been said to overindulge, and the twenty-first had a significantly younger wife, whose only comfort was to be found in a bottle.'

Her awkward little laugh floated up to his ears, and he couldn't keep from smiling down at her.

'Would you like to hear more about the estate?' he asked, as he led her in a slow promenade around the perimeter of the room, their closeness and his dark look keeping others at bay.

She lifted her chin and said primly, 'No.'

He allowed them to continue in silence, and several minutes later it was she who spoke next. 'It's rather a short distance from town, all things considered.'

Brick looked away for a moment to hide his smile. 'Half a day. It's an easy journey with a good road.' He left space for her to reply, and when she didn't, he added, 'As a child, I always begged my papa to bring me to London whenever he had business here, using the short distance as the cornerstone of my argument, but now I resent every letter that takes me from home.'

'You do not care for the season?' Her question was asked with equal parts curiosity and doubt.

'I like the theatre, musicales, seeing friends, dancing with a beautiful woman, but it's all playing a part.' When he looked down at her, he noticed a faint stain on her cheeks he could not account for.

'You think I'm playing some sort of role?' The question wavered, just at the very end, the effect unsettling him, although he couldn't be certain why.

'You speak to me in a way I've never heard you speak to anyone else. You put on an act, but not for me. Not with me.'

Vivienne had been holding his stare, but with those words, she dipped her head and hid herself away from him. It took effort not to frown at her mysterious reaction, and even more restraint when Lord Lansbury limped to stand in their way as they neared the door through which they'd first entered.

'Hazelhurst, Miss Emory,' Lansbury said, his hungry eyes resting a second too long on the low neckline of Vivienne's dress. Brick's free hand curled into a hard fist. 'The tables begin to fill. You won't want to wait too long to take your places.' Turning to Vivienne, he added, 'His Grace is known to enjoy a good wager.'

Brick's jaw clenched. 'We only wait for you to take your seat so we know which table to avoid.' With that, he steered Vivienne around the man but to nowhere in particular.

'He offered for me, once,' she stated, in her forthright way.

It was clear to Brick she meant only to share the piece of information, not to solicit a reaction of any kind. 'I'd heard something to that effect.'

'Oh?'

There was a trace of surprise in her voice, and his eyes, bright with mirth, dropped to hers. 'You've a reputation for devastating men and leaving their broken hearts behind when you leave a room, or didn't you know?'

'Hardly that,' Vivienne replied, through an amused smile. 'You may still break mine.'

Lady Linden saved Vivienne from the burden of replying by coming over to see them settled at a table with another young couple, set a little apart from the others.

Loo, which Brick had never much enjoyed, became the most pleasurable of activities with Vivienne seated near him, her tinkling laugh ringing in his ears, her attention as much on him as the game. There was only one way in which the evening might improve. Brick had surveyed the room after his turn to discover Lansbury watching them, a grim grin twisting his mouth.

'You seem distracted. Bad cards?'

He looked to Vivienne, studied her clear, intelligent eyes, her pert mouth, and thought how much he would miss the privilege of looking at her, feeling her near, when she cast him off.

'Perhaps the champagne has worked wonders after all,' he said, with a levity impossible to feel at that moment.

She lifted a perfectly arched brow and tried to prevent the corners of her mouth from curling upwards. 'I'm only interested in whether I ought to pass or play.'

'Pass,' he said, his voice firm and full of challenge.

'Play it is.'

His smile then was genuine and just for her, and his knee knocked hers under the table. The gesture flustered her a very little, but he noted with pleasure that she didn't move her legs further away. Still, the damage was done, and an implacable heaviness settled in his chest. The whole of the rest of the night he thought what an absolute fool he'd been ever to accept Lansbury's wager.

21

'*B*rick William Thomas Vesily!' his mother thundered from the entryway as she rounded into the library where he was enjoying brandy and rereading some of his favourite passages of *First Impressions.*

Brick closed the book, his finger tucked between the pages still, and cast a dispassionate glance at the dowager, who was white with fury, as he expected she would be. 'You know, Mother, I can't recall you ever stringing together all my names.'

'That you are teasing at a time like this is only another measure that you belong in Bedlam. What have you done, you foolish boy?'

'How is my aunt, ma'am? I thought you were to remain with your sister in Wimbledon some days yet.'

'She knows the joy of children not half so disobedient as you've proven to be,' she barked, jowls quivering. 'Tell me this is some joke done in poor taste—that you've convinced the printer to do this especially for you and it's not the thing being talked about in every drawing room in Mayfair.' As if she needed to clarify what she'd spoken of, she walked over to where he was still seated and tossed that day's paper at his lap.

Brick let his finger slip from the book, retrieved the paper, and without looking at the pages, stood to hand it back to his mother. 'Surely people are more interested in the rising cost of grain than my engagement.'

'It is true, then?'

'If you feel your eyes deceive you, you ought to be at the oculist and not in my home.'

'Brick!' The dowager screeched his name in such piercing tones, he glanced at the vase on one of the side tables near the sofa.

'Are you telling me you've not heard of my duel?'

His mother teetered and braced herself with a hand on the chair directly across from the one in which he'd been sitting. 'What's that to do with it?'

Brick went to refill his glass, saying as he did so, 'Lansbury made an unpardonable comment about her virtue.'

'Which is not yours to defend and certainly no reason to tie yourself to the girl.'

'Perhaps not, but I'd like to tie myself to her, all the same.'

'How can you say so? She's no match for you.'

His expression remained unconcerned, but the muscle in his jaw pulled tight. 'If you feel Lady Felicity is the better match, I can only lament how much you misunderstand me.'

The dowager snorted. 'I misunderstand nothing. You're thinking like a man and not like a duke with more responsibilities to shoulder than the king himself.'

'I'm thinking of my happiness and how much easier it will

be to shoulder the weight of the world when I've a partner by my side, and not some insipid wife who's just another thing for me to manage.'

'That's what being a husband is.'

'That's not the kind of husband I wish to be nor the kind of wife I wish to have. Vivienne is as intelligent as she is beautiful, as sharp as she is sweet. She is not cowed by my title, does not bend to my wishes, will not excuse my bad behaviour to purchase favour. You may think of her however you wish, but it matters not to me. Now, I must ask you to leave. I've a meeting at half past.'

'You will regret this, child.'

'On that we must disagree,' he replied with equanimity, as he took his mother by the elbow and steered her from the library. When the door was closed behind her, he turned on his heel and made for the stairs.

As he entered his chamber, rather than turn left towards the dressing room, as was his habit, he paused and looked right at the closed door standing between him and the suite of rooms reserved for his wife.

His wife.

At Huxley House, he'd told Vivienne they could break their engagement over the summer, when no one was left in town to gossip over the news. People would be visiting friends or family, catching up on estate work, readying for fox hunts and shooting parties. Their interest would wane as quickly as it had been piqued without a dozen events in one night at which they could discuss what had happened.

There was just one problem with Brick's plan: he had no desire to break their engagement. He wanted to open that door and know Vivienne was on the other side. He wanted to breathe in and taste notes of jasmine on his tongue. He wanted a lifetime with her and was beginning to feel that without her, he might cease to exist.

22

'We ought to host a dinner for you and the duke, dear one,' Lady Lane said, as she ran a needle through the fabric of her husband's handkerchief, where a very pretty flower was taking shape.

Vivienne, dropping the book she was reading into her lap, said flatly, 'No.'

'Let me put it another way. I've sent out invitations to a dinner party celebrating your engagement to the duke.'

'Aunt! You haven't!'

Still, without stopping or even looking up from her work, her aunt replied, 'Certainly I have. How backward it would look if we didn't.'

Vivienne groaned and let her head fall against the back of the sofa.

'You act as if finding yourself engaged to a duke is the worst possible thing in the world.'

'Not truly engaged, may I remind you, and you know *exactly* why it is the worst thing in the world. You think a man like that would let me have a profession, much less one with such potential for exposure?'

Her aunt made a tight, interested, humming noise. 'How fascinating you did not begin your rebuttal with a statement about the egregiousness of marrying a man you've no feelings for.'

'Of course, I—'

'I'm not interested in whatever lies you've been telling yourself that you hope to pawn onto me. You have not confided in him, then?'

'Goodness, no.' Vivienne was shocked her aunt would even suggest such a thing. Lady Lane's concern regarding the revelation of Vivienne's identity had always been much greater than Vivienne's herself. Her aunt worried prodigiously about her future. To Lady Lane, marrying well, advancing in society, and being accepted by the *ton* was the only option. To oppose expectations so openly as to have a profession and to refuse eligible offers of marriage was something Vivienne's aunt couldn't understand. Not only this, but she feared the consequences of such behaviour. It was anathema to everything Lady Lane had been taught as a young woman herself. In that way, she could not have been more different from Vivienne's own mama.

'He seems quite taken with you,' she said.

'That's not enough. Nothing will ever be enough.'

'Quite an extreme point of view.'

'It's too great a risk, and I am surprised you of all people are encouraging it. If we choose to accept that most things are possible, then of course it is conceivable he might not care. However, even the most liberal man finds himself less so when his wife courts unwanted attention. To say nothing of his pride. Unless one is the king or queen, there is not enough money and power to stand up to a duke determined against you. He might not care, or he might out me, or openly oppose me, see to it that my work never hangs in the Royal Academy again. If he did so, what choices would I have? Move to the continent? Leave my friends and family behind? It's too great a risk.'

'So you said. My mistake for misjudging how much trust you had in him.'

Something awfully close to a snort came from the couch where Vivienne sat.

'You have enough trust in him to commit to an engagement—'

'A false engagement.'

'Exactly my point—an engagement everyone else believes is real. Should he wish it, he could make things very difficult for you, which I am certain you know. Therefore, I am surprised you outwardly trust him with your person and your future without, so it would seem, genuinely trusting him with your person and your future.'

Vivienne pressed the tips of her fingers to her temples, rubbing firm circles, and hoping to expel the headache coming on.

'Thursday.'

'Hmm?' she murmured, eyes still closed.

'Thursday, dear, is your dinner.'

It was Tuesday. Vivienne bolted upright, the motion sending the blood rushing from her head and making it swim for several seconds. She pressed a hand to her forehead, and the room stopped spinning just as it occurred to her there was nothing she could do about the dinner or the engagement at present, and so sank back into the couch once more to question everything she'd ever done that had brought her to this point.

Two days later, the throbbing in her head had yet to cease. Under normal circumstances, Vivienne would ask her uncle to call a physician. Presently, however, she thought severe illness or sudden death might be a welcome reprieve from the dreadful, undeniable fact that she was engaged to a man who, despite her best efforts, she was coming to like very much.

Even the cold lavender-scented compresses Maria continuously rotated every half hour failed to relieve any of the pressure pushing on Vivienne's skull, the space behind her eyes, her heart.

'I'm sorry, miss,' Maria said, on her fifth trip to the room, this time arriving without a fresh cloth, 'but if we wait any longer, we'll not have time to complete your toilette.'

'So be it.' The words came out harsher than intended, and Vivienne apologised swiftly.

'No slight taken, miss. You're not yourself, I daresay.'

'No, and I will apparently never get to be myself again.' It wasn't true, but her life hadn't felt like her own since the night she went to Almack's.

'It can't be as bad as that, miss. I've seen the way you two look at each other. If nothing else, I don't think I'd mind looking at him for the rest of my life.'

Vivienne looked sideways at her sweet little maid and wondered for the first time if she were right in the head.

'Come and sit. I will not be rushed and send you looking like a mopsey to your betrothed.'

With a sigh, Vivienne heaved herself out of her bed and over to sit in front of the mirror.

'Have you selected a dress? That green is so light. Ethereal, even.'

Vivienne's aunt, who, despite her desire to see her niece settled well, had gone so far as to refrain from appearing as if she took pleasure in the odd situation in which her niece found herself, had given up that façade entirely by the day of the engagement dinner. As if by magic, the woman had left three new dresses in Vivienne's room, new slippers, and several cases of jewellery—diamonds, sapphires, and emeralds, some of her aunt's most exquisite pieces—paired with them.

'The green is fine.'

Maria brushed Vivienne's hair till it shone, using just the right amount of rouge on her cheeks to make it seem as if the bloom appeared from happiness and not from a little pot; if Vivienne smiled, one could almost believe she was pleased to have landed the biggest matrimonial prize of the season.

Tilting her head first to the right, then to the left, Vivienne examined herself in the mirror as her maid fixed the delicate diamond combs in her pale copper strands. The woman looking back was unfamiliar, not in appearance but in feeling, or rather by virtue of being lost among so many conflicting emotions, it was impossible to give more weight to one than another.

'Cerulean.'

A flicker of surprise dashed across Maria's face. 'Beg pardon, miss?'

'The cerulean dress with the silver and gold embroidery. Not the green.'

Vivienne, determined to ignore her maid's wide, round stare, closed her eyes, pulled in a long breath, and focused on what was certain to be a trying evening ahead.

When the duke arrived, she kept him waiting long enough that it pushed the boundaries of what was considered polite, only leaving her rooms when Maria came round once more to warn her of the pinched look on Lady Lane's face.

'You look radiant, Miss Emory,' said the duke, once she finally came down.

While getting dressed, Vivienne had worked on any number of short quips, ready to employ them at a moment's need, but then she saw him waiting for her at the foot of the stairs. He was clad all in black, except for the white silk cravat that shone like a polished pearl in the candlelight, a large diamond pin nestled in its centre. The black should have minimised him, but instead, his thighs appeared even more muscular, his shoulders impossibly broad.

Vivienne could feel his eye on her, like fingers grazing her spine, as her foot found the final step. Every hair on her body prickled in its follicle.

'I'm quite in agreement,' said her uncle, giving Vivienne a start. She'd noticed no one in the entryway beside the duke. 'Shall we go through? Guests will begin arriving any moment.'

Anabel, her parents, and her brother were the first to arrive. After felicitations were given, received by Vivienne and her intended with credible smiles, Vivienne was pulled aside by her friend, who used the quiet moment before others arrived to say, 'You're out with the duke so often, this party was the only way I could be certain of finding you at home—though, of course, I can readily understand why you find his company preferable to my own.'

Vivienne held in a little snort and returned the tease with one of her own. 'Interesting you should say so. I quite think you prefer Lord St Germain's company to mine or anyone else's. He's expected tonight.'

The two moved nearer the long windows overlooking the street, and Anabel ran a length of the heavy brocade drapes through her thumb and forefinger. 'Hardly that.' Her gaze settled on something beyond the glass pane.

'Oh? For a moment at Miss Kent's you'd almost convinced me of your ignorance of how pall-mall is played. You looked quite cosy with him, but you need not say anything if you don't wish.'

Anabel turned, a fleeting moment of uncharacteristic sadness playing on her face. 'I would if there were anything to say. What you deem cosy was only a spot of kindness.' The tense smile she offered couldn't fool Vivienne in the least. 'Lord St Germain sees me as nothing more than one of Frederick's many sisters. Even the keenest eye would be challenged to find anything his in instruction that even came near flirtation. No lingering caresses, no long looks, not even a perfunctory compliment. Besides, how many men who are interested in a lady nick their chins and say, "Well done, you"?'

Vivienne was debating whether she ought to say more when Anabel turned the topic.

'I did not arrive early to talk of his lordship. Tell me, is this all because of the duel? You *will* be happy, won't you?'

Concern threaded through her friend's words and prevented Vivienne from replying with anything but candour. 'Yes, only we are pretending it's not.'

'Of course.'

'As much as we are *pretending* to be engaged.'

'No!' Anabel's cry caught the attention of both her mama and the duke. The latter raised an eyebrow before returning to his conversation, and something in the familiar, private gesture made Vivienne feel a little silly for speaking so of their betrothal.

'Come summer when everyone is from town and gossip cannot so easily pass from drawing room to drawing room, we'll call it off.'

'Oh.' Anabel pursed her lips and tried to hide what Vivienne could only describe as disappointment. 'Only, you two seem well suited.'

'You cannot believe that.'

'I do. I know your stance on entering the matrimonial state, but you forget how long I've been a friend to you. This is not to say you would change your mind, only that I've seen you together.'

'If you are about to say I light up when he enters a room—'

'Hardly that, although you've had a glow about you.' When Vivienne glared at her, Anabel pulled a quick smile and continued, 'You are determined in your dislike of him, and yet you are more yourself around him than others. Most people wouldn't notice, because most people aren't treated to the version of you that I am—that he is.'

Vivienne's brow creased. 'Anabel, did you ever discover what he and Lansbury duelled over?'

Anabel scrunched up her lips to one side, something she did often while thinking. 'No. I suppose I'd assumed like everyone else you had something to do with it—not directly, of course. Only, I mean, it's not as though His Grace goes running about with a gun in his shirtsleeves. Just that it seems if one wants to protect one's mortality, then one ought to pretend any lady who's captured the duke's attention simply doesn't exist.'

The fine hairs on Vivienne's nape rose, and she looked over to find the duke's cool, inquisitive stare pinned on her. 'Of course,' she said, squaring her shoulders. 'He's shot a man over a woman before.'

Her friend replied through a chuckle, 'You need not look so put out, particularly as you very nearly needed smelling salts when I told you of the first. Besides, on the outside they may appear to have happened for the same reason, but I am quite certain *he* feels a distinction.'

Vivienne was both vexed that he'd fought a duel and vexed he'd done so before over some other woman. She struggled to make sense of why the former should matter to her as much as the latter.

The door at the far end of the room opened, and the butler announced Lord St Germain. At her side, Anabel stiffened. Vivienne heard the sharp hitch of her friend's breath and gave her hand a firm squeeze before moving to greet those who'd just arrived. Although she could not share the experience of pining for an elder brother's friend, Vivienne understood all too well what it was to desire something she could not have.

23

*T*he duke had presented himself at Huxley House an alarming number of times since their engagement—that is to say, every day. He took Vivienne for ices, for drives in the park, to Fortnum & Mason, and currently, they were wandering between the high hedges of a maze that had appeared in the little park near Grosvenor Square.

'I've told you something of my life before,' she commented as they reached a dead end. 'Now it's your turn.'

'What would you like to know?'

'Why you killed that man.'

'If he didn't want to be shot, he shouldn't have absconded with my bride.'

'Did you love her?'

'Not even a little.' He moved in that graceful, unhurried way of his to close some of the space between them.

'And still you feel no remorse?'

He stood directly in front of her, and yet she felt as if she were being circled before capture.

'Is that what you want? You wish me to feel badly, or at the very least to excuse my behaviour on account of some deep, inexplicable feeling that drove me to madness? I would give you anything within my power, but to give you that would be false to who I am.'

'Who are you?'

'I am a man who is impulsive, who does what he pleases, who gets what he wants.'

Her pulse pounded, the heat of the day suddenly stifling and pushing in all around her. 'You're spoiled.'

'Very.'

The caressing tone he used twisted her up inside. 'Had you been in a duel previous to that one?'

'Several. Some men are poor losers, exceedingly so where cards are concerned.'

'Did you hurt them, too?'

'Their pride more than anything.'

'Would you do it again?' The whisper of her words was barely loud enough to be heard over the rustling leaves caught in a breeze.

His body leaned closer to hers, blocking out everything but her and him. 'With the right provocation, I would do anything.'

'For cards or women? There is no difference then for you between the two?' She was pushing but couldn't stop and couldn't work out the answer she hoped to hear.

'There didn't used to be. Now, there is only you and everything else.'

Vivienne's mind went instantly and entirely blank—every thought she'd had replaced by a refrain of his words: '*There is only you.*'

The duke reached out, slipping two fingers under the ribbon of her bonnet, his knuckles skimming her jawline.

'Your Grace,' she said, on a throaty sigh.

'Hazel,' he whispered back.

She closed her eyes and focused on how his name felt in her mouth as she repeated it. 'Hazel.' With the rustle of satin gliding against satin and the slight pressure on the crown of her head, she felt him remove her bonnet and let it tumble to the grass.

Vivienne squinted against the bright light of sun, finding first his eyes and then his lips. His hands claimed hers, and he pulled them up to his chest, bringing her so close, not even the charged air around them could fit between. He ran his thumbs over her fingers, wrapped tightly around his own, and his head inclined in silent question. She swayed into him, lifting her chin in a wordless sign of permission. The seconds it took for him to close the distance were interminable, as if she'd been waiting the whole of her lifetime for him to kiss her.

His mouth, warm and full, covered her own in a gentle kiss that sent an ache of longing through her body. His tongue traced her lips with tantalising slowness, urging them to part, to let him taste her more fully. She yielded, surrendering her mouth to him and letting herself slide into the unrelenting depths of desire from which she would never be able to escape.

Brick moved her hands to the nape of his neck, where her fingers caught in his soft curls. Giving over to primitive instinct, she held him to her, nipping his full bottom lip, using her tongue to graze and tease and tempt his senses. His guttural moan vibrated through her bones and coaxed her to deepen the kiss. She savoured the wild awareness overtaking her body—every nerve, every follicle, every limb had come alive in response to his touch.

When he finally pulled himself from her, the husky way he

murmured her name turned her heart over in her chest. 'Vivienne.'

His hands were at her waist, and his forehead rested on hers. She could feel the tenderness, the desire in the word as it caressed her mouth as his lips just had.

'I can't,' she stated, although her tone was more wistful than confident.

'You can. Let me give you everything.'

'I have everything I need.'

'Everything you *want.*'

Her hands had dropped down to the lapels of his coat, but to those, she still clung tight.

'Don't,' he said, his voice raw.

'Don't what?'

'Deny me. Deny *us.*'

His voice cracked with an ache so deep, Vivienne felt a wound, irreparable and incurable, rip open inside her. She reached up to explore the planes of his face, his strong brow, his perfect nose, his stubborn chin. She skimmed her fingers over his carved cheekbones, the perfect peak of his upper lip and the pout of the bottom. Hazel watched her, his hooded eyes probing and intense. As her thumb slid along his bottom lip, he kissed it, the movement surprising a little gasp from her.

In one fluid motion, she was back in his arms, the soft curves of her body fitting to the hard ridges of his. He kissed her with such hunger, a shiver rippled through her, unearthing a need she couldn't sate.

'No.' She pulled herself away. 'I can't.' And this time when she said it, Vivienne didn't allow her hands to stay tangled with him. She turned and bent to retrieve her bonnet, which was on the ground at her feet.

'Allow me,' Hazel said, taking the bonnet from her loose grasp.

Vivienne stood still as stone as he placed it on her head and began to tie the very ribbons he'd undone, his long, skilled fingers gliding along the flesh of her neck and over her skittering pulse.

'There's something I need to tell you.'

His voice was serious, and she responded a little breathlessly, 'I'd rather you didn't.'

'Vivienne, please. It's not what you think.'

'No.' The word cracked as it left her mouth. He was dangerous, and not because he'd shoot a man for looking at him the wrong way. His hands grazed her arms as he dropped them from the ribbons, and Vivienne sensed two things: first, there was nothing so important as putting space between herself and him; second, there was nothing so hard as putting space between herself and him. 'Not now. Not today, please.'

He nodded, but by the grim set of his mouth, she got the sense his silence was costing him something dear.

24

'*A*re you quite prepared for this?'

'For what, Your Grace?' Vivienne cast a sideways glance in his direction. She had only just begun calling him Hazel, and with her aunt in the carriage the diminutive felt too intimate.

'We've not yet attended a public event as an engaged couple.'

'The loo party came close, did it not?'

'Whispers fuelled by rumour are always quieter than those fuelled by truth.'

Vivienne settled further against the plush velvet with a deep breath meant to shore up her resolve. 'Certainly the *ton* have talked their throats raw by now.' Even as she said so, she knew how silly it sounded. The *ton* needed gossip to survive, much as she needed air. The duke's crooked brow, visible in the moonlight streaming through the windows, and the gentle upward pull of his mouth, told her he knew it as well as she did.

'Can you tell me something more intriguing than the biggest matrimonial catch and an infamous spinster announcing their engagement?'

With a pinch of her lips and one second of silence, followed by another, she was forced to own she could not, at least not at that moment.

'A very good thing you're made of stern stuff,' Lady Lane chimed from across the carriage.

'Just so,' replied Vivienne, covering with ease the fact she'd momentarily forgotten her aunt's presence.

What she discovered when they passed between the colonnades of the theatre and into the entrance hall was that even the duke had underestimated the interest their engagement had stirred up among the other patrons. As they came through the doors, everyone stilled, as if unsure what they were seeing was real, unsure if the notice in the paper had been nothing more than some odd jest or prank. When the duke threaded her hand through his arm and held out the other for her aunt, the noise that erupted reached deafening proportions.

He tipped his head to hers. 'They would, of course, be less interested if you were half so beautiful or I half so rich.'

'My part could very easily be done with a little dirt and a dash of creativity, but for you, I believe half so rich as you currently are is still quite rich.'

The sound of his laughter sent a warm current through her, and the soft smile tugging at her lips was unstoppable. For onlookers, this little exchange was all the confirmation they needed to determine the duke had indeed found a shocking match and the spinster a mighty prize—onlookers, that is, who were not one of the many men whose proposals had been rejected. Some looked on with wide eyes, others with frowns.

As they moved through a crowd that parted before them, Vivienne caught snatches of words and phrases: 'Suppose I ought to have been born a duke.' 'Didn't we all know she was waiting for a fortune and grand title?' 'She's a beauty, but her best years are behind her already.'

Her teeth came down hard on her tongue.

'Jealousy makes people behave in ugly ways, Vivienne.'

With a sharp jerk, she looked up at the duke, noticing only then that her aunt had excused herself at some point and could now be seen smiling among her friends.

'I'm not used to being the object of jealousy.'

'No? That's quite surprising.'

'You're teasing.'

'Not at all. Your face is exquisite, your manners flawless, and you've received offers from nearly every eligible gentleman in London. Long before I took your hand in mine, you were an object of envy. Perhaps it's just that people were not so open as they are now, which is my fault.'

'How so?'

'People always wish to cut down the things they find threatening.'

His words brought a faint flush to her cheeks, but if he noticed, he didn't let on.

By the time they'd made their way to his box, her uncle had arrived and was waiting outside it with her aunt.

A footman held the curtain open, and the duke gestured for Lord and Lady Lane to precede him and Vivienne. There were two sets of chairs on either side of the wide doorway. Her uncle sat at the far end of the box, her aunt next to him. The duke guided Vivienne to the chair along the wall opposite, effectively sequestering her in the corner. She leaned forward a little to look out and down towards the stage but started when his leg brushed hers. There was a slight tremor on his lips, and with so subtle a movement as to go undetected by the two others in the box, he knocked his knee into hers.

Vivienne looked at him with what she hoped was a warning and was caught off guard by the guileless expression upon his face, but the amused glint in his eyes gave him away. The provoking man was teasing her.

'I've yet to absolve you for putting me in this position, sir,' she whispered, hoping she sounded more upset than she felt.

'No,' he returned. 'I doubt you will anytime in the near future, if ever at all.'

'Then perhaps you will consent to being less vexatious.'

'And perhaps one day you will consent to being my wife.'

'I believe I already have.'

'Not of your own accord and not truly.'

His fixed stare, bold and full of longing, made her feel dizzy, breathless. Behind him, she could see that neither of her relations was paying them any mind.

'What is the point of speaking so?'

'Your happiness is the point.'

'Why do you—?' she broke off, her voice cracking. 'Why do you persist?'

'Because, Vivienne, I have never met another woman like you, and'—he lightly fingered a loose tendril at her cheek, tickling her flesh as he did so—'because I think you want to marry me as much as I want to marry you.'

Her name on his lips rolled over her like a wave pulling her out to sea. If she let herself go, it wouldn't be long before she couldn't see the shore. He had awoken within her a need that wasn't driven by logic or reason; there was something deeply unsettling about him, about the way he made her feel, the things he made her want to do.

Despite knowing she could never be with him, when his gaze raked over her body and paused for a fraction of a second on the swell of her breasts, when his finger caressed the soft bit of flesh behind her ear, when he spoke aloud the truth she desperately wished to ignore, she couldn't help but imagine what it would be like to give herself over to him.

She blinked back tears. 'I can't.'

The line of his mouth tightened a fraction of a second before his face settled into a placid expression. At the edge of her chair, she felt his little finger reach out, his knuckle rubbing along her own. Whether it was because she wanted some relief for the pitiful feelings welling up inside her or because she could never have as much of him as she wanted, she pressed back. His finger linked around hers, and instead of pulling away, she curled her own to keep his close.

WHEN THE SMALL group exited the theatre, Vivienne assumed they would return home the same way they'd arrived. But Lady Lane, with a little wave of her hand, said, 'You are no young miss fresh out of the schoolroom, and it's hardly a long enough ride for you to put a point to his existence, tempted as you may be to extract yourself from your current situation,' she added, her placid tone at odds with the pointed look in her niece's direction. 'You two can follow behind.'

She watched her aunt and uncle board their own carriage before Hazel handed her up into his own and she settled against the velvet squabs, her body wound tight as she struggled against the emotions running through her like a band of wild horses. He took the seat next to her, his long legs falling apart at the knees, and even in so spacious a carriage, it made the very little distance between them feel impossibly small, like she was closed in a room with him and a thousand butterflies, their wings feathering every inch of her skin. The heat from his body washed over her, permeating every layer of clothing she had on before kindling in her belly.

With a shaky inhale, Vivienne attempted to steady herself, but her nostrils filled with his scent—charred cedar wood, tobacco, something warm and sweet like vanilla—the heady notes reminding her of their kiss in the maze. She wondered what his skin would taste like beneath her lips, and the very idea made her head spin, as if she'd consumed too many glasses of iced champagne.

'Are you all right?'

The deep timbre of his voice scraped against her like crisp, dry bristles on a fresh canvas.

No. The word lodged in her throat, her body unwilling to release that one syllable: 'Quite.'

'I wish you would tell me what's wrong, my love.'

Her heart winced. Danger had never been so near at hand as it was now. Visions of her future had always been clear and pure—until Hazel offered her something different, something she had never before bothered to imagine.

He was so many things to so many people, but to her, he'd simply become Hazel. Time spent in his company had the familiarity of a dream, one that came to her every night, but which she could never remember once the sun rose. Finding herself in the intimacy of the closed carriage, of a world where nothing beyond the two of them existed, was like waking up and remembering the dream, only to wish she hadn't. It revealed to her a life she could not have.

'There is nothing the matter.' Her voice was weak, tremulous, despite her effort to sound composed, and one single tear ran down her cheek.

Hazel turned on the bench to face her; she knew by the swishing sound of satin against velvet, the gentle sway as his weight shifted, the familiar feeling of his eyes pinned to her.

He reached out a bare hand, his fingers briefly sliding up into her hair before skimming the back of her neck and round to the exposed flesh of her shoulder. The delicate touch sent waves of awareness through her. His thumb traced the wet track on her cheek.

'What's all this now, my love?'

Her response was a shallow shake of her head, and with her eyes closed tight, she tried to focus on anything but the vital man next to her, his words that knocked the wind from her, and the overwhelming desire to curl herself into him.

Those long, strong fingers grazed along her jaw and turned her head towards him. The warm pad of his thumb traced her bottom lip, and when he parted them, she let a tormented little exhale escape. Her heart fluttered wildly as a violent shiver of wanting rippled over her.

'I'm afraid, too.'

Once more she shook her head, almost imperceptibly this time. Her hands burned with the urge to touch him as he was touching her. At her side, she curled her fingers into the fabric of her dress. His thumb still rested on her lower lip, and he dragged it along once, twice, before pressing the very tip of it into her mouth.

Instinctively, she closed her lips around it and held on gently with her teeth. When her tongue massaged the little bit of him inside her, he groaned with unrestrained arousal. The logic holding her together began to fragment as desire for him flooded her veins.

'Look at me, Vivienne.' Hazel pulled his thumb from her mouth and dragged it in a straight, hot line from her chin, down her neck, and along her front where it arched over the swell of her breasts, peeking out of her dress, before tracing her whole curve.

Her breath hitched as his whole hand palmed her breast. With a gentle squeeze, he pinched her nipple between his thumb and forefinger, and she let free a sound between a cry and a moan.

'Do you like this, my love?'

Vivienne licked her lips but said nothing.

'Look at me.'

His voice was smooth, commanding. Vivienne blinked open her heavy lids, and Hazel came into focus as her eyes adjusted to the dark. She reeled at the passion she found there, the certainty he was going to eat her whole and she was going to let him.

Over her dress, he teased and rolled her other nipple until it peaked to match its mate. Her eyes fluttered closed.

'Look at me,' he demanded again in a hoarse whisper. 'Tell me you like this.'

The intensity of his voice wound through her, and she trembled.

When she spoke, her voice was low and raw, the one word choked as if it ached from a place deep inside only he could touch. 'Yes.'

His mouth found her collarbone and the hollow behind it, the pocket of pleasure where her earlobe met her neck, and she focused on the exact right combination of sucking and nipping that made her forget everything except him and this moment.

'This?'

His touch bewitched her. She mewed her agreement, and a moment later found herself settled on his lap, his hardness throbbing against her, her hands pressed into his muscled chest.

He caught her panting breaths as his mouth met her own. He tasted like wine and spice and inevitability. She felt his tongue tracing her lips and she parted them, trying to fill herself with him in every way possible.

'Open for me.'

Vivienne parted her legs, unsure how she'd ended up straddling him or when her dress had been hiked up enough for her to do so. His fingers grasped hungrily at the hot flesh of her hips, and her whole world tilted as he began to rock her against the hardness between his legs. The silk of his satin knee-breeches glided along her centre. She knew she should be terrified, should have demanded he stop at once, but her mind was clouded by the pleasure coursing through her, the pleasure *he* was giving her.

With a little tug on her dress, the puff sleeve dropped down her arm, setting free one of her breasts. She arched hard against his mouth as the rough surface of his tongue teased the rosy peak of her nipple. One hand was at her back, the other pulling at the opposite sleeve, and she had a hazy sense of awareness of moving all on her own, chasing some feeling that was burning and building inside her.

'That's right, my love,' Hazel said, his words feathering the hairs on her neck between kisses, 'find your pleasure.'

His words encouraged her, and she began moving her hips a little faster, alternating between bearing down on him and grazing the hard ridge between her legs with her own throbbing core. The tip of a finger at her entrance surprised a little yelp out of her, and she paused a moment as he stroked her opening.

'Christ, you're wet, Vivienne.' She didn't know what that meant, only that his voice vibrated with a hunger she knew was all for her.

'Put your hands behind me.'

Vivienne slid her palms up the velvet back of the carriage a little above his head, and in doing so, stretched herself out, bringing her breasts closer to his mouth. He growled as he devoured one and then the other.

'This, my love?'

Hazel had slipped a very little bit of his finger inside her, and she felt her muscles clench and pulse around it. He edged it out before gliding it back in, again and again.

'Yes.' Her voice shook like her legs were beginning to do. 'Yes, Hazel.'

His other hand had come once more to her hip, but she still controlled the pace, the friction. The mistake she made was in looking down at him. His eyes were full of desire and devotion. When he whispered, 'Give over to me, my love,' she felt the supplication in her bones.

Her lungs compressed erratically, a faint sheen of sweat dappled her skin, and her whole body coiled fierce and tight before she shattered. She held his heavy gaze with her own as she abandoned herself to the sensations mounting within her.

'Oh. Oh.' She panted the word over and over as she spasmed, a feeling of complete ecstasy thrumming through her like a hundred violin strings just plucked.

Hazel's finger trailed her sex, and she seized, tender with pleasure. He took her hands in his own and placed them on his chest. His heartbeat was as wild and erratic as hers, and she stared at his waistcoat as if his heart might burst out at any moment. He leaned forward to reclaim her lips, but the kiss wasn't demanding or frantic with passion, but slow, caressing, gentle. An acknowledgment of what was shared, of what she'd given to him.

'I—I—' She struggled to find a single word to follow the first as her thoughts whirled in an infinite number of directions.

'*You* are perfect,' he stated, pulling out his handkerchief and dabbing at the little pearls of perspiration on her hairline, before sliding the sleeves of her dress back over her shoulders and helping her re-pin the curls that had come loose. When she tried to slide off his lap, he held her tight to him.

He seemed content to let the rest of the carriage ride pass in silence, but his hand curled around hers and remained there until they reached Huxley House. For a fleeting moment he released her as he exited the carriage first, but he reclaimed her hand at once and assisted her up the steps to the door of her home as if it were the most natural thing in the world, as if they would go through together and not just her alone.

Hazel ran his thumb over the back of her gloved hand, pressed his lips to the crest of her knuckles. 'Good night, my love.' His hushed words were as soft and caressing as the kiss on her temple that followed.

'Good night, Hazel.' She stepped inside, refusing to look back but knowing he was watching her, all the same.

That night, alone in her room, Vivienne fell all to pieces. Her thoughts were so disordered and confusing that no sense could be made of them. For one wild moment she imagined revealing her secret. But painting wasn't a profession for a gentlewoman, let alone a duchess. The very idea of telling him and watching him walk away from her forever caused her chest to tighten as though she'd run too far, too fast. It wasn't concern for her reputation that prevented her from taking him into her confidence—it was deep, terrifying dread of his rejection.

25

*S*leep had not come easily for Vivienne after the theatre—after *that* carriage ride—and so she was up with the sun, dressing herself as best she could, hoping to make use of the hours before breakfast to finish the painting of Hazel. She stepped from one side to the other, got on her knees, stood on a chair, everything she could think of that might offer a different perspective on the man. The work had been easy in the sense that the background wasn't as detailed as many of her other pieces, but she was struggling with the expression on his face. Or she had been until the night prior.

She moved to the little table in the corner to mix up her colours, picking up the cobalt blue first before adding a little black and a little white. She lifted the palette, selected a brush with a fine point, exhaled her nerves away, and faced her canvas.

She was as close to feeling satisfied as she suspected was possible when her uncle knocked on her door almost three hours later.

'I was growing concerned. It's unlike you to miss breakfast.'

Vivienne sighed. 'This painting. I can't tarry over it any longer, but there's something I feel I can't get right.'

'May I have a look?'

She stepped back, allowing her uncle to enter her room and through the door to her studio. He came to stand shoulder to shoulder with her, and with her lower lip caught between her teeth, she watched his profile for a reaction. Wide eyes, the brief rise and fall of his eyebrows, and a deep breath, was all she was afforded.

'It's very good.' His tone was measured, and Vivienne was familiar enough with her uncle to know when he was placating her.

'That's not enough. You need not be reserved with me. Is it unworthy of submission, do you think?'

'Not at all.'

'Then what is it you aren't saying to me, Uncle?' It was one of the only times Vivienne had ever seen the man look uncomfortable.

He started and stopped several times before committing to whatever it was he wished to say. 'By his expression, whatever he's looking at has taken up all his attention, become his only focus. It leaves the viewer feeling, ah, exposed in a way.'

Vivienne crossed her arms, tilted her head a little, and rolled her lips together as she often did when thinking something through. In the earliest hours of light that morning, she had put the final touches to the most challenging part—his eyes.

'It is a bold choice, painting this particular subject, and one that won't sit well with your aunt.'

'You think I ought to leave this painting out?'

Lord Lane reached out and gave her cheek a little pat. 'You are twice as talented as many of the painters so often discussed in salons and well worthy of being grouped with all the rest. That is why people have begun to take notice of your work.' He turned back to the painting. 'Something like this, you cannot expect it to go unnoticed—by him or by anyone else. Your aunt's concerns and fears if you are discovered as the artist aren't unfounded, as you know. If this makes it into the Exhibition, there may be no going back for you. If that is what you want, you know you have my full support. We can always retire to Scotland for a time—or Italy. I've longed to return,' he added, with a smile.

Vivienne turned to hug him, only hoping after the fact that the paint on her apron was dry. 'Thank you. I'll be down in a quarter of an hour.' As her uncle reached for the handle of the door, she called out, 'You think it's done, then?'

He gave her a rather singular look and said, 'Yes, I think he's done,' before nodding once and leaving her alone again, without another word.

Her uncle would see the painting sent to his man of business, who would put it in the hands of a trusted and discreet art dealer, who in turn would submit it to the Royal Academy. Her uncle's words were worth consideration, and a little part of Vivienne knew it would be better if the Academy rejected this piece—or better still if she consigned it to the flames—but she was certain, deep down in her very core, they would take it and it would likely set off a fire she couldn't control. It was a prospect both thrilling and frightening.

There was nothing so terrifying to her now, however, than how *he* might react. Whether he would love it, hate it, look at it with little more than indifference. She wanted him to see in himself what she could, and the chance he might dismiss her work caused her heart to stop for a few perilous seconds. He could ruin her career and crack her heart in two with one disdainful sniff.

Vivienne went to the armoire in the corner of the room, retrieved several boxes, and set them on the floor at her feet. She knelt and opened the lids, lifting out scraps of paper, whole catalogues, scattering them around her until she found what she was looking for.

'From an unknown artist comes an example of the kind of inter-esting genre painting we'd thought could not exist on a wall with more serious history pieces, the kind of painting certain artists and critics have long believed could elevate British art to that of the Old Masters. I am here to put forth another idea: British art will never succeed if that should be its goal, so ought we not to give more wall space to pieces that celebrate our country, its inhabitants, in all their beauty as this one does?'

For every bit of praise her work received, there was always someone who didn't like it—who criticised her for being pedantic or afraid to take bold risks.

Amidst these words were the catalogues from every year her work had hung in the Royal Academy's Summer Exhibi-tions, beginning with *Joie*.

It was seven years ago that she'd sold her first painting, before she was even out, a piece inspired by a tenant's daughter whom Vivienne remembered from when she still lived with her parents in Cornwall. The young girl was dressed plainly in a grey-brown dress, sitting on the slope of a gentle hill set a little distance from her home, her legs tucked to one side, the bright blue of a calm bay in the background. She was making a flower chain. The girl, despite the certain knowledge of having much to do at home, looked peaceful, content in a way Vivienne hadn't understood until she began painting.

She wondered where *Joie* had gone—where all of them had gone. Whether she were hanging in pride of place somewhere, or consigned to a long gallery, or a little salon at the back of a house where a dowager knitted. Vivienne hadn't yet learned to let go of her work as an artist must, and although it made her feel silly, she hoped her paintings were cared for, wherever they landed. Every painting she had exhibited had been purchased, but she never knew by whom. Her uncle's solicitor handled the transactions on her behalf under strict confidentiality, and even if the solicitors for the buying parties revealed who they represented, she didn't want to know—that knowledge felt too dangerous.

26

A piece of business brought Brick to Upper Wimpole Street, a little removed from the *tonnish* part of town where he passed most of his time. The weather was uncommonly fine, but Brick hailed a hackney, impatient to call on Vivienne. It had been three days since the theatre. He had debated with himself over whether to appear the very next morning in her drawing room or to allow a little distance for her to think over what had happened between them. In the end, he'd settled on sending her flowers the day afterwards—a lush bouquet of roses, apple blossoms, myrtle, ivy—and a note expressing his intention to call. As he stepped up into the carriage, a movement a little down the road caught his attention. A young woman stepped into the flag-way. Her graceful movements, the copper glint of her hair, stopped his heart cold.

'Where to, m'lord?' the driver asked, with some impatience.

'A moment.'

Brick stood half in the hackney, his mind racing with possibilities, and for once feeling uncertain what he ought to do next.

'Far be it from me to rush ya, m'lord.'

'You don't, but I've no need of you.' Brick flicked a coin to the driver, stepping back out to the road as the hackney pulled away empty.

Miss Emory was keeping a brisk clip, and from the distance, he could tell she was carrying a rather awkwardly shaped parcel, almost like a portfolio case. With only a moment of hesitation, he trailed after her, and with each step that brought him closer, he determined not to give himself away but to wait and see where she went.

He paused a moment in front of the nondescript townhouse she'd stepped from and noted the number. It was insignificant to him, but his man of business could make discreet inquiries.

Twice she stopped, and he ducked into the portico of a business just as she turned to look behind her. Brick observed that before she did so, she ran her hand up to her neck—a curious little movement that struck him as rather odd.

A quarter of an hour brought him within a few steps of Huxley House. He watched her sail through the doors of her aunt and uncle's home, and he leaned against a tree in the smallish park at the centre of the square. The debate happening in his mind was short-lived, and he pushed off the tree and in the direction of the house, without another thought.

'If you will wait in the morning room, Your Grace, Miss Emory will be with you directly.' The elegant and elderly butler directed Brick to a room he was fast becoming familiar with.

When Vivienne appeared, less than ten minutes later, she was in a fresh dress, but her hair was still in a low, simple bun, different from any other time he'd seen her at home or outside of it, and she seemed a little flustered.

'To what do I owe the pleasure? I had not thought to see you for some hours yet.'

He noticed her closed expression, how she tucked her hands behind her back, the way she stood at a little distance from him, a chair between them. 'I was in the area.'

'You live in the area.'

'I wished to see you.'

A look of wariness passed over her face, and her eyes, still vibrant from the exercise, were cautious as she watched him.

Brick drew in a steadying breath. 'What were you doing in Upper Wimpole Street?'

Vivienne gasped. 'You were following me?'

'Business took me in that direction.'

'And *then* you followed me?'

He said nothing, his lips setting into a thin, hard line.

'How dare you!' Her nostrils flared and fury lit her features as she stalked nearer. She squeezed the back of the chair till her knuckles were white.

'You forget yourself, madam. You are my intended, and I've every right to know how you spend your time. If you're involved in something unsavoury, we would both be better off if you make a confession now.' The very thought she might be doing something even he wouldn't approve of made his stomach churn and bile rise in his throat.

'I'm not your intended, not by any definition.'

The strong emphasis on the word knocked the wind from his lungs. 'If I had my way, you would be, but you remind me again how repugnant the idea is to you.'

'You put words in my mouth.'

'Tell me in your own, then, why you won't consent to be my wife?'

'Why did you shoot Lansbury?' She held his stare, her eyes hard and hostile, her face pale with anger.

'Why are you asking a question to which you already have an answer?'

'I don't have *your* answer, the *real* answer,' Vivienne countered, her chin tilting.

'What can it possibly matter now?' Brick showed no other sign of frustration than the subtle flex of his hand at his side. With a resigned sigh, he said, 'He questioned your virtue.'

A deep shade of red suffused her neck and cheeks, and he was certain she was replaying their carriage ride home from the theatre. 'It wasn't your place to defend me.'

He repeated her words back to her with a hint of a snarl as he came around to where she stood. 'Not my place to defend you? There is no world in which I would let an attack on your honour go unchecked. You may never consent to being my wife, but I will protect you, champion you, until my last breath.' A faraway expression cast a shadow over her face, like a cloud passing over the sun. It was gone just as swiftly, too. 'You have not told me what you were doing in Upper Wimpole Street.'

'And I will not, so you may save yourself the trouble and cease your bullying.'

'You'd rather my imagination fill in what you won't provide?'

'I'd rather you relent and relinquish all idea that my concerns are yours.'

'As long as society believes us engaged, you are my

concern. If you are embroiled in some scandal, some scheme that will bring shame, I'd rather have it out now.'

She faltered. Only for a moment. He saw it in her eyes, a fleeting look of worry, of trepidation.

'So you can very publicly cast me off?'

'Surely you know I would never do such a thing.' With those words, he did away with the remaining distance between them, his hands hardly leaving his side to take hers.

'It's easy to promise when the scenario is only hypothetical.'

His thumb ran over the back of her hand. 'Then make it real, Vivienne.'

They were staring at one another, his eyes pleading, hers cloudy in a way he'd never seen them before. 'Vivienne,' he whispered, resting his forehead against hers, letting the tips of their noses brush.

'I can't. You know I cannot. Not the way you wish.'

He inhaled as she spoke, the warmth of her breath filling him as though he'd swallowed the sun. 'I won't stop asking. I will never stop asking you to be mine.' All the fight had left him. The fact was nothing she could do would make him want her less.

Against him, he could feel the unsteady rise and fall of her chest as she worked to pull in air. He ran a hand up her back, rubbing it in slow, calming circles. She sagged a little in his arms, as worn from carrying something she refused to share as he was from trying to persuade her to do so. Minutes passed, and Brick knew there was nothing else to be said, so he placed a soft kiss on her brow and took his leave.

BRICK SAT in his library sipping a tot of brandy, feeling as if he were bound for Bedlam. He couldn't discern the exact moment he'd gone from feeling all thirteen of Miss Emory's other suitors had made a lucky escape to wanting nothing more than to be her choice, but that he wanted her to choose him was certain. Only he had not the slightest clue how to make that happen, particularly after their tense exchange a few days previously.

It was the small hours of the morning, but the room was awash in the soft glow of candlelight and he stared at the painting, wondering what piece of advice his younger sister might have for him had she still been part of this world.

He hadn't even had time to determine where to hang the artwork before he left England, but when he left, he'd given his man of business strict instructions to purchase any other pieces the artist chose to exhibit, whether they were offered for sale or not. He now boasted a growing collection by a painter he was certain would one day hang with the masters. It had taken years, but society at large had finally begun to wonder who was behind the funny askew 'W' and his pieces, which year by year were commanding better positions on the walls of the Great Room.

He swirled the brandy in his glass and had lifted it to take another sip when his whole body froze. He rose from the sofa, crossed the space between it and the mantle, and stopped only a few feet from the painting. He had seen the view in this painting before, only the sea had been churning and there had been no fair-haired girl on the cliffs. It was the same prospect shown, near identical even, as in the painting hanging at Huxley House. The only piece he and Vivienne had ever discussed for which she seemed in possession of startlingly little information.

Trading his glass for a candle he came within inches of the painting. Even in such low light, he could make out the signature, the 'W'. He tilted his head a little, reaching out his free hand to trace the letters. He couldn't believe he'd never noticed before—it wasn't a W and never had been. It was a VC. *'My mother was a Cornwall Caldicott.'*

27

The truth knocked the wind from him. His emotions varied wildly from anger to hurt to confusion, and at moments, fascination, pride, and a desperate wish for her to tell him the truth, a wish that ached deep within his chest.

He reasoned there was an infinitesimal chance he was wrong, but there was so much that made sense once he'd realised his secretive love was the artist behind not just his favourite painting, but several others he owned. First and foremost, there was her extensive knowledge and interest in art. But also the paint behind her ear, which she'd waved away as pomade or some such thing. The little rough spot of skin on her right ring finger. Her refusal to marry anyone, even him— and he was more than certain she was at least as half in love with him as he was her.

'Dear god,' he said aloud, to no one in particular, being alone in the library. The house he'd seen Vivienne come out of in Upper Wimpole Street. He'd asked his man of business to look into who lived there, but the information returned revealed little. A widow had inherited it from her husband, who had owned a bank in the City of London. She was, as far as his man could tell, a respectable, retiring woman who offered instruction in drawing and watercolour. Brick was certain Vivienne had never mentioned an interest in either of those things to him, and he let it rest, feeling a bit of a brute for cornering her and making demands, but also because, despite his immediate panic, there was nothing untoward to concern him, no trouble she was in from which he would gladly extricate her.

Suddenly he had so many questions, but more than anything, there was a gnawing wish that she would trust him.

WHEN HE NEXT CALLED, his intended was laid up with a headache, or so she instructed the butler to say. That happened twice, but when he tried a third time, she was sitting in the morning room with a book. Despite the closed expression on her lovely face, it was as if there had never been a moment of discord between them, and she accepted his invitation to a private gallery.

As his curricle came to a stop in front of a large townhouse in St. Martin's Lane, he scrutinised her countenance for any sign of recognition of the place but saw none.

'Have you been here before?' he asked.

'On the street? Yes. The Boytons live near here, but this residence is not at all familiar to me.'

'It's the Earl of Bayworth's home. He's one of the most prodigious art collectors in the country, and I thought perhaps you might enjoy viewing his private collection.'

When they entered, the housekeeper greeted them and led them up two flights of stairs to the gallery, which was situated along the west-facing side of the house and stretched its whole length. There were at least three dozen paintings of all sizes and subjects arranged, not by artist or theme, but seemingly to the taste of the collector.

'There are placards at each work, and as I understand it, you have no need of my limited insight, Your Grace. Ring the bell when you're ready to depart, and I'll see you out myself,' the housekeeper said, making a show of pushing the door as wide as it would go and leaving it that way.

'Decidedly not a fan of Wollstonecraft.'

Vivienne flashed him a grin before turning towards the miniatures decorating a side table just inside the gallery.

'The names listed are nearly all women,' he remarked, in what he hoped was a casual sort of way.

She agreed, but added, 'Mrs Robert Barron, Mrs Edward Baschet, Mrs Waldo Stevenson. Do you suppose they had names of their own at one time?'

'Does it not speak to the forward-thinking nature of the husbands that the work is here at all?'

'It's hardly a feat, or a surprise. This kind of work is prolific. That is not a criticism of the work itself—it's all very good and I recognise some of these artists from the Royal Academy, but for a woman who wishes to paint and display her work publicly, becoming a miniaturist is often her only option. Who will object to a little portrait of a friend or family member or one of the king's many children? To become an artist, any artist, is a risk to how others see them in their roles as women, and yet, in conforming to the expectations set forward through marriage, they have lost their identities as artists.'

'What of Le Brun and Villers?'

'French.'

She said it as though it explained everything. 'Different country, different culture, but men will always have names for women who dare to shift from their place; they will always make it hard to cast off the idea of what we ought to be.'

'Moser and Kaufman?' he asked, referencing two of the founding members of the Royal Academy.

'How many women have they let in since? None. Not a single one in more than forty years.'

She turned to move further into the gallery, and he followed. The first painting they came to was a great beast of a canvas featuring men and women naked from the waist up.

'Even when they do achieve success, at whatever cost, they're restricted from the same education as men. Kaufman and Moser weren't allowed to sit in the life-drawing classes. At best they had paintings, books perhaps, to copy what had already been done. I'm half convinced they each married in the latter half of their lives simply to have access to the male figure.'

'You believe women should be given entry to sit and stare at a naked man?'

Her lips turned down in a little frown and her chin dimpled, a sure sign she was considering his words, determining what *his* answer would be and if she would agree or be displeased. 'Gently bred females are expected to be shocked, fearful, of the nude form—the male as well as their own. When we aren't, the other sex begins to lose some of their power.'

'Is that what you see in painting? Power?' He'd kept his voice even, or so he thought, but she turned and pinned him with a sharp, assessing look.

'I see opportunity. Men are capable of considering only one perspective—their own. In art, whether they realise it or not— and surely they must not or they would have long banned women outright from picking up a brush—they are forced to see a person, a place, a thing, from a different viewpoint. It is like that painting at the British Institution. As much as you may have preferred to maintain your original feeling when viewing it, learning the work was painted by a woman forced you to reconsider what was transpiring on the canvas, regardless of whether you wished it to be so. Rather than seeing a young woman flirting with a man, you saw an old man leering at a woman simply trying to do her work.'

'What I wish,' Brick began, stepping close enough to run his hands down her arms, 'is that you would tell me the truth.' He watched her expression shutter.

'I've told you as much as I wish to.'

'You're keeping something from me.'

'Everyone has at least one secret. Surely you do, too.'

'I've plenty, but I would tell them all to you if you asked me to.' As he said the words, he immediately recalled that night months ago in White's, when he'd accepted the bet to win her hand, and swallowed the bile that rose in his throat.

'You and I are two very different people.'

'With common interests and shared passion.'

In her presence, it was easy for him to forget how upset he was by her significant omission as he trailed his fingers along the curve of her neck and collarbone, teased the curls at her nape, nipped her earlobe with his teeth. When she leaned into him, when she expelled a yielding sigh and a low moan, it was easy to forget everything except how badly he wanted her.

'Tell me,' he whispered against the soft skin of her neck.

'There's nothing to tell.'

'Tell me, my love.' Brick felt the chills as they poured over her body, and her flesh bristled beneath his hands and mouth. 'Trust me with your secret.'

'I haven't one.'

The lie pulled him from the deliciousness of her scent and taste. He looked at her, at the mix of fear and defiance in her beautiful green eyes.

'Very well.' In frustration, he let his hands drop from her and moved along the wall, where he would pretend to enjoy the paintings in front of them while wondering what else he could possibly do to prove himself worthy of her confidence.

28

*P*review Day at the Royal Academy had come quickly, and Vivienne's composure was under attack. Every year, the day before the exhibition opened, select members of the *ton* were invited to enjoy it before everyone else. Hazel had invited Vivienne. She'd accepted with the utmost reluctance because she could not do otherwise and had subsequently spent several days wondering if she ought to feign illness, or else throw herself into the Thames. Guilt was eating her up. She hated lying on principle, but deceiving Hazel made her stomach churn, and the peculiar look in his eyes as he took her through the private gallery had caused a wave of apprehension to course through her.

Even worse than the guilt, however, was the despair she'd felt once she understood what it was truly to choose between two things one loved. Only that morning her aunt had remarked on Vivienne's wan countenance, the circles forming under her eyes, and once again had pressed her to tell Hazel everything. Had they been friends and nothing more, maybe it would have been possible for her to take him into her confidence, but he was a man who possessed her heart. She was already grappling with losing his touch, a great liberty she'd allowed herself while playing a part in a charade that must come to an end when the engagement did. She could not bear to lose his esteem, his good opinion, his affection.

The man who occupied all her thoughts was at that moment seated next to her, and she struggled to pay attention to what he was speaking of as he drove his curricle along the Strand, drawing them closer to Somerset House by the minute.

She had been a fool to submit the painting of him, and just the thought of being present when he saw it was causing a very thin film of sweat to bead down her spine. Even if he could never know she was the one who had wielded the brush, at the same time she desperately wished for him to be pleased with the work.

They left the curricle in the hands of his tiger and began the long ascent up to the main gallery of the Academy, each step causing Vivienne's heart to beat harder and faster. Although there were fewer people than there would be on opening day, they still numbered more than she could count.

Over the heads of those gathered, she could only see the uppermost works displayed, nothing at the centre line. She had spied *Woman at Water's Edge* as soon as they came through the anterior room, hanging three rows down from the ceiling on the back wall, but saw no sign of *The Stranger.* In her focused determination to seek out her pieces, she hadn't immediately noticed the deadly silence that fell over the grand room when they entered it. The sound of someone sniffing echoed in her ears.

Her hand was tucked into Hazel's arm, and she instinctively moved a little closer to him, seeking the security of his person even as a primitive warning rang out in her brain. He dropped his head to her ear to whisper, 'Ought we see what this is about?' and led them further into the room, where the crowd grew larger by the minute.

It felt as though the entire room were holding its breath, a sense of disquiet permeating the air. The group parted as they walked, and long before the last of the viewers had moved out of the way, Vivienne knew which painting they would come upon.

There, on the centre line, in the place of honour, was *The Stranger*.

She swallowed convulsively, her eyelashes fluttering faster than a hummingbird's wings to keep the tears at bay. Everything she had ever wanted was right here in front of her. The very idea of looking at the man by her side, knowing his expression could shatter her, was enough to send bolts of terror coursing through her veins.

The distinct sound of boots on the hardwood floor rang out, and before she could look to see who was approaching, she heard the deep timbre of the duke's voice as he said, 'You may mark this one sold.'

Vivienne swayed a little on her feet, panic beginning to swell within her.

'I beg your pardon, Your Grace,' a member of the Hanging Committee began, 'but this piece has not been marked to indicate it's available for sale.'

For a moment, Vivienne had entirely forgotten that she hadn't planned to sell the painting, unable to stomach the idea that anyone else would have a piece of him in their home. She was too scared to look up, but could imagine the glacial, haughty stare upon Hazel's face, because the next words spoken were, 'Yes, of course, Your Grace. We'll speak with the artist. Certainly he would be lucky to have you as a patron.'

'Or she.'

Blood rushed to her ears, drowning out the general cacophony that erupted with those few words, from both the Academician and the people around them close enough to have heard. The significance of the moment was so great, Vivienne didn't even notice the vice grip with which she was holding fast to his arm to keep herself upright.

The duke led her further along the wall at a rather quick clip. When she chanced to finally peek at him, she noticed he was looking at the paintings only long enough to note whose work it was before moving on.

'Ah. Here we are. My man of business said there were two by this artist present at the exhibition. We've seen the first; here is the second.'

Vivienne's eyes didn't need to travel up the wall to know he referred to *Woman at Water's Edge*.

He gestured for the Academician once more, signalled his intent to purchase the piece, and when once again left in relative privacy, said, 'For someone so learned and so vocal about art, my love, you've said not a word since we arrived. What think you of this painting?' When she remained silent, shock causing the few words she could think of to wedge in her throat, he added, 'I find her genre paintings and landscapes superior to her caricatures, which although clever, are not to my taste.'

Vivienne couldn't feel her legs, or her arms, or any part of her body for that matter, except for a slight tingling all over. He wasn't upset with her, that much she could discern from his gentle tone, the relaxed smile that tipped the corners of his mouth, but her mind failed to make sense of what was happening. That he would be angry or disappointed or disgusted had all seemed certain at some point in time or other. That he would purchase her paintings, use the endearment that was as intimate as his touch—*tease* her—seemed impossible.

'Hazel.' Her voice quivered as she said his name on a strangled breath.

His hand came up to cover hers where it gripped his arm. 'Yes, my dear girl?'

'Hazel.' It was as if his name were the only word her mouth could form, and she hoped he heard in it her apology, her joy.

'As much as I adore the sound of my name on your lips, perhaps you've another word for me? Something closer to *husband*?'

Every emotion she'd stored up these last weeks, months even, threatened to burst out of her. She didn't trust herself enough to try any word but his name.

'I haven't had the pleasure of offering my felicitations on your pending nuptials.'

As one, they turned at the interruption to see Lord Lansbury swaggering up to them. She felt Hazel's hand tighten over hers. His body went rigid at her side, and when she glanced up at him, the light on his face was gone and his mouth had hardened into a tight line.

'Entirely unnecessary for you to do so.'

'How backward you must think me not to wish my cousin and his charming betrothed happiness and health.'

Vivienne said nothing as an eerie, unsettling feeling washed over her.

'You may have the credit for the sentiment and go.'

'It's perhaps a trifle unfair you won our little wager by shooting me, but far be it from me to stand in the way of true love. Your Grace, Miss Emory.' He bowed and made his exit much as he'd made his entrance—careless, unhurried—but with the damage taking mere moments to inflict.

Hazel remained stiff, unmoving. She stared at him, the tension between them growing with frightening rapidity. Every contrite thing she could think to say to him about *her* secret flew from her mind.

'What wager, Hazel?' she choked out, struggling to keep hold of her fragile control. The longer he stared up at *Woman at Water's Edge*, the more tenuous the thread holding her together became.

'It's nothing. I should have told you.' He still wouldn't look at her.

'What wager?'

'I wanted to tell you. I did try, that day in the maze.'

There was a flash of clarity in her mind, the two of them standing among the tall hedges. He had wished to say something to her, and she asked him not to. It didn't matter. That was one day, one minute among countless others they'd spent together before and after. Other moments crowded her mind: the first time she'd held his hand in hers, the day at the British Institution, the carriage ride after the theatre.

The urge to be sick was so powerful, the muscles in her stomach spasmed.

When he finally pulled his eyes from the painting, she could barely stand to look at him, and her words came out as a growl. '*What wager,* Your Grace?'

'That you would accept my proposal.'

Her free hand came up lightning fast—as if by its own accord, and before she could think better of it—her kid leather glove muting the sound as it connected with the flesh of his cheek, but not enough to avoid drawing horrified stares. His jaw clenched, but his expression hardly registered her action.

By the time she walked away, her reputation would surely be in tatters. None of it mattered to her anymore.

'You'—she gave a strangled little sob as ice spread through her veins—'disgust me.'

Without another word she turned and went from the room, leaving a sea of stunned faces in her wake.

---

29

*B*rick was already pacing in the cosy back parlour of Huxley House, practising his apology, long before Vivienne returned from the Royal Academy. Her aunt and uncle were away from home, and he'd asked the butler to send her straight to him when she returned, and without mentioning who was waiting for her; he'd felt only a momentary stab of guilt at the knowing flicker in the old man's eye. The butler, no doubt, thought the surprise would be a pleasing one.

He pulled out his pocket watch, checked the time against the clock on the little side table, and ground his teeth as he suppressed the bit of worry that had begun to creep in. He had no idea how she planned to return home. A flower vendor had promised on her dead mother's grave that she'd seen a young lady matching Vivienne's description enter a hackney, but a hackney driver nearby on the Strand swore up and down he saw her walking in the direction of Mayfair. Brick didn't care for either of those possibilities, but walking would be the worse. The only thing buoying his hope that the flower vendor was in the right was Vivienne's lack of presence along the most common and populous route to Mayfair. Brick had taken his curricle the direction he imagined she would walk, if she had, and had seen no sight of her.

Another five minutes passed, now thirty in all, and his concern was turning into panic when he heard the bell for the front door. His relief was short-lived as apprehension knotted inside him. He stood in the middle of the room, next to a sofa the colour of sunlight at dusk. He rested his hand on the wood frame a moment before pulling it off, putting it back, and removing it once more, before taking a step in the opposite direction. Never before could he recall a time it was so hard to breathe, as if all the air in his lungs had solidified.

There was a soft clacking as the heels of her shoes knocked against the polished marble floor of the hallway, and then she was there in the doorway. Her exquisite face was pale, her nose and eyes red, and the mask of composure she'd put on for whoever it was she would find in this room slipped the moment she saw him.

'No.'

'Please.' He took a tentative step towards her.

'No. No, no, no.'

She had begun to back out of the room. Without thinking, he rushed to her, pulling her further into the parlour and using one hand to close the door part of the way, not that the entire household wouldn't know what had happened soon enough. Vivienne flung his hand off her arm, shouting as she did so, 'No!'

'Dammit, Vivienne, listen to me.'

Her chin quivered as she spoke, her words filled with wrath and rancour. 'Don't you dare. I have finished with listening to you. I've done nothing but listen to you for weeks, and for what? The pleasant discovery everything you've said to me is a lie?'

'No,' he insisted. 'I've not lied to you about anything.'

'Except that this has been nothing more than a game to you, a way for a bored, arrogant scoundrel to entertain himself. Tell me, Your Grace, has shooting people lost its amusement?'

A vein in his neck throbbed, but he would not retaliate. 'You have never been a game to me, Vivienne, you know it.'

'What I know is everything you've said, everything you've done, it's all based on a lie.'

'Vivi—'

'How dare you make sport of my life. What were the terms? Was I at least worth a fine price?'

His stomach roiled and he forced down the sourness rising at the back of his throat, but he would not defend himself. It didn't matter that he hadn't known her so well when he accepted the wager or how little he'd thought it would matter to her. He should have never agreed to it in the first place. 'Lansbury offered to return Milwell Lodge if I won. It was my favourite place to go with my father as a boy, but one of the few properties not entailed. My father left it to his brother upon his death.'

'Was it? Returned, that is.'

'The deed is with my solicitor.'

'And if you lost?'

'Lansbury has long wished for my signet ring.'

Her eyes shimmered with anger, but on those words, confusion flashed in their green depths.

'You must know. Everyone else does.'

'I don't take your meaning.'

'Come now.' His voice was quiet, tender even. Any trace of

desperation or frustration gone in an instant. 'Why keep one last secret between us?' He paused, measured her a moment, and said, 'You know I am a Vesily in name, but not by blood.'

'Then why does that ring matter more than me?'

Without thinking, he twisted the weighty band of gold round his little finger. 'To my father, there was no difference.'

Those words smothered the fire in her eyes, but the sorrow that replaced it tore him in two. He took a step in her direction, needing to feel her closer to him, needing the comfort only she could provide. 'Vivienne,' he whispered.

All the crackling tension in the room that characterised the beginning of their exchange had been exhausted, and what was left was his longing for her and her determination not to have him.

She shook her head, her posture unyielding, her lashes wet with unshed tears.

Brick came forward to stand in front of his betrothed. She refused to meet his gaze, her eyes anchored on the folds of his cravat. He reached out, taking her hands in his own and running his thumbs over her warm, bare skin, leaving a trail of goose-pimples behind.

'Go, please.' The only consolation was that she didn't immediately tear her hands from his grip, but then when she did remove them, he felt the loss all the more.

Brick was a man with every resource who could do whatever he pleased, but he could not make her listen and he could not make her forgive him.

He stood before her, transfixed, wishing she would look up at him, reach out to him, anything, to give him some little sign all was not lost. He couldn't bear to think this was the way things must be from now onwards, him aching for her love and she unable even to stand the sight of him.

Her body lilted, time slowed, and for a glorious moment it seemed as though she would fold into him. Instead, she brushed past without a glance and moved towards the bell-pull.

'No need to ring,' he said, as he made for the door. He paused on the threshold, and a painful tightness rushed through his chest and up his throat when his gaze landed once more on the top of her bowed head. 'I beg you will believe how very sorry I am.' And because there was nothing more for him to say and nothing else he could do, he retreated on heavy, trembling limbs.

'WHEREVER TO BEGIN WITH YOU, CHILD?'

Brick didn't bother looking up from his paper as his mother stormed into his breakfast parlour.

'Why did you not tell me you were having a portrait done? Who was it that made you look so *ordinary,* no sash or pins, nor anything marking your distinction or rank. The disgrace! My carriage remains outside. I will not have that degradation in a position where all can see.'

'You will attempt to bully the entire Hanging Committee into removing it?'

'They should never have put it on those walls in the first place!' the dowager thundered, her jowls shaking with rage.

'I did not sit for the painting. It's from the artist's view-point, an artist I happen to know and whose works I collect,' he said, with calm indifference. 'I've also made known my intent to purchase the painting, so I rather think you'll be undertaking a fool's errand if you storm the Academy to seek its removal.'

The moment his mother recognised she was losing the battle, she switched tactics. 'While we're speaking of the Royal Academy, I knew no good would come of you cavorting with that Emory chit.'

'You said nothing of the sort. You called her an ape leader, which she is not. Either way, I have to request you stop using such language when speaking of my betrothed.'

'Your betrothed? Ha! She's besmirched her name, behaving like a hellcat. She will be lucky to outrun the damage to her reputation even in the far-flung parish in which she lives. It wouldn't surprise me in the least to hear her poor aunt and uncle have taken her out of the country. *Those* people I feel sorry for. To have their generosity for taking her in all these years repaid with such a crass display of ungratefulness, their standing in society felled with one stupid action.'

Brick knew that wasn't quite the case, but withheld the truth from his mother, understanding she had no interest in it anyway. 'None of that matters.'

'Of course it does. Don't be a dolt, Hazelhurst.'

'It doesn't matter, because when I marry her, everyone will conveniently forget her display of temper, which was well justified, mind you. If she had pulled a pistol out of her reticule and shot me, it wouldn't have been anything less than I deserved.'

'You will not marry her!' bellowed the dowager.

'We are engaged. I am not printing a retraction.'

'You will browbeat her into being your wife?'

'I will spend my life proving my worth to her, either as her husband or the man who desperately wishes it were so. I am not even a little sorry you do not care for the match. She is my choice.'

'You would choose her—the idea of her, more like—over

duty to your family, your name, your father, God rest his soul?'

'I would choose her over everything.'

His mother stared at him, perhaps measuring the sincerity of his words, and turned to leave, but as she reached the door, he stopped her with the following words: 'You have forgotten, ma'am, my father chose *you* over everything.'

The previous duke would have been well within his rights to seek a divorce from Brick's mother. It was rare, but not unprecedented, and doing so would have prevented Brick from receiving the title, the estates, the Vesily name. Brick's mother wasn't an easy woman to love, but his father had done so from the moment he had met her and never stopped.

Her tight mouth arced downward, her brows knit together in a frown, but she didn't trouble to reply, and with a long look but without another word, left. Unfortunately, Brick wasn't able to enjoy the quiet very long. Hardly a minute after the door had closed behind the dowager, it opened again to reveal Lord St Germain.

'I can't help but feel somewhat responsible.'

Brick used his foot to push out the chair to his left. 'You only witnessed the wager. I am the one who accepted it and then kept it concealed, when I should have told her the whole truth. If I had, her reputation wouldn't be in tatters.'

'It's not so bad as that. It's not good, but not so bad. There is talk, of course, but you know how the *ton* is. A new scandal next week, and all will be forgiven—forgotten, even, if you stand by her. Ellena is desperate to know if you will, by the bye.'

Brick didn't think something as shocking as a duke's intended slapping him in a public place would blow over as easily as that, but he only said, 'I rather think the odds of her wanting anything to do with me are slim.'

'You would make a wager again so soon?' St Germain's countenance remained serious, but Brick appreciated his friend trying to tease him into better spirits.

'Is it bad form to call Lansbury out a second time?'

'It was bad form for him to mention any wager made in the club, never mind in front of the lady herself. I've already been to White's, Watier's, Brooks', and Boodle's. He is unwelcome at all of them, at least for a time.'

'Hardly a fitting punishment for a man cruelly satisfied to embarrass a lady.'

'Lansbury is not one to forego an opportunity to cause hurt. The moment he saw his only chance at that ring slip away, he was going to wreck it all one way or another, so your happiness will have to be retribution enough. Well, your happiness and an heir. What will you do? I am too familiar with you to think inaction even an option.'

Brick shook his head. 'I've not the slightest idea.'

'm sorry.

It wasn't enough, but it was something.

Vivienne ran her thumb over the words on the card that came with the flowers, which were now nothing more than ash in her fireplace. She wanted to consign the stupid little note as well, but each time she held her hand over the flames, her fingers wouldn't let go.

She was furious with him, with Lord Lansbury, with all the people at the Academy who had borne witness as her life burned as fast as the petals of the flowers he'd sent. Mostly, she was furious with herself. She'd agreed to a false engagement to protect her reputation, all to destroy it by herself in a fraction of a second. Even worse, she'd let herself get caught up in a game of pretence. Vivienne hadn't thought herself alone in playing pretend, not with the way he'd looked at her, kissed her. But it was clear to her now she knew nothing—nothing of him or his feelings, or of what was real and what was shaded by her wishes and desires. She tipped her head to read the card again, noticing the words were blurred by tears she hadn't realise had formed.

There was nothing anyone could say that would erase the memory of her vulgar behaviour, and short of the Prince Regent running off with a chambermaid, probably nothing that would make people soon forget it, either. Neither her aunt nor her uncle had made any mention of retiring to their country home, but Vivienne was certain it was coming. She had made it impossible for them to stay in London.

The idea of leaving town, however, of leaving him, sent a fresh set of tears spilling down her cheeks. She let her knees buckle and dropped to the floor from actual fatigue of spirits. She was furious at him—enraged, infuriated, hurt, disconsolate, and whatever other words existed to describe the awful depression that had wrapped her up tight and refused to let her go—but she loved him. She loved him whether or not he loved her. She loved him, and she couldn't determine which fate was worse: remaining near enough to watch him love someone else, or never seeing him again.

Anabel had come every day to check in on her, but Vivienne had refused to see anybody. Still, she was not the least surprised when she heard the door to her room open, felt the bed dip under the weight of someone sitting upon it, and cracked one eye open to see her dear friend.

'You shouldn't have come.' Her voice was hoarse from disuse.

'With nine children and grandchildren appearing at regular intervals, my mama can hardly keep track of our names, let alone whatever the scandal of the week is. Besides, as you are kind enough to remain tucked away in your tower, I'm not even put through the awkwardness of avoiding you in public.'

Vivienne put her hand on Anabel's and gave it a squeeze.

'People are struggling to decide what is more scandalous: you slapping him, or the *reason* for it,' Anabel drawled, wiggling her eyebrows as she did so. 'The speculation, as you might imagine, was exceedingly dull in the beginning—you, who had finally deigned to accept a proposal, discovered the truth about his father. As if everyone didn't already know, as if that would make you any less of a duchess. Ridiculous, no?'

Vivienne bit her lip, unwilling to admit she'd managed to remain naïve to that truth until days ago.

'But the *ton* is nothing if not excessive and imaginative when they so wish it. He wouldn't buy you a matching pair; he refused to fill St George's with a thousand roses in full bloom; he's Irish.'

'Goodness,' Vivienne said on a laugh, the noise and feeling of it almost unfamiliar as it rattled out of her.

'Would you want to know if I've seen him?'

After a few moments' reflection, Vivienne nodded, preparing herself to hear of him dancing with Lady Felicity or taking some other proper and demure young lady for a ride in the park.

'He approached me at Sir Jackson's picnic.'

Vivienne's eyes went wide and her breathing became immediately and infinitely harder.

'He asked if I had seen you and appeared disappointed when I said I had not been successful in my attempts. That is all.' Anabel cast a concerned glance at her friend, and added, 'He looked worse than you do. You know, for all the rumours, I've not heard anything with a hint of truth about what precip-itated your disagreement.'

Disagreement was the most generous euphemism.

'I am not asking you to tell me—'

'He had made a wager with Lord Lansbury for my hand.'

Anabel's gasp sucked in all the air around them. 'He never! That scoundrel.'

Vivienne loved her friend for the instant and unequivocal disapproval of the duke but felt compelled to add, 'It's rather more complex than that, I'm afraid.'

'Yes,' Anabel agreed on a gentle huff. 'You said Lansbury. My mind is quite capable of filling in the rest.'

With an awkward, harsh, clearing of her throat, Vivienne added, 'There is something more.' Anabel's eyes were wide and sympathetic, and Vivienne could only hope they would remain so when she told her dearest friend in the world her secret. 'Something I'd kept from him—and you, and from everyone else, really.' She drew in a deep, quivering breath. 'He has learned the truth, and so should you, but you may feel —well, if being here with me now is seen as a risk…'

'You're scaring me, Vivi. I'd prefer it if you just tell me whatever it is. No more preamble, if you please.'

'The painting of him in the Royal Academy is mine.'

Anabel's brows scrunched together; her head tipped to one side. 'I'm not certain I understand. You mean to say you purchased it?'

'No.' Vivienne's heart hammered so hard in her chest, it felt as though her body were jumping with each beat. 'I *painted* it.'

Her friend went frightfully still except for the comical dropping of her jaw. For several minutes, the only sounds in the room were those floating in from outside beyond the window: the coo of doves, the crunch of carriage wheels, a door opening and closing.

'You—'

'Are a painter, yes.'

'You—'

'Have been displaying work for some years now. Oh, and I

also do caricatures from time to time, like the one of the dowager duchess several months ago.'

Anabel's eyes rounded with surprise and recognition. 'The animals?'

Vivienne gave one concise nod to confirm. As silence settled between them, she was beginning to regret her decision to tell her friend, until a sudden bark of laughter caused her to jerk and slop coffee out of the cup she'd just plucked from her tray.

'My mama laughed—nay, cackled—for five whole minutes when she saw it. She *loathes* the dowager. Something about the woman tutting my mother at some charity event and embarrassing her in front of her friends.'

'You aren't upset? Planning to flee my chambers and my life?'

'I do wish you had told me sooner, but between slapping the man and painting *that* picture of him, you are easily *the* most interesting person I know, Vivienne.'

Her friend remained above an hour, and when she rose to take her leave, said, 'Oh, I almost forgot. Your aunt wished me to give you this.' Anabel reached towards the foot of the bed and handed Vivienne the *Morning Chronicle*, then placed a kiss on her cheek and left her alone with her muddled feelings.

The paper was folded curiously, and it took a little manoeuvring for Vivienne to set the pages in the right order. Her breath caught when she saw the front page: '*Scholarship Fund Established for Female Artists by His Grace the Duke of Hazelhurst*'

She read the words of the accompanying article almost faster than she could comprehend them. Because the Royal Academy had banned women from the classes afforded male artists, the scholarship would provide funds to hire preeminent masters and for travel abroad, should the recipient be desirous of furthering her talent in France, the Netherlands, Italy, or another locale of her choosing.

Vivienne rubbed a hand over her chest to ease the physical ache in her heart. It wasn't just what he'd done, but how swiftly he'd done it. She slipped from her room to her studio, not bothering to change out of her dressing gown first.

In the days since he'd left her standing in the little parlour at the back of the house, she'd done little else besides wallow —wallow, and compulsively draw the duke. There was an entire stack of sheets tucked into a nook of her desk which were images of him in charcoal. She drew him with ferocious fury in his eyes, with disappointment turning down his lips, with desire pulling every muscle taut. More and more, she drew him as she wished most to remember him: his face rigid with passion, his eyes glowing in the dark of the carriage, his lips swollen from kissing her until she radiated with pleasure.

In slow, caressing strokes, she trailed her fingertips along her exposed collarbone, imagining it was his mouth and remembering how gentle he had been, despite his own body pulsing with need. Her nipples peaked beneath the fabric of her dress and heat rippled through her, a knot of it throbbing at the hollow between her legs. She traced the outline of his mouth, relived the sensation of his tongue exploring her ear, her breasts, her neck. The memory sent chills down her back, arms, legs.

Before that moment, Vivienne had known something of raw, compelling desire in concept if not practice. There were books at her disposal no gently bred young woman even knew existed; there were paintings and sculptures and artworks she'd seen on the continent that showed her what it must be like to chase divine ecstasy, to give over oneself and yield to passion.

Hazel had brought her to the edge of the world she knew and pushed her over in a storm of hunger, pleasure, possession. She couldn't pretend to be ignorant of what she'd experienced, what she'd felt when he lit a fire within her and let it burn everything she believed about herself to the ground. Only now she was left with vivid, unbidden memories and uncertain how to go on when wanting spiralled through her as easily as fear or hope or sadness. She palmed her own breast, the sensitive bud of her nipple pressing against her hot skin through the thin muslin fabric of her dress. An idea began to dip and dart in her mind as she reached for a pencil and blank sheet of paper.

31

S t Germain, as it turned out, was exactly right when he called the fallout for Vivienne 'not good, but not so bad.'

There were murmurs when Brick entered a room, and of course everyone in it had something to say. The worst of it was the sympathy he received, as if he were the one who deserved any of it. No one knew exactly what had happened, although their dearth of knowledge didn't stop them from speculating— doing so was one of the *ton's* most favourite activities, after all. He wouldn't tell them, and he doubted she would either. Her hiding away, however, was making it worse. He had been to Huxley House several times, spoken to her aunt and uncle, and had it confirmed by Saint, who heard it from Ellena, who heard it from Alice, one of Anabel Boyton's sisters, that it wasn't just him she was avoiding, but all of society.

'You can do better than the niece of a viscount, Your Grace,' the elderly Countess of Brookside croaked out, while boring him to tears at a salon hosted by a friend of his mother's.

'There is no better woman than Miss Emory, ma'am, and

while I thank you for your concern, it's precipitate. We remain engaged. I'd be an odd male indeed to untie the knot binding me to a woman with that much passion, do you not think?' The countess flushed, sputtered on the sip of wine she'd just taken, and when her airway was clear, stammered nonsense into the glass shaking in her hand as Brick looked on, the churlish pleasure he felt buried under a face void of all emotion. 'May I secure you more wine?'

With a hand on her chest, she shook her head and moved away, with little more than a bob of her head.

The men were more forgiving, but whether it was because they *did* think he'd be better off in Bedlam than to give up a gently bred lady who managed to retain even an ounce of spirit or because they were terrified of being shot, he cared not, so long as they carried on as if the incident at the Royal Academy had never happened. Several went so far as to ask him to pass on their wishes for Miss Emory's speedy recovery and commiserated over ailments Brick was certain did not exist.

'My youngest sister, you know, suffered from acute fading agitation of the phalanges—a quick, passing thing,' St Germain said, his eyes so bright with laughter they could replace the candles. 'No lasting effects. In fact, no real effects of any kind except a lack of sleep, which can lead to unexpected fits of passion. Easily treated with a week or two of rest.'

Brick, amused, a little impressed, and entirely grateful for a friend like Saint, raised an eyebrow. 'Phalanges?'

'Not much interest in anatomy at Cambridge. Shocking, really. Nearly as shocking, in fact, as the number of gentlemen who appear to have afflicted sisters or wives.'

'You've outdone yourself.'

'As much as I'd love to claim all the credit, I must give

some to Ellena. I spoke out about it, but it was her very convincing retelling of her own experience with acute fading agitation of the phalanges that made it so believable. By the end, I was chiding myself for missing all the tell-tale signs and thinking I'd failed her for not sending for the physician.'

The ludicrous statement made Brick laugh for the first time in days.

32

'Y ou cannot remain in here forever,' Lady Lane said, as she took the seat across from Vivienne in the little sitting room off her bedchamber.

'I can try.'

'Vivi, my dear one, I won't pretend to know the embarrassment from which you are suffering, but do not deny the truth of it. A young lady cannot behave so in *such* a public place and not feel some little bit of shame, no matter what the provocation or justification. You know I would never condemn you for such, and I own to feeling a great deal of disappointment in the duke. As little as you care to hear it said aloud, despite the origin of his interest in you, he wouldn't have shot that horrid Lansbury boy if his feelings weren't true, and he certainly wouldn't be here every day leaving you gifts.'

'Gifts?'

'Perhaps that's not the right word. Your new brushes, the bladders of colour, the poppy oil.'

''Tis all what I normally purchase from the paint shop.'

'Just so, except he's been purchasing it all and bringing it by himself. In addition to the flowers, of course,' Lady Lane added, casting a fleeting glance around the room, but saying nothing when there was not so much as a petal to be seen of the half dozen bouquets brought round.

Vivienne's nostrils flared, although her heart clenched.

'I suggest you take better care of the paints than the blooms. Not that we can't afford it, but why replace perfectly good paints and tools?'

Her aunt made a sound point, and Vivienne hated it. Besides, there were several ounces of blue ultramarine in this delivery, which should have alerted her to the duke's involvement. The colour was the superlative blue among serious painters, but the cost was prohibitive for many, and the paint itself was not always so easily obtained, as it came to London all the way from Afghanistan. For years, she'd asked the proprietor of the paint shop for an ounce, and for years he'd always told her it was too dear for her, despite her insistence she could pay for it. Once, she'd even tossed an unholy number of guineas on the counter, and he still refused. 'Despite the name,' he'd said to her in a patronising tone, ''tis not for watercolour.' It wasn't that he thought it too dear to sell her, but the idea of the colour itself being used up by a woman.

'The scandal is not so bad as it could have been. We've suffered from being given the cut direct by Lady Sussfield, but I daresay she'd cut her own children should she take offence at how they sneezed. There is gossip, but there always is. A few friends have put some distance between us, but my charity event with the soprano Catalani is in three days, and *all* of us will be in attendance. You were prepared to risk your reputation for painting, and you did. Now you must hold your head high.'

There was nothing startling in this rousing speech. Lady

Lane was equal parts romantic and pragmatic, which was how, as a young lady with roots in trade, she was neither insensible to the offer from a titled gentleman nor willing to accept it without there being some affection. She very much had the mind of a businessman like her father—she knew how to read people, how to convince them about something they didn't know they wanted, and right now, what she wished was for the *ton* to forget her niece's brief lack of decorum. The best way to do that was to remind them of her beauty and her pretty manners, and she said as much to Vivienne.

'I'll send water up for a bath. Maria, too,' her aunt said, rising. 'It will take days to get those tangles out of your hair.'

Vivienne did little else while the maids filled the great big copper tub in her dressing room besides stare up at the canopy over her bed, but when she finally sunk low into the steaming hot water, her aunt's words rolled over her like the bath water: *despite the origin of his interest.* They replayed over and again in her mind.

She wished her painting of him was still two doors away in her studio. The look in his eyes that had taken her so long to capture was a challenging mix of appraisal, fascination, and wonder.

It didn't absolve him from the deplorable wager he'd made, but it did cause her to slip from the maids and into the water, where her tears wouldn't be noticed.

There was something else her aunt had said that continued to knock about in Vivienne's mind—that she had been prepared to risk her reputation for painting. In the end, though, she'd wrecked her reputation for a man, which was so much worse.

For days after fleeing the Royal Academy, she'd remained dull and listless in bed, thinking only about how much her heart hurt, how much she missed him. Then she'd had an idea, left her bed, and had begun painting. Her heart still hurt, but the pain drove her to work more, work harder, work differently. At no point since she left the Academy had she thought about anything besides Hazel.

'Maria? Maria!'

There was more animation, more urgency, in Vivienne's voice than there had been in more than a sennight, and when Maria rushed through the door between the dressing room and the bedchamber, the maid's eyes were wide with panic.

'My dressing gown,' requested Vivienne, steam rising from her skin as she stood up, water running in rivulets down her body. Once settled by the fire to dry her hair, she added, 'The newspapers, from Preview Day onward, can you bring them all to me?'

Maria bobbed her head and disappeared, returning with such haste, Vivienne wondered if perhaps she'd actually run.

'Which would you like first, Miss?'

'Just set them all on the floor, just here,' Vivienne said, tipping her head to the side of her chair, further from the fire.

With a disapproving look in her eye, Maria first set the papers on an upholstered chair nearer the window, before moving a little end table to Vivienne's elbow and setting the papers there instead.

Vivienne snatched at the first one and tore through it to the section dedicated most often to the artistic world. There, at the top of the page, in large print: '*Who Painted the Duke?*'

There was a wild fluttering in her chest, as if her heart were getting ready to fly away, and her head began to spin. Setting the paper down, she didn't even need to turn the pages of the next. On its cover: '*On the Line: The Artist Behind This Season's Darling of the Royal Academy*'. Each of the five papers had some variation on this theme, and when Vivienne went back to read the articles that accompanied the bold headlines, all were searching for the same answer: *'Who is W? Is it even a W? What is his relationship to the Duke of Hazelhurst? Does he even know the duke?'* There were also phrases impossible to ignore: *'Record Numbers Flock to See* The Stranger*'*; *'Stunningly intimate portrait'*; *'W limns a different duke to the one we have all seen and feel we must know, if only by reputation'*; *'Masterful composition'*.

Of course there was criticism, which always grew proportionally to an artist's popularity. A critic notorious for hating everything called it self-indulgent, and a writer in the *Gazette* didn't care for the direct perspective, feeling it too harsh an angle for even the most hardened subject.

Vivienne wondered if Hazel had seen it all, what he made of the reviews, if he were angry she'd made him into a subject of even more interest than before. She knew herself to be terribly cross with him, but while that emotion rose alongside her affection, it didn't quell her longing for him as much as there were moments she wished it did. How could she still hold dear someone who thought so little of her as to wager on her happiness? But hold him dear she did. And yet, and yet...

The paper she'd been clutching between her hands dropped to her lap as she looked up and towards nothing in particular as everything clarified in an instant: the only way forward was through.

33

'Tis going to be all right, miss.'

Vivienne reached a little behind her to where Maria was standing and groped for her hand, giving it a squeeze so hard the maid yelped. Together, they stood at the entrance to the Royal Academy, a place Vivienne had not dared enter since Preview Day. It was too early for most of the *ton* even to consider rising from their beds, but the gallery was bustling with other artists. She reached for the delicate necklace she was wearing, pulling it away from her throat as though that was the thing strangling her, and not sheer terror at the magnitude of what she was about to do.

'Come now, miss. All will come right.'

An erratic little shake of her head was Vivienne's only response.

Historically, the Royal Academy held one varnishing day— a day before the exhibition opened where artists were permitted to come and touch up their work in full view of whoever else happened to occupy the space. Of course, Vivienne had never attended one of these days, although she'd read about the antics that sometimes went on, the squabbles between painters, jokes she would never be part of, well-known painters who used the day to complete their work.

The week after the exhibition opened, a young sprig of fashion tripped on the train of some lady's dress, the motion sending the contents of his open flask flying into another canvas hung on the centre line. The outraged painter had demanded an opportunity to fix his piece, and, naturally, all the others refused to be excluded. As a result, for the first time in the Academy's history, there was a second varnishing day taking place. One which Vivienne heard about and knew she must attend.

People passing by were already staring at her, as she hovered in the Academy's entryway, everything but her worn and dingy dark blue dress speaking of her quality. At Maria's feet was a heavy basket filled with an apron, brushes, colours, palette, turpentine, water jars, rags, drop cloths. Everything Vivienne needed to make a slight change to the painting. *Her* painting.

If she entered—when she entered—and set about her task, there would be no retreat. Her aunt had valiantly refrained from weeping when Vivienne first mentioned revealing herself. Lady Lane's eyes had been red and watery, but not a single tear had dropped. Lord Lane, on the other hand, had quite swelled with pride. Vivienne had felt relief and reassurance when he hugged her tightly to him, repeating the same words as Maria: *All will come right.* She couldn't be sure it would, and it was that uncertainty that had kept her from ever daring to go even this far.

But she knew something now she had not known then: herself. It was easy to feel content with her decision to remain unwed when there had never been a man she wished to marry, just as it was easy to remain anonymous. For years she had said there was never a true choice because had there been, she would always side with her first love. But the duke had forced her to consider her path forward with sombre deliberation, and if she was going to choose painting, then she must *choose* painting.

'I've had quite enough of this. We go now, or I give you a little pinch and we go then. Either way, we are going in.'

Several seconds ticked by, and Vivienne remained as frozen as a lake in winter.

'Ow!' She whipped around, her hand darting out to the back of her arm, where a little patch of skin throbbed.

'You were warned. Would you like another?' Maria asked, picking up the basket. 'Your uncle's man has already been down to speak with Mr York and whoever else.'

Vivienne nodded. Mr York was the man who coordinated the current Summer Exhibition, and her uncle had told her of the exchange, although she could not recall a single word.

'And Mr York is, at this moment, inside awaiting us, should you have need of him.'

Meaning should any of the men who ran this fine establishment, or the male artists who would gawk and guffaw and accuse her of touching work not her own, take umbrage with her presence, Mr York was there to intercede on her behalf.

An unsteady nod was all she felt herself capable of, but with a thick swallow and a hammer in her chest, Vivienne took her first step into the Royal Academy as more than a patron.

Mr York, it seemed, had been waiting just inside for the pair, and rushed over to take the leaden basket from Maria, whose form was bowing under the weight.

'Welcome, Miss Emory. Or perhaps I ought to address you

as Miss Caldicott, if you'd prefer?' he asked, with an approving lilt of his lips. 'After you.'

Vivienne walked through the foyer and paused to look up at the staircase that swirled higher and higher above her head, a circle of light streaming through at the top, despite the grey skies outside. She pressed a hand to her belly, determined that if nothing else she would not cast up her accounts, and began the ascent.

The very top floor of Somerset House was set aside for the Grand Salon, and despite the lengthy climb, Vivienne was no more prepared when she stopped between the two pillars of the antechamber preceding the Great Room than she had been on the ground floor.

'Go on.' Maria placed her hand at Vivienne's elbow and gave it a gentle nudge. 'Don't forget to enjoy this moment. It's unlikely there will ever be another where you get to inflict apoplexy on an entire roomful of men.'

Despite herself, Vivienne smiled, and the exhale that came after was both audible and determined. There was no going back. In truth, there hadn't been since the moment she laid eyes on the duke.

She thought perhaps somewhere in the large gallery there was a woman touching up a miniature or a portrait, or perhaps a lovely painting of flowers, but at large, they were excluded from the camaraderie that developed within the walls of this august institution. Which is why, when Vivienne entered, a few men took notice, and when she spread her drop cloth, donned her apron, and picked up the turpentine, the spacious room fell as quiet as a crypt.

Mr York had stepped back but was not far, and Maria was near at hand to assist however she could, but Vivienne knew every artist, every spectator, every single person in that room was watching her, waiting to see what she did.

She took a rag, dipped it in the turpentine and, feeling as if her chest might burst because she'd not taken a breath in at least a minute, she swiped at the space around *The Stranger*'s left hand.

Mayhem ensued.

There were shouts from those who thought she was ruining some esteemed artist's work. There were cries of indignation from those who had already made the leap from her work to her caricatures and were steeped in displeasure for how they'd been portrayed. There were those who recognised her from drawing rooms and were too surprised to do more than stare, and there were those so scandalised at seeing a woman of the gentry in work clothes varnishing a large oil painting, they could do more than sputter and gape. In the chaos, Vivienne failed to ignore the one word she had known was coming: *whore.*

An Academician pounded on the wood floors with his walking stick to draw the men to order. Mr York moved a little closer, as if to create a physical barrier between Vivienne and the rest of the occupants in the Great Room. Her hands trembled. Her maid, standing at her left, with both their backs to the room, looked over, a satisfied smile on her lips, and said, 'Delicious.'

'I'd no notion you thrived on anarchy, Maria.'

'I thrive on people getting what they deserve. You deserve to be acknowledged for your talent. They deserve to have a woman get the better of them.'

Vivienne squeezed Maria's hand and, with extreme effort, swallowed the lump in her throat before mixing a little blue ultramarine with chrome yellow for the unusual blue-green colour she would need. It wasn't often she painted anything without sketching it first, but this was too important not to do. She'd practised a dozen times at home—working through the angles, how much of the cover would make sense for the perspective, how much *he* needed to see to understand—till she felt she could get the little book in his hand just right, without the pencil underneath.

She'd allotted two hours for her work, an hour longer than it would take her at home if she did more intricate detailing on the marble-like cover, and she was nearly done when all the fine hairs at her neck rose. Hazel was there. Vivienne could feel it but refused to turn around—she hadn't since she first stepped up to her canvas, even when the discord reached a crescendo around her.

There was little more than a hint of the spine left—just a reddish-brown line standing between her and escape—and she finished with little fanfare but agonizing determination to avoid searching out a most beloved face.

At home, she often cleaned up after herself, only leaving the task for Maria when she'd remained far too long in her studio and had to be somewhere with her aunt and uncle. Today, she could not countenance looking anywhere but at the painting in front of her. Her courage had brought her this far, but she had not yet learned to think it wholly infallible.

The time it took Maria to empty the water jar and clean up the workspace was torture. Vivienne was half hope and half agony that the duke would appear at her side. Whether she wished him to or not she could not decide, but when Maria gave word they were ready to depart, her stomach dropped with disappointment.

'I'll escort you out, Miss Emory,' Mr York said, from somewhere a little behind her. 'Your work has been garnering quite a bit of attention, even before today.'

Vivienne wasn't sure what he was hinting at and so remained silent.

'You may have noticed His Grace, the Duke of Hazelhurst, in the Grand Salon this morning.'

'Was he?' she asked, although she always knew when he was near.

The man nodded once. 'He often begins his day on the bench in front of your painting.'

Her heart swelled with a wistful feeling. 'I see.'

'I wonder if you do. Do you keep records of who purchases your paintings?'

Vivienne stepped onto the stone flag-way in front of Somerset House as the carriage that would carry her home came to a stop, conscious they were having this conversation within hearing distance of those passing by. 'My uncle, Lord Lane, has his man of business handle transactions on my behalf.'

'Ah. Well, let me perhaps be the first to congratulate you then on so fine a benefactor as His Grace. He's purchased half a dozen paintings of yours that I know of, including *Woman at Water's Edge* this year, along with the one you just now touched up, if you'll let it go, in addition to several others. Forgive me, I cannot recall their names at present.'

The gentle, early summer breeze felt enough to knock Vivienne over. Dazed and disoriented, she struggled to recall where she was and what she was doing. With a baffled 'Thank you, sir,' she mounted the steps of the carriage.

Maria said nothing, for which Vivienne was grateful, as emotions whirled and skipped through her. The worst of them, hope.

34

*E*very day since *that* day, Brick appeared at the Royal
Academy before it was open to the public and
remained for several hours, doing little else besides staring at
the painting of himself and marvelling at the hand that had
completed it. It mattered not how many days he returned, how
long he sat, the angle from which he examined the work, he
could not see in himself what she did.

He'd noticed the intense hush falling over the room before
he noticed her in it, walking with her shoulders back, her
proud chin in the air as she approached her work. He was startled to see her at the gallery; he was also full of pride and
yearning for the beautiful, brave creature in front of him, and
grateful he'd been examining the painting at a distance, from
across the room, as she arrived. She wasn't looking anywhere
but at the wall directly in front of her, and he watched with
interest as she and her maid spread her drop cloth and set out
her supplies.

While Vivienne was one of several dozen artists present to
touch up work, she was the only woman. When the cries came

crashing down after the turgid silence, it took every ounce of restraint not to quiet them all with one roaring word. Brick knew her well enough to be certain she wouldn't appreciate the gesture from him. That knowledge was the only thing pushing back against his natural impulse to do so.

She was doing this without him, and he wouldn't interfere.

'Whore!' the artist next to Brick shouted, before returning his attention to the sloppy portrait with his name in the corner. Brick recognised the man, being familiar with both his objectionable reputation and derivative work—work that wouldn't even be shown if not for the man's father, who'd hoarded all the talent and left none for his son.

With a dangerous lilt in his voice and without taking his eyes off Vivienne, Brick asked, 'Who do you suggest she's whoring with?'

'The duke in the painting, of course. How else would a chit like that convince the Hanging Committee to put *her* work on the line?' The man paused to step back before dipping his brush in brown and moving towards a little ship in his painting once more, caring so little about the impact of his words, he didn't bestow so much as a glance at the man with whom he spoke.

'Here I believe they place work based on the talent displayed, although I suppose that's not *always* the case.'

The artist scoffed. 'I've had plenty of time to examine the piece up close. I'll own on first impression it's striking, but knowing it was painted by a female'—the word *painted* said with almost as much sarcasm as even the duke himself was capable of delivering—'there are limitations impossible for ladyfolk to overcome.'

'How gratified I am to be standing so near a man with such expertise,' Brick replied in a deadly, even voice.

At his side, the artist, preening from what he mistook as a compliment, straightened his back and finally turned to look at Brick. The man went whiter than the shirt he was wearing.

'It's only a shame I've already made an offer to purchase the piece.' Brick turned to fully face his victim. 'I don't doubt Miss Emory's success selling her work in the future. Your future income, however, is less certain.'

'I—I—it's just that—'

Brick left the man stuttering and moved to a different corner of the room, where he could better watch Vivienne as she worked, being both curious and fascinated by her process. And, if he were honest with himself, he was a little concerned about what changes she sought to make.

He edged closer, without realising it, until he was just fifteen feet away, but made no move to speak with her. He'd apologised, sent flowers, sent paint supplies. He'd begun a programme for female artists. In short, he didn't know what else he could do, but he knew that pushing her wasn't the answer. Not here, not while she was working on a painting of him under the hard stares of dozens of curious onlookers. Still, his eyes never wavered from her and remained at her back as she packed up, left the room, and disappeared entirely out of his sight but not his mind.

Those who had been fixated on her turned their attention to him as he made his way over to the painting. Her hand had worked slowly, methodically, on something at his side and in the bottom half of the painting, but from a distance he'd been unable to determine more than that.

The fresh blue-green paint of the little rectangle was bright against what was long dried. The pattern looked as if someone had poured colours out, each on top of the other, until they swam and swirled together. Brick would recognise the object anywhere. It was the cover of *First Impressions.* For the first time since he'd left the house in Grosvenor Square, he felt the stirrings of possibility. He sank down on the nearby bench, the weight of relief too much to bear.

A quarter of an hour passed, with his head bowed and resting firmly in his hands, before he felt capable of looking at her work again—the little sign she'd left for him and only him. It wasn't much longer before hope and relief collided in confusion over what the book meant. That she was softening, certainly. That he was forgiven, maybe. But neither meant she would marry him. She'd been adamant for so long that she wouldn't—no, couldn't. Those were her words: *I can't.*

She was afraid—nay, terrified—of losing the thing she loved and losing herself in the process. Everything made sudden sense for him, particularly her determination to remain alone.

His unfocused gaze sharpened in an instant. He could see her in Goldfinch Park, beautiful in a worn work dress and drenched in soft morning light, palette in hand, attention not on him but on the canvas in front of her.

The idea came to him in an instant.

35

*A*ll of London came out to see Angelica Catalani, fêted opera singer and famed soprano.

'It's a very good thing your aunt had the foresight to bring in Catalani for the charity,' Anabel said, the hand looped through Vivienne's arm giving a squeeze.

'Why is that?'

'Because the *ton* will be too awed by her voice to be awed by *you*.'

With a half laugh that turned into a little sigh, Vivienne replied, 'I don't recall thanking you or your brother for your offer this evening.'

'It's nothing. You know that.'

It wasn't quite nothing. Lady Lane had insisted on Vivienne's attendance. She would have insisted regardless of the event but was adamant that the worst thing Vivienne could do, after turning up at the Royal Academy that morning, was to hide away during her own aunt's charity event. Vivienne had agreed but stood firm on arriving late so as not to take away from the night itself—something she couldn't have done if

Anabel and Mr Boyton had not offered to bring her, in lieu of her arriving with her aunt and uncle.

'I suppose I ought to discover the whereabouts of my aunt before the performance.'

'We passed my mama on the way in. Will you be all right?'

With a nod, Vivienne pulled away from her friend and began to make a path through the throngs of people crowding the rooms at the home of the Viscountess Allen, who'd offered her Brook Street house for the occasion.

'*You.*' The word was low and raspy, and in the crush of people, it took Vivienne a moment to realise it was the Dowager Duchess of Hazelhurst speaking to her. 'I heard about your little scene at the Royal Academy.'

'Which one?'

The dowager's brows pinched in confusion. 'Which Academy?'

'Which scene, ma'am.'

'You mean to tell me there was more than one? Was the second also held in front of that ghastly painting?'

'You find something wanting in that piece?'

'Of course I find something wanting! I don't want it hanging there at all. It's a degradation to my son's name, his title. No medals. No coronets. No dogs or horses, or anything to distinguish him, and what is he wearing? A common waistcoat?'

''Tis hardly common if His Grace is the one wearing it.'

The dowager scoffed—a coarse, rough sound that surprised Vivienne. 'You will tell me next you agree with those fools who called the composition masterful or make a case for some unknown who's proven why he deserves to fade into obscurity.'

'Something much worse, in fact. I am also the one who painted it.'

A funny little strangled noise came from somewhere deep within the dowager, and for a moment, Vivienne wondered if she might have caused the woman to suffer a stroke.

'You lie.'

'I am only surprised you have not already heard the truth of it. I went this morning to touch it up. Now you must excuse me as I continue the search for my aunt.' The lightness she felt as those words slipped from her mouth was unexpected. Vivienne veritably floated past the dowager, biting the inside of her lip to keep from smiling, and feeling heartily disappointed she would not be present when that woman one day recognised her as the source of a certain caricature as well.

Across the room, Lady Lane's elegant aubergine turban caught Vivienne's eye, and she squeezed herself between two groups: one proclaiming their excitement and eagerness to hear Catalani, the other bemoaning the crush despite being part of it. As one of the latter turned, Vivienne jumped to the side to avoid being knocked back by an elbow and found herself steadied by a familiar hand.

'Lady Ballentine! What a pleasure.' Vivienne dipped an elegant curtsey, noticing as she rose that the woman was surrounded by several of her friends, some of whom Vivienne recognised and others she did not.

The lady cast a comprehensive look over Vivienne. 'You look well, Miss Emory—and how nice to see you out.' She dropped her voice and added, 'We'd heard about the display at the Academy, of course—I, myself, was there to bear witness —but rest cures all manner of ills, does it not?'

'Certainly, but as it's said, no rest for the wicked—or artists,' Vivienne replied with a smile that was for the entire group. Every woman in the group looked on with blank or confused stares, as Vivienne was sure they would. 'Oh, I beg pardon. I believed you referring to my painting. If you were present on Preview Day, perhaps you've seen it? *The Stranger*? This year I'm lucky to have several hanging, but that particular piece is on the line.'

After a long, silent pause, Lady Ballentine offered an odd half smile, while several of the others around her tittered.

'Such an unusual sense of humour, Miss Emory.'

'A kind compliment, ma'am.' Vivienne continued past the group, who would think little else of her strange jest until the papers revealed her identity. There had been too many people at the Royal Academy when she appeared that morning. Too many men stunned into shocked silence or surprise, or full of disgust or jealousy, to expect them to do anything less than make it known who had dared breech their domain. No doubt word had already begun to circulate.

Her aunt, when Vivienne reached her, turned from the women she'd been speaking to and held out a hand.

'Truthfully, I wasn't sure you would come, but I am glad to see you here, all the same. You presenting yourself for public inspection will do much to temper interest in you.'

Vivienne bit her lip and peeped through her lashes at her aunt as she made her confession. 'Perhaps, although I just took credit for the painting when speaking to both the dowager duchess and Lady Ballentine. The former was furious, and the latter understood it to be a jest.'

'And you were equally amused by both responses?' Lady Lane asked, an eyebrow raised, a smile fighting for a place on her face.

'What other choice do I have if this *is* my choice?'

Lady Lane studied her a moment, before turning the topic. 'He's not here.'

'Who, ma'am?' The artifice would fool no one, least of all her aunt.

'You can hardly keep your head from turning this way and that. Your uncle has already gone through to the ballroom to reserve seats. We'll begin moving people that way presently, if you care to join him before the rush.'

With a nod, Vivienne headed for the ballroom, collecting Anabel as she went. Despite her friend's chatter, she couldn't keep her focus on even one of every ten words. It had been more than a fortnight since she'd seen Hazel. A fortnight since his eyes had pleaded with her to understand, since his words nearly undid her, since she'd felt anything resembling happiness.

When Maria had been helping her get ready for the evening, Vivienne had tried not to think about crossing paths with him but found the effort of putting him from her mind fatiguing. She couldn't decide if she were ready to see him or not, what they would say to one another if they did meet, or whether or not they'd even have the opportunity—if she hoped they did or didn't. Even now, she couldn't determine if the feeling knocking around in her stomach was relief or disappointment.

TWO DAYS LATER, when Vivienne arrived at a fête at Carlton House with her aunt and uncle at which there must have been at least two thousand guests in attendance, she knew he was there. Her body was always certain of him. Despite the din of conversation and the music ringing in her ears, the oppressive heat of the rooms, the awareness that every other person was either whispering about her behind a fan or gaping at her without a hint of shame, the fine hairs on her neck rose like a hundred tiny antennae attuned to his being.

She tried to put the knowledge aside. Despite numerous sleepless nights, Vivienne was no closer to determining what she'd say when or if she came face to face with him again. Lady Lane weaved a hand through Lord Lane's arm and led their small party further into the crush, Vivienne trailing one step behind, chin held high.

'Quite an accomplishment,' Lady Sefton said, as Lady Lane brought the three of them to a halt, 'to have at least some share of attention from more than a thousand people. I can think of half a dozen women who would pour spite on you for nothing but that.'

A footman was passing with a tray of champagne. Vivienne took a glass and forced herself to sip rather than toss back the entirety of it. Lady Sefton raised her own glass to Vivienne's.

'Tell me, how can I get my hands on one of your paintings? You know, I tried to purchase one several years ago—what was it called?—oh yes, *Ship Caught in a Cornish Storm*. 'Twas already sold, despite being only the second day of the Exhibition. My own fault for missing the preview, I suppose.'

'You're too kind,' replied Vivienne, with only one ear on the conversation, the other being busy trying to pick out a rich, deep sound that could roll through her like a summer storm.

'Mrs Drummond-Burrell has had much to say on the subject of a lady painting for public consumption and enjoyment, in addition to money, as I'm sure you can imagine.'

'We can *all* imagine.'

Vivienne turned to see who had spoken, her mouth dropping a little when she took in the man in front of her.

'Miss Emory, you must know Mr Farington?'

She did—but only by name, by face, and by his meticulous accounts of what was transpiring socially in town, particularly in artistic circles, himself being a well-known painter.

'I've not had the pleasure of an introduction,' Vivienne said, with a curtsey.

'Believe me when I say the pleasure is all mine,' Mr Farington told her. 'I've been following your career for some time, and I can tick off the number of things that have ever amused me half so much as the diverting little scandal you've created. To hear Smyth renounce your work as amateur, without merit, when earlier this month he called *The Stranger* audacious and praised the artist for finding a soul under the coal. Delightful.'

He moved on with an amused smile and an impish light in his eyes, leaving Vivienne feeling a little overwhelmed by the attention, the blatant acknowledgment of her as an artist and of her work.

'I'm going to take some air, Aunt.'

Lady Lane nodded, and Vivienne weaved through the guests to the terrace, which, although crowded, had several stone benches at the far end that remained unoccupied.

'He was at a card party some days ago. I heard him tell Rudford they remained engaged.'

There was a sharp gasp followed by an incredulous, 'No!'

Vivienne looked around a moment before realising the voices were coming from the bench below her on the other side of the balustrade.

'I was shocked when it was first announced, with her being on the shelf and everything else, but never more shocked than to hear he intends to proceed with it.'

'Well,' the other young lady said, with a heady sigh, 'that's very honourable.'

'As if anyone would fault him for calling off a wedding to a hoyden who dared strike him.'

'He must be very much in love.'

Vivienne caught what sounded like a soft scoff before the girl replied to her friend.

'In love? She wore a *work* dress—and in public no less. Do you think she might even wear an apron, like a common maid? He'll come to his senses. Any man would.'

Vivienne hadn't meant to eavesdrop and turned to retrace her steps, but for the rest of the evening her mind only had room for one thought—why had he told anyone they remained engaged?

36

The conversation Vivienne overheard at Carlton House left her with a nagging question. One that could only be answered by the duke himself, who, it seemed, planned never again to reappear at Huxley House.

Unable to face another day without knowing what he thought of her, or if there was any possibility for a future in which there was space for both her art and him, besides having a reputation already in tatters, she waited until her aunt and uncle had left for the theatre before donning an old, hooded cloak and slipping out of the back door of the house.

'Honestly, miss,' Maria said, as they slunk around the square, 'you've quite ruined me for any other. How boring the life of an ordinary lady's maid must be.'

'All part of my nefarious plan. You've been a part of my household in some way or another almost as long as I can recall. I could never part with you.'

They reached Hazel's home only a minute later, and the door opened just as Vivienne let go of the knocker, casting a warm glow of light over her and her maid.

'Miss Emory for His Grace, if you please,' Maria said, standing firm by Vivienne's side.

The footman looked more fearful than anything but showed them to the library just off the main hallway.

It was the first time Vivienne had been in the duke's house, and the first thing she noticed, besides the rich, warm colours and suggestions of him in every little item inside the house, was *Joie*. Her eyes misted, and she was still staring at the painting when Hazel entered only moments after her.

'Vivienne!' He sounded surprised to see her, and his face was etched in concern. 'Are you all right? You shouldn't be here.'

'Maria is with me.' The look he gave her said he knew that wasn't enough, and that so did she.

'James.' It was the only word he spoke to the footman, who had lingered at the open door of the library. James nodded and a second later was gone, as if he'd never been in the hallway to begin with.

'Why haven't you run the notice announcing the end of our engagement?'

'I beg your pardon?'

'It's been weeks.'

'The gossips are busy enough trying to determine which is more salacious: you being an artist, you painting a very handsome man, or you striking the subject of your painting in front of the painting itself. I'm certain if I add to that list a very public castoff of my intended, I will be held liable for hundreds of fits and convulsions throughout Mayfair.'

The space between Vivienne's brows crinkled as she tried to make head or tail of what he was saying. Whatever she had expected, it wasn't that.

'You've stopped coming to Huxley House—and I think

you've been avoiding me. I know you were at the Academy, and at Carlton House, too.'

'I began to doubt whether my presence was doing any good—whether it was doing anything at all to prove how much you mean to me—or whether it was just making everything worse.'

Pain flitted across her face. 'Hazel.'

'Since you are here, may I show you something?'

'All right.'

'It's upstairs,' he said carefully.

Vivienne understood. She walked to the doorway and glanced at Maria, who had already made her way to a little bench against the wall. The only sign the maid was aware of anyone else in her vicinity was the sly wink she gave her mistress before once more training her eyes on the empty space in front of her.

Hazel took the first step, and Vivienne followed. On the first-floor landing, he turned left and led her down to a door at the very end, stepping back as he pushed it open.

One wall was all windows. There were no drapes hanging, allowing soft blue light from the almost-full moon to stream in unimpeded. Near one side of the large room was a deep, plush sofa with several chairs and tables scattered around it, and on the other, row after row of mahogany shelves, some empty, most filled with stacks of paper, charcoal, pencils, dozens of paintbrushes, and jars.

It was what stood in the centre of the room, however, that caused Vivienne's vision to blur. A hot tear found its way down her cheek and she freed the sob imprisoned in her throat. Even as her body shook with emotion, she felt that familiar sensation cascading down the back of her neck.

'I hope this means you like it.' Hazel's voice was rich and caressing.

She swiped at her tears, trying to focus on the scene in front of her—the easel, the stool, the blank canvases of all sizes lined up neatly against a stark white wall.

'This room gets the best light in the house. Nash was here a few days since, before I sent him on to Goldfinch Park. He'll send over designs for two studios in the coming weeks for your review—one here, one there.' His tone was pitched low. 'You may change them however you see fit, or toss them aside and direct him in whatever ways you'd like. There is plenty of space to build whatever you desire.'

Chills ran down Vivienne's spine, and goose-pimples dappled the skin of her bare arms. She turned to face him, her legs trembling beneath her.

'What I desire cannot be built.'

Hazel peered at her. His body seemed to loosen with relief while intense pleasure glinted in his clear blue-grey eyes. He stepped back, dropping to one knee, and she waited, unable to blink or breathe or think.

'I have not run a notice calling off our engagement for one very simple reason. Without you, I cannot exist. As long as I walk this earth, draw breath, know that somewhere you are doing the same, there is no other for whom my heart will beat. Vivienne, my love, say that you'll have me now, always, forever.'

Her heart hammered away in her chest—beating in happiness, disbelief, anticipation. 'What's longer than forever?'

His face split in a wide smile, and a moment later she was swept up in a strong embrace, her whole body crushed to him and held as if he never meant to let go. When he did, it was to take her face between his hands. Her cheeks glowed under his touch, and she laid her much smaller hands over his, revelling in the feel of skin against skin.

He brought his lips to hers with slow, tantalizing tenderness. He tasted warm and sweet, and the way his mouth lingered on hers—coaxing her, savouring her—left Vivienne feeling weak and eager.

Hazel pulled away first, and she could think of nothing but the pleasure that emanated from within her and the desire for more of the same. But he moved away and towards the candle he'd brought up with him, using it to light a dozen others around the room before setting it back down on a table.

When he came back to her and wordlessly took her by the hand, her stomach clenched with excitement, and she felt her nipples peak against the soft fabric of her dress. He led her to the stool, and she sat, her need for him sending pulses of excitement coursing through her.

He walked several feet from her and stepped onto a small dais she hadn't before noticed. There was a dizzying little moment when she realised he wore no shoes. She looked up at him, a question in her eyes. His gaze, bold and absorbing, never left hers as he shrugged out of his tailcoat and let it fall to the floor.

---

37

*B*rick watched as Vivienne's bright eyes darkened as he let the fine, heavy fabric drop from his shoulders down to his feet.

His fingers slipped his buttons through their holes, one at a time, until he was free of his waistcoat. His betrothed's mouth had opened a little, and she licked her lips as she watched him add the article of clothing to the growing pile just beyond his stockinged feet.

The knot on his cravat was snug, but he worked it open with the deftness of a man filled with overwhelming and unbearable urgency. He imagined her mouth, her tongue, in the silky feel of the fabric against his sensitive skin as he tugged it off.

When he worked his shirt from the waist of his breeches, pulling it loose and tugging it over his head, he heard an audible gasp that made his cock twitch.

He watched her eyes roam greedily from his navel upwards, his chest broad and the muscles of his abdomen hard and well-defined from years of boxing. When she brought her gaze back to his he was startled and more than a little aroused by the hunger in it. Her eyes dropped as he let loose the fall on one side of his breeches and then the other, his pulse pounding and throbbing through every part of his body, keenly aware of what came next. There were five buttons left between her and all of him.

'Vivienne, look at me.' His voice was soft but insistent, and he waited until his eyes held her appraising green ones before releasing those last five buttons with painful patience, his manhood stiff and aching for her touch. He pushed his breeches to the ground, taking his stockings along with them, and stood, revealing every hard part of his body to her.

Even in the low light of the candles, he could see her swallow.

'Paint me. Sketch me. Study me. My body is yours—for art, for pleasure.' His heart hammered erratically as her eyes raked over him. In all his life, he had never felt so vulnerable as he did in that moment.

She stared at him, studied him, the uneven rhythm of their breathing the only sound in the room. There was no regard for time, no thought of propriety. In that moment, it was him and her, and nothing else could exist but the unyielding, intense connection between them. He'd known from the moment he'd seen her in Bond Street not just that she was beautiful, but that she was different, special, made for him and he for her.

He thought he might explode with anticipation when she stood. She repositioned the easel, the stool, and retrieved one of the pencils before reclaiming her seat. Brick remained still, listening to the lead scratch the paper, each stroke landing on him like a whisper of a kiss.

'Turn,' she said, without looking up from the paper.

Her voice was decisive, and Brick did as he was bid,

glancing back over his shoulder in time to see her bite her lip, her eyes intent on his backside. A quiet minute or two passed, and he had begun stroking himself without realising it.

'Turn,' Vivienne said again, much closer this time. He could feel her at his back, heat rippling under his skin in response to her nearness.

He shifted on the dais, rotating to face her. She was inches from him. Her beauty, her boldness, robbed him of his breath. Her face was upturned, her countenance radiant, and she kept her focus on him as she tipped her head forward and placed a searing kiss in the middle of his chest.

Brick groaned and his member jumped, the tip flicking the muslin of her dress. 'Vivienne.' Her name ground out of him in a husky, guttural sound.

She stepped up on the dais, her breasts pressing flush against his chest, the folds of her skirt tickling and teasing his cock.

'Vivienne, my love.'

His soon-to-be wife kissed the scar on his left arm made by the bullet he'd taken defending her honour. She brought a finger up to trace the little ridges and let it roam to another scar across his collarbone, enjoying the prickle of his skin as it came to life at her touch. Her fingers followed the light trail of dark hair that curled on his chest and ran down his middle, guiding her hands over the ridges of muscle and to his most sensitive area.

She wrapped a hand around him in a touch that was curious, a little uncertain, but not shy. He felt his muscles begin to quiver as he fought for control.

'Tell me you like this, my love,' she whispered against the heat of his skin, her lips hovering a hair's breadth above his hammering heart.

Brick's eyes closed as she began to pump in long, slow movements, the loose grip of her hand just barely teasing the soft flesh within it.

'Look at me.'

Her touch was exquisite, but the way she spoke to him nearly sent him over the edge, as he forced himself to do as she wished.

'Tell me you like this,' she demanded, a teasing, seductive curl to her lip as she repeated to him his own words from the carriage. The candlelight was reflected in her eyes, dark and dilated with pleasure.

Brick managed to choke out, 'Too much.' His breath becoming shallower, faster, as she played with different rhythms, different holds. 'I don't know how much longer I can maintain control,' he said, sensing how close to release she was bringing him.

'Then don't.'

'Vivienne.' His fraying constraint choked the word.

She looked him right in the eye, her hand slowing but not stopping. 'I've everything I need, Hazel. Give me everything I want.'

He said her name once more. This time it rumbled deep in his chest and was punctuated by her surprised squeal when he swept her from her feet and deposited her beside the gilt-edged velvet sofa, as deep as it was wide.

'There is no turning back from this moment. Are you sure?' He didn't want to ask. He wanted to crush her beneath him and claim her as his own, but he would only do so if she was certain in her choice—it cost him nothing to be a man. Vivienne had changed his life, and this would change hers.

She laid a hand against his cheek, letting her fingers catch

on his stubble before dragging a thumb across his lower lip.
'Please.'

That one word, full of longing, sealed her fate and his.

He spun her round, and took care as he undressed her,
teasing the curve of her shoulder, the long, narrow valley of
her spine, the sensitive skin at the back of her knees. With delicate care, he exposed every part of her until she was as naked
as he.

Brick pulled her flush against his front, his cock pressing
hard against her back, and felt her chest expand with a gasp.
His lips scattered kisses like light rain showers over her shoulders as his fingers teased a slow trail down her arms, her
warm skin tingling and burning in their wake. His hands
cupped her breasts, luxuriating in their weight and fullness as
his thumbs massaged delicate circles over the pink buds
already peaked.

'Vivienne.' His voice was ragged with desire, emotion. He
knew she was giving him so much more than her body.

She groaned and uttered his name on a breathy moan.
'Hazel.'

He moved one hand down the flat plane of her stomach,
tangling his fingers in her patch of curls and searching out the
centre of her pleasure. She pushed back against him as he
stroked her, and when he used two fingers to glide down
along the inside of her lips until her bud met the crux of his
fingers, she quivered in his arms.

Reluctantly he released her, and without a word, she
crawled onto the luxurious sofa and leaned back against a
pillow. He followed, and with slow, gentle movements, guided
her legs apart to make space for himself between them. His
lips found hers in a kiss that was both agonising and insistent.
He savoured the feeling of her mouth against his, the taste of

her sweet and heady. He moved to her earlobe, nipping it before working down her neck and across her collarbone. At her breasts, he paused, mesmerised by the rise and fall of her chest and letting his own unsteady breaths cascade over her. With slow, tender care, he pressed his tongue to her nipple, flicking and swirling as Vivienne jerked at the unfamiliar sensation. Her moan delighted him as he worked one and then the other, his hand teasing her when his mouth wasn't.

He feathered kisses down her stomach until he came to the soft curls at the juncture between her thighs. Her hips bucked as his lips captured her centre. She was slick with wanting, and far from recoiling at the sensation of his mouth there, she pushed against him as if chasing a feeling. There were so many things he wanted to do to her, every part of her body he wanted to cherish and explore, a hundred ways he wanted to give her pleasure. Every airy moan she released into the candlelit room made him harder.

Brick forced himself up and watched her watch him as he settled at the hollow between her legs, letting his cock rest on her mound and teasing her with several long, slow strokes. He wanted her to know pleasure, to burn with divine euphoria as he did, and he was certain holding onto his control once inside her was going to be an impossible feat.

'Last chance, my love.' His eyes held hers, and he searched for any sign of hesitation or concern.

'Without you, I cannot exist. Everything I am, everything I have, is yours.'

Her words were soft, solemn, floating like a vow between their bodies. He bent to place a slow, reverent kiss on her lips, warning as he lifted his head, 'It may hurt.'

With a hand on his cock, he traced it up and down her opening, wetting the tip before positioning himself at her entrance. He pushed in only the head. Vivienne gasped as her body tensed at the intrusion and fought to adjust to his width. He bowed his head to kiss her once more as he withdrew, before entering her again with more length. He repeated the action once, twice, three more times, the controlled, measured motion exquisite agony for him. Her body began to relax beneath his, and when it did, he used one forceful thrust to bury himself in her.

Vivienne released a sharp cry of pain, and he whispered apologies in her ear as he pulled out and pushed back in, inch by slow inch. When he withdrew next, he took himself in hand and ran his sex over her pearl, his arousal growing painful when he heard her breath hitch and then quicken as pleasure began to overcome the initial discomfort.

Sliding both hands under her backside, he lifted Vivienne a little and sunk his whole hardness into her on a desperate groan as her tight core swallowed him up to the hilt. He held her to him, moving in slow circles, the patch of curls at the base of his cock grazing against her own and that tender little spot nestled within. Her legs quivered, and she panted his name, half question, half demand. He knew she was close and, with deep, even thrusts, he drove into her core, his base rocking against her bud each time she took his length.

Brick was desperate to hang on until she claimed her pleasure, his body shaking against the restraint. When her release came, he felt her spasm against him, her centre bearing down on his full length in a frenzy of erratic pulses that was more than he could withstand. The feel of her sex tight around his as she gave herself over to him was too much. With a growl, he withdrew once more before burying his arousal in her core, his cock pulsing as he spilled into her.

38

*V*ivienne's mind was blank—or perhaps too aware with the significance of their actions for there to be any space left over for any other thought. Giving herself to Hazel felt as natural to her as holding a paintbrush, but to come to his house, to engage in such an act before they were wed, the magnitude of this compressed every last bit of air from her chest.

'Vivienne?' When he said her name, it vibrated against the warm skin of her temple where his lips rested.

A little humming noise was all she was capable of.

'Vivienne, my love, we cannot remain much longer.'

He'd rolled a little to the side after they were both spent but had taken her with him—her leg and arm draped over him —and had kept their connection.

'I disagree.' She would never forget that first moment, the first seconds as he entered her, his eyes locked on her own. It was a feeling unlike any other—foreign, uncomfortable at first, a little painful. But then, to be joined physically with a man to whom she'd already given all the rest of herself, it was as though her whole being had expanded so they could become one. She couldn't say how she knew, only that she was certain everything was exactly as it should be, and she wanted to hold that feeling for as long as possible.

'By your side is the only place I want to be, and if I thought less of you—if you meant less to me—I could remain there now.' His hand came up to brush back a curl stuck in the light sweat dappling her forehead. 'Even more than I wish to take you again, I wish to get you home without anyone being the wiser. Soon enough we'll be wed, and we can love one another on this sofa, in your bed or mine, the library, the music room, anywhere else we wish, whenever we wish it.'

An image of herself sitting upon his lap on a bench at the pianoforte came clearly and immediately to her mind, heating her already flushed skin and causing her core to clench. She could feel his cock, still sheathed inside her, react with a throb of desire. On a groan, he forced himself to withdraw and pulled her up and off the sofa.

As much care as he'd taken to undress her, he took twice that to set her to rights.

'You have no regrets, I hope?'

He was standing behind her in front of the window—the only bit of reflection she had to check her appearance—and she turned to face him, surprised to see so much concern in his fine features.

'Besides meeting you, finding myself quite in love despite my best efforts, and lying with a man to whom I am not married?'

His eyes went wide before he noticed the twitch of her lip giving away her teasing. She ran a hand through his hair, then brought it round to his cheek, where she used her thumb to trace his lips.

He nipped at it before placing a painfully tender kiss on the pad. 'Minx.'

When Hazel escorted Vivienne downstairs, a clock in the hall alerted her to the fact that the night had progressed well into the small hours of the morning, and she was a little startled to see Maria on the bench where she'd left her, with James, the footman from earlier, and the two of them in close conversation.

'So you see, James, what Swift was saying about human nature—'

Vivienne swallowed a little smile. *Gulliver's Travels* was Maria's favourite book and a source of endless conversation for her.

Whether or not James did see, no one would ever know. The footman noticed them before he could reply and sprang to his feet, a frightening shade of white overcoming his handsome features.

'Be easy, James.'

Vivienne admired the steady way Hazel spoke. The magnitude of what she'd done settled upon her, and although she didn't regret a moment of what had just happened between them, her cheeks pinked a little when it occurred to her that both the footman and Maria very likely knew *exactly* why she'd been gone so long.

'Neither of you need a reminder of the importance of discretion if you wish to retain your position in this house or any other. Or do I assume incorrectly?'

Maria bristled. 'I beg your pardon, Your Grace! Are you insinuating that my mistress has been anywhere these last hours besides tucked away in her bed? You believe her capable of sneaking out in the night, like a thief making off with the silver, when she has suffered enough mortification for a lifetime? How long must she repent her actions? I daresay those vile words speak more about your character than hers.'

'You terrify me, Maria.' Hazel chuckled, the sound warming Vivienne from the inside out, and she darted over to place a swift kiss on her dear maid's cheek. Even James looked impressed by the performance. 'Now, we must get you home. We'll go out the back of the house and along the mews.'

'We?'

'Yes. James will attend you, and I'll stay some paces behind.'

Hazel dashed off and was back before she even thought to ask where he was going, but she had a lingering suspicion if she ran her hands over his person, she'd discover a pistol within easy reach, despite the fact they were going no further than across the square between their houses.

'Come, let us be off.'

As they sneaked out of a back entrance, James and Maria first, Hazel grabbed Vivienne by the hand, pulled her to him, and caressed her mouth with his own. His lips lingered and his tongue spent a luxurious minute exploring her mouth before a subtle cough reminded them where they were and who was watching.

Vivienne patted her hair, joined Maria and James, made easy work of the short distance between their houses, and, after one lingering look at her intended that unfurled a deep need within her, regained the safety of her own home once more, although everything felt and looked somehow different. It was more than the act of giving herself to Hazel; it was the knowledge of what her life would be like with him, his support for her work, for the work of any woman who wished to be an artist—a future she'd never thought to imagine, because the very idea felt impossible.

'Well, miss,' Maria said, as she helped Vivienne out of her dress and into her nightclothes. 'I for one am looking forward to working in His Grace's home.'

'Yes.' Vivienne climbed into her bed with a smile on her face, a full heart, and a vision for a painting that would set the *ton* on their ears. 'I daresay you are.'

EPILOGUE

*B*rick saw no need to secure a special licence and rush the wedding, particularly when, between the two of them, they'd given the gossips more than enough to keep them tittering over their tea till it grew cold.

The day after Vivienne came to him, they set a date for the wedding, and despite his suggestion they marry from her aunt and uncle's estate, Vivienne preferred to remain in town and nearer her studio until one at Goldfinch Park could be completed. As a compromise, or so she called it, they wed in town and followed this with a fortnight at his family seat in Hertfordshire, during which she spent the days compiling a list of changes for her suite of rooms and drawing up new plans with Nash for a bright, airy studio on the south-facing side of the house. And she spent the nights in his bed, which he began referring to as their bed in no time at all.

London in the summer was a miserable place; the heat rolled in, the air grew thick, and the company thin. Brick offered the builder twice what he'd been quoted to finish the studio twice as fast. The autumnal months at Goldfinch Park were the finest, in his opinion. His wife often traipsed out of doors with an easel and pencils, asking him what shade of orange he saw in the leaves of the trees or how he would describe the blue of the lake at exactly ten in the morning on a cloudy day. Not long after they'd retired to the country, she packed a picnic and asked him to show her his favourite prospect.

He took her on horseback to Kell Peak, the kind of remote spot one could only reach if one knew where to find it and how to follow the path. They came through a swathe of poplar trees at the top of a crest, all of the county rolling and dipping and sprawling below them. Much to his surprise, Vivienne did not pull bread or meat or cheese out of her basket, but a thin quilt, which she spread out with a teasing twinkle in her eye.

Despite his insatiable appetite for his wife, he often spent himself outside her and suspected he would continue to do so while she first found her balance as an artist and a wife. Vivienne had confided to him the eve before their wedding that although her vision of their future together included children, and she wasn't insensible to his wish for an heir, she hoped it might take some time. It was the only time he had seen her look worried, her brow creased with uncertainty, and after explaining how they might prevent her from becoming with child, he suggested they not even think of it for six months or more.

They returned to London from time to time to attend exhibitions or private showings, and for a longer visit during the season the following year, remaining, of course, for Preview Day. As Brick walked through the doors of the Grand Salon at the Royal Academy with Vivienne on his arm, a deathly hush fell over the room.

'There,' she said in a low voice, with a nod to the wall opposite them.

Together, they walked in step to the painting, the crowd in their way coming undone like a poorly stitched seam.

'Is that truly what it looks like?' Brick cocked his head a little to one side and then the other as he studied the work that was nearly as tall as he was.

'Delectable? Edible? Oh, yes. That and more. I daresay this could be my highest sale to date.'

Brick lifted his free hand to cover the one resting on his arm and bent his head low to whisper in his wife's ear. 'Keep talking like that, and you'll be lucky if I can contain myself till we reach the carriage.'

Her cheeks pinked, and he savoured the moment, relishing the fact that after nearly a year of marriage he could still make his wife blush.

The sound of boots on the wood floor interrupted their private moment, and they turned as one to see a gentleman from the Hanging Committee coming near.

'You may mark this one sold,' Brick said.

The man looked a little confused. 'My apologies, Your Grace, but this piece is not for sale.'

Brick turned to his wife. 'Then I suppose I'll have to plead my case with the artist herself.'

'Oh, I am very sorry, sir,' Vivienne began, as the other man cleared his throat and backed away from the exchange. 'But in truth I could never bear to part with this piece, unless perhaps you are willing to stand in as my subject for another?'

His mouth lifted in a sensual, satisfied smile. 'Minx.' Vivienne's laugh filled him with intense pleasure, as he squeezed her hand where it rested on his arm.

'As if I'd let this piece hang anywhere but in our home.'

The large painting was one she'd completed several months after their wedding. It was a masterpiece of the male form—his male form, specifically the back of it. His wife often made him recreate the night she came to see him, much to his own delight. When she painted this piece, she'd sketched out only a fraction of his profile, as if he had just begun to look back over his shoulder. It was hint enough to make people wonder, and perhaps most wouldn't have felt so certain had there been no further clue. Her signature in the corner, however, all but confirmed her husband as the subject. Those who wished for a more scandalous story ignored the obvious and put rumours about that the duchess was sleeping with her sitter.

'It's much worse than that,' she said, when she overheard two ladies gossiping, unaware Vivienne stood just behind. 'I married him.'

One lady's mouth fell open. Vivienne smiled sweetly at her, and Brick, laughter in his voice, said, 'Come, my dear wife, let us continue so you may educate me on why *that* particular piece is superior to all others, and correct all my wrong opinions on this year's set of landscapes.'

'Keep talking like that, dear husband, and you'll be lucky if I can contain myself till we reach the carriage.'

Her cheeks glowed with happiness, and her countenance was alive with mirth and something else he couldn't determine. His eyes raked over her, stopping for a moment on the fullness of her breasts as they peeked from the bodice of her dress. He felt a tightening in his breeches and had to remind himself where they were.

'Hazel, my love,' his wife whispered, so quietly he almost couldn't hear her even as he tipped his head towards her. 'My courses have not come this month.'

His head whipped back in shock, and he studied her, determined to smother his reaction until he was certain of hers. He stared at her, too afraid to move, to speak, to breathe, and everything faded around him except her. Time slowed, then stopped altogether as the two of them stood there facing each other, expressions matched in their uncertainty. Then, starting with just a little lift of the corner of her lip, Vivienne broke into a wide smile and swiped at her eyes, which had begun to glimmer.

Without giving it a second thought, Brick dropped a quick kiss on his wife's sweet lips, scandalising those present at the Academy for the second time in hardly more than a twelve-month, before promptly leading her out to their carriage.

ALSO BY GEORGINA NORTH

The Rake of Tamarix Hall

ACKNOWLEDGMENTS

A second book! Wow. It doesn't feel any more real than the first, and a part of me hope that never changes. The amount of support I've received since the release of *The Rake of Tamarix Hall* —so often from surprising corners—has turned me into a sniffling, sobbing, happy mess more times than I will ever admit to anyone.

This book took me to London, not nearly for long enough, but being able to sit on a bench in the same space where Vivienne's paintings would have hung—to see her in my mind's eye strolling on the duke's arm, striding past the curious stares of men and setting out her drop cloth in front of *The Stranger*—is a memory I'll have forever.

There were books, so many books, that helped me understand the climate of the art world at the time and the challenges Vivienne would have faced. Several I returned to again and again: *Broad Strokes: 15 Women Who Made Art and Made History (in That Order)* by Bridget Quinn, *Art on the Line: The Royal Academy Exhibitions at Somerset House 1780-1836* edited by David H. Solkin, and *In Her Own Image: Women Working in the Arts* edited by Elaine R. Hedges and Ingrid Wendt.

A special thanks to Sarah Pesce my editor, Helena Fairfax my proofreader, and Robin Vuchnich who creates these stunning covers. To my Auntie Reen who is equal parts beta reader and cheerleader, and Joanna Hinsey who is a little bit of everything—editor, sounding board, confidante—and always ready with the wine when I'm trying to write a steamy scene but can't stop giggling.

As always, my husband, Keola. In order of things he loves the most it goes golf, our cats, my books, which is a big deal if you know how much he loves golf.

And of course, you, my dear readers. You all are truly amazing. It's a dream knowing people around the world are reading my books. I loved writing *Painting the Duke* and hope you enjoyed reading it even half so much as that.

ABOUT THE AUTHOR

Georgina North lives in Southern California with her husband and their two cats. When she's not curled up with her laptop and a cup of coffee, you can find her daydreaming in her favourite chair, eating fish tacos, or adding more books to her to-read pile. *Painting the Duke* is her second novel.

Be the first to know!
Sign up for Georgina's newsletter
to receive updates
on new releases and more.

www.georginanorth.com

instagram.com/georginanorthauthor

Printed in Great Britain
by Amazon